With a roar, he yanked me toward him with a speed I never could have mustered on my own. My body screamed at me to do something to stop the burning, anything to ease the acid eating through me. As Pestilence held me directly over his mouth, Lark yelled at me.

"Tell me you know what you're doing."

"I know"—I yanked my sword upward, slicing through Pestilence's tongue—"what I'm fucking doing." The tongue flew away from me and I dropped, landing with a foot on either side of the demon's head.

I held my sword over my head, poised to drive it straight through him when I saw the laughter in his eyes. "You will never win, Tracker. Even if I die now, you will die later. And I will be free again."

With everything I had, I tapped into all the good in my life, the love I had for my daughter and Liam, for Alex and Pamela, Eve, and maybe even Faris. The emotions flowed through me, calming the rage. In my hands, my sword began to glow, as if lit from within. I didn't think about this new development, couldn't; there was no time.

"Demon, go back to your home."

PRAISE FOR SHANNON MAYER AND THE RYLEE ADAMSON SERIES

"If you love the early Anita Blake novels by Laurel K. Hamilton, you will fall head over heels for The Rylee Adamson Series. Rylee is a complex character with a tough, kick-ass exterior, a sassy temperament, and morals which she never deviates from. She's the ultimate heroine. Mayer's books rank right up there with Kim Harrison's, Patricia Brigg's, and Ilona Andrew's. Get ready for a whole new take on Urban Fantasy and Paranormal Romance and be ready to be glued to the pages!"

—*Just My Opinion Book Blog*

"Rylee is the perfect combination of loyal, intelligent, compassionate, and kick-ass. Many times, the heroines in urban fantasy novels tend to be so tough or snarky that they come off as unlikable. Rylee is a smart-ass for sure, but she isn't insulting. Well, I guess the she gets a little sassy with the bad guys, but then it's just hilarious."

—*Diary of a Bibliophile*

"I could not put it down. Not only that, but I immediately started the next book in the series, *Immune*."

—*Just Talking Books*

"*Priceless* was one of those reads that just starts off running and doesn't give too much time to breathe. . . . I'll just go ahead and add the rest of the books to my TBR list now."

—*Vampire Book Club*

"This book is so great and it blindsided me. I'm always looking for something to tide me over until the next Ilona Andrews or Patricia Briggs book comes out, but no matter how many recommendations I get nothing ever measures up. This was as close as I've gotten and I'm so freakin happy!"

—*Dynamite Review*

"Highly recommended for all fans of urban fantasy and paranormal."

—*Chimera Reviews*

"I absolutely love these books; they are one of the few Paranormal/urban fantasy series that I still follow religiously. . . . Shannon's writing is wonderful and her characters worm their way into your heart. I cannot recommend these books enough."

—*Maryse Book Review*

"It has the perfect blend of humor, mystery, and a slow-burning forbidden-type romance. Recommended x 1000."
—Sarah Morse Adams

"These books are, ultimately, fun, exciting, romantic, and satisfying. . . . Trust me on this. You are going to love this series."

—*Read Love Share Blog*

"This was a wonderful debut in the Rylee Adamson series, and a creative twist on a genre that's packed full of hard-as-nails heroines. . . . I will definitely stay-tuned to see what Rylee and her new partner get up to."

—Red Welly Boots

"*Priceless* did not disappoint with its colourful secondary characters, unique slant on the typical P.I. spiel, and a heroine with boatloads of untapped gifts."

—*Rabid Reads*

BLOOD OF THE LOST

Books by Shannon Mayer

The Rylee Adamson Series
Priceless
Immune
Raising Innocence
Shadowed Threads
Blind Salvage
Tracker
Veiled Threat
Wounded
Rising Darkness
Blood of the Lost

The Rylee Adamson Epilogues
Rylee
Liam
Pamela

Rylee Adamson Novellas
Elementally Priceless
Tracking Magic
Alex
Guardian
Stitched

The Venom Series
Venom and Vanilla
Fangs and Fennel
Hisses and Honey

The Elemental Series
Recurve
Breakwater
Firestorm
Windburn
Rootbound

Contemporary Romance
High Risk Love
Ninety-Eight

Paranormal Romantic Suspense
The Nevermore Trilogy:
Sundered
Bound
Dauntless

Urban Fantasy
A Celtic Legacy Trilogy:
Dark Waters
Dark Isle
Dark Fae

BLOOD OF THE LOST

A RYLEE ADAMSON NOVEL
BOOK 10

SHANNON MAYER

TALOS

New York

Talos Press books may be purchased in bulk at special discounts for sales promotion, corporate gifts, fund-raising, or educational purposes. Special editions can also be created to specifications. For details, contact the Special Sales Department, Talos Press, 307 West 36th Street, 11th Floor, New York, NY 10018 or info@skyhorsepublishing.com.

Talos Press® is a registered trademark of Skyhorse Publishing, Inc.®, a Delaware corporation.

Visit our website at www.talospress.com.

10 9 8 7 6 5 4 3 2 1

Library of Congress Cataloging-in-Publication Data

Names: Mayer, Shannon, 1979- author.
Title: Blood of the lost / by Shannon Mayer.
Description: First Talos Press edition. | New York : Talos Press, 2017. | Series: A Rylee Adamson novel ; Book 10
Identifiers: LCCN 2017006747 | ISBN 9781945863080 (softcover: acid-free paper)
Subjects: LCSH: Missing children--Investigation--Fiction. | Psychic ability--Fiction. | Paranormal romance stories. | GSAFD: Fantasy fiction. Classification: LCC PR9199.4.M3773 B585 2017 | DDC 813/.6--dc23
LC record available at https://lccn.loc.gov/2017006747

Original illustrations by Damon Za www.damonza.com

Printed in Canada

ACKNOWLEDGMENTS

The end of the Rylee series feels like the end of an era for me. When I started the first book I wasn't even a published author yet. I played with the idea for a long time before I started down the path Rylee's story. From first publishing *Priceless* to ending the series with *Blood of the Lost*, it has been almost three years to the day. In those three years I have had many editors, copy editors, proofreaders, and beta readers. I've had friends come and go. I've had family members arrive and leave this earth. My life has gone from working full time to writing full time, from being a wife and writer to becoming a mom. Each step in my life in the last three years gave me the focus, and the emotion to write Rylee's story and truly bring her to life.

I hope that in reading this final book (and the series) that you take away from it what I tried to impart. That there is always hope for the future no matter how dark it looks. Love is strong enough to survive the worst things that life throws at us. Our friends and loved ones can bring us through the darkest hours of our life if we let them. And when all else fails . . . just say Yuppy Doody and get the job done.

CAST OF CHARACTERS

Rylee Adamson: Tracker and Immune who has dedicated her life to finding lost children. Based near Bismarck, North Dakota.

Liam O'Shea: Previously an FBI agent. Now he is a werewolf/Guardian as well as lover to Rylee.

Giselle: Mentored Rylee and Milly; Giselle is a Reader but cannot use her abilities on Rylee due to Rylee's Immunity. She died in *Raising Innocence*.

Millicent: AKA Milly; witch who was best friend to Rylee. Now is actively working against Rylee for reasons not yet clear.

India: A spirit seeker whom Rylee Tracked in *Priceless*.

Kyle Jacobs: Rylee's personal teenage hacker. Human.

Doran: Daywalker and shaman who helps Rylee from time to time. Located near Roswell, New Mexico.

Alex: A werewolf trapped in between human and wolf. He is Rylee's unofficial sidekick and loyal companion. Submissive.

Berget: Rylee's little sister who went missing ten years prior to *Priceless*. In *Raising Innocence*, Rylee found out that Berget is still alive. In *Shadowed Threads*,

Rylee discovered Berget is the "Child Empress" and a vampire.

Dox: Large, pale blue-skinned ogre. Friend of Rylee. Owns "The Landing Pad" near Roswell, New Mexico.

William Gossard: AKA Will; panther shape shifter and officer with SOCA in London. Friend to Rylee.

Deanna Gossard: Druid, sister to William. Friend and help to Rylee.

Louisa: Tribal shaman located near Roswell, New Mexico.

Eve: Harpy that is now under Rylee's tutelage, as per the Harpy rule of conduct.

Faris: Vampire and general pain in the ass to Rylee. He is in contention for the vampire "throne" against Rylee's little sister, Berget.

Jack Feen: Only other Tracker in existence. He lives in London and is dying.

Agent Valley: Senior in command in the Arcane Division of the FBI.

Blaz: Dragon who bonded (reluctantly) with Rylee in *Shadowed Threads*.

Pamela: Young, powerful witch whom Rylee saved in *Raising Innocence*. She is now one of Rylee's wards.

Charlie: Brownie who acts as Rylee's go-between when working with parents on all of her salvages. Based in Bismarck, North Dakota.

Dr. Daniels: AKA "Daniels"; a child services worker and a druid Rylee met up with in *Raising Innocence*. Rylee and Daniels do not like one another.

"Thus shall one Tracker stand between Orion and the darkness he brings. She shall be our destruction or our salvation. No matter the outcome, her blood will be taken, drained to the last drop."
Book of the Psychic's Prophecies *(Green Book)*

1
RYLEE

I knelt on the edge of the grave, staring into the six-foot hole, and wondered if it would be me in the dirt the next time we faced Orion. We'd wrapped Milly's body in one of Giselle's quilts—the one with the blue-and-yellow triangles that had been on Milly's bed when she'd lived with Giselle and me. I brushed a hand over the quilt. Years, so many years we'd been friends and sisters . . . and now she was gone.

Taking a handful of dirt, I held it over the grave, and let it sift through my fingers. "Be at peace, Milly. Wait for me on the other side, my friend."

A hand touched my shoulder and I knew without looking it was Lark. She was the one we'd been fighting to free only hours before. Lark was an elemental tied to the earth and the final key to taking out Orion once and for all.

"Are you ready for me to cover her?" she asked.

I stood, nodded, and stepped back from the edge. Lark held her hands out and waved them across the front of her body in a single smooth motion. The pile of dirt beside the open grave slid into the hole with a sound not unlike rushing water. The cascading patter of pebbles and dirt hitting the quilt, covering Milly, was too much and I stumbled backward. A set of muscular arms caught me.

Liam, or Faris (depending who was in charge of the body they currently shared), held me against his chest. "She truly did love you, Rylee. And she wanted you to succeed against Orion. That is something to hang on to."

Again, all I could do was nod as tears slipped down my face. But I was not the only one grieving. Beside Milly's grave was a second hole. One for Frank, the young necromancer, nephew to Agent Valley, and most recently, Pamela's first love.

Pamela sat beside Frank's body, touching his hair, smoothing it back as tears wet her face. I sat on the grass beside her.

"Pam, it's time."

"I know." She hiccupped a sob back. "I think I loved him a little. Is it bad to say I didn't love him a lot?"

I slid an arm around her shoulders and hugged her to my side. "No, it isn't bad. You were both young. Loving him at all is a blessing, I think."

Lark crouched on the other side of Pam, her dark brown leather vest and khaki pants blending with the soil piled to the side. "Rylee is right. Love is a blessing."

"He died because of love," Pamela spit out, and I felt her anger rising like a living creature inside her.

I tightened my hold on her. "Yes. The same as I would lay down my life for any of you. Love makes you bold in ways you might not ever be otherwise. Like you tackling Orion when he came for me. You saved my life almost at the cost of your own."

Seconds ticked by, and slowly, she began to lean into me, her body sagging as the anger in her eased. "It hurts so badly, though. He was too young."

I looked over her to Lark. Like me, Lark's eyes were not normal in any way, shape, or form. One was gold, the other green. Unblinking, she gave me a tight nod.

The time for grieving was over; we had a world to save and a demon to stop.

"Pamela, it will get better. Right now, though, we have to go. We have three days before Erik gets here with Marcella and Zane. Three days to kill Orion and make him pay for everything he's done to us."

Her body tensed. She leaned forward and kissed Frank gently on the lips. "I'm sorry I didn't love you more, Frank. But thank you for fighting for me. For saving me when you didn't have to."

She stood and stepped back, brushing my arm off her shoulders. Holding her hand out, she wove her magic around Frank and lifted him into the air, carefully lowering him into the hole Lark created. "Goodbye, Frank."

Lark held her hand out, but Pamela beat her to it, shifting the dirt into the hole. The elemental stared at Pam. "You have a lot of our blood running through your veins. After this is done, would you consider training with me?"

Pamela blinked at her. "But I'm a witch."

Lark laughed softly. "All supernaturals are derived from elementals. Our bloodlines mixed with the humans and we got witches, Trackers, Readers, Harpies." She waved her hand in the air as if to envelope everything.

I'd suspected something along those lines, but hearing it outright and from an elemental . . . .

And the Blood of the Lost? I wanted her to say. Maybe even needed her to say.

"Spirit elemental blood is the most formidable in many ways." Lark let out a sigh before going on. "It boosts the powers already inherent to a bloodline. Whatever the powers are. In your case, Rylee, it made you a Tracker. All Trackers carry Blood of the Lost."

"Which is just another word for a Spirit elemental?" Pamela asked.

The three of us walked across the yard toward Giselle's home, Peta following at Lark's heels. Looking like an ordinary gray and white housecat, she was Lark's familiar. She could shift into the form of a snow leopard when needed, which was rather handy at times. Since they'd been reunited, Peta hadn't left Lark's side.

Lark nodded. "Yes, in a way. The other elemental families wiped out the Spirit elementals because they were so strong, and able to manipulate things to their will. After they were hunted down, there was a little of their blood here and there, diluted at best. Except in a few cases. Rylee and I are the last of our bloodline."

My feet froze to the ground. "*Our* bloodline?"

Lark glanced at me. "Yes. Do you not realize we are related?"

My eyes about dropped out of my fucking head. "How?"

She frowned, thinking hard. "I'm not sure where exactly our ties are, but I think you are a cousin. My mother's brother had one child with a human. Your grandmother is my understanding. So, yes, we are cousins."

Too much information all at once for me, yet I had a feeling there was a reason behind this sudden deluge. "Why are you telling me this now?"

Her mouth quirked upward into a big smile. "Final confession. We are going to war, Rylee. If I die, I want to make sure you know exactly what you are. We are the last two."

I shook my head, chills rippling through me. "No, not the last. I have a daughter."

Lark's eyes flashed wide and then she laughed. "Then that is a blessing. Our story won't end if we die. She will carry it forward for us."

Pamela gave a huff. "Rylee isn't dying."

I couldn't help the warm fuzzies that flickered through me. I stopped on the threshold of the door and looked into the backyard at those left standing with me against Orion.

Blaz, his wings healed by Pamela, was the first who caught my attention. His eyes found mine and my connection to him told me he was incredibly happy.

You'd be happy too if you went from not being able to walk ever again to being put back together.

"I know," I said softly.

Berget stood quietly off to one side of Blaz, her bright blonde hair catching the last of the starlight as it faded. My sister, the one I'd fought so hard for, had her happy ending. Though she was a vampire, she was no longer under the thrall of those who controlled her. A gentle laugh rolled from her lips and Eve squawked a laugh in response.

Eve and Marco sat by each other. They were quite possibly the last two Harpies left in the world, and yet they came with us, even if it meant the extinction of their species. They knew the stakes.

Then there was Charlie with his peg leg and unfailingly-cheery attitude, despite being taken prisoner by Orion and almost killed. The brownie stood barely three feet in height, yet he would fight at my side.

Cactus was Lark's best friend, and a fire elemental. While he was powerful, he'd been hidden away from the world for a long time. His imprisonment meshed with what had happened to Lark, and why she'd been confined in the oubliette for so many years. Yet he, too, was here, ready to fight to the death.

The newest and oldest of my friends was the six-foot-plus gangly teenager with jet black hair and golden eyes. He glanced at me.

Alex.

If I squinted and looked at him with my second sight, I could see the werewolf he'd been, trapped between forms until Pamela healed him. He grinned at me, a wide, white-toothed grin, and gave me two thumbs up, mouthing two words.

Yuppy doody.

God, I loved him. He was my heart, like the brother and best friend I'd always wanted rolled into one goofy, show-stealing, hairy bundle.

Then there was Liam. The first and only love of my life.

His spirit was trapped in Faris's body, until they found a way to separate. And yet if they did, he might be lost to me forever. He stood beside Alex, talking about something quietly. But like Alex, he felt my gaze and looked my way, blue eyes rimmed with silvery gold filled with a heat so strong I had to turn away in order to keep it together.

Until it was only Liam, I couldn't look at him with the same heat. Faris was a beautiful man, and while he held Liam's spirit in his body, the temptation was too fucking great. Fucking being the word, indeed.

I thought of our friends on the other side of the water in England, waiting for word from us. Doran, Will, Deanna, India, Louisa, Crystal, Calliope, and Mer were amongst the last of the supernaturals. All waiting for me to give the battle cry. Time to lay down their lives in the hopes I stopped Orion.

No pressure.

Pamela touched my arm, pulling me out of my thoughts. "Where do we go from here? Do you know?"

I let out a slow breath and would have answered, but Lark interrupted. "We have one more team member to add to this ragtag group before we go any further."

That was news to me.

"We do?"

She crossed her arms over her chest. "Yes, and he's on the West Coast, so I suggest we get moving."

Of course he was on the West Coast—he couldn't be next door, that would be too easy. "How important is he?" Pamela asked.

Lark looked from her to me. "He will help Rylee decide if she's going to live or die in the battle with Orion. So I'd say pretty damn important."

Well, hell. That certainly changed things.

2
LIAM/FARIS

He stood by Alex, still struggling to believe the kid was no longer trapped as a werewolf. "You think you can shift?"

Alex gave a shrug. "I think so. But I'm kinda freaked out by the idea of trying. What if I get trapped again?"

Faris pushed his way forward and took over. "You remember anything from when you were stuck?"

Alex tipped his head to one side. "No, seems like I went to sleep and had really vivid dreams. Now I've woken and the dreams are over."

"It'll be like that again. The people around you— Rylee—will suffer more than you."

The once-submissive wolf glared at him. "That's got be Faris talking."

Liam took back control and drew in a deep breath, scenting the air. Faris didn't like when Liam ran the show, but they'd come to a basic understanding. Until the shit with Orion was done, they would have to work together, handing off the reins if one of them would deal better with things than the other. In this case, Liam knew he was better off dealing with Alex. "You don't smell submissive anymore. I think you should try now. You try when you're in a situation where it's do or die and you might—"

"Die," Alex finished with a nod. "Okay, here goes. Tell Rylee I'm sorry if I can't shift back." He slipped out of his clothes, a lopsided grin on his face. "For after."

The kid closed his eyes and his skin shimmered a split second before his body slid downward, black fur sprouting over him. His joints popped and tendons snapped as he shifted to the werewolf body he'd had before. Stuck somewhere between man and wolf.

Liam sucked in a sharp breath. Fuck, what if he'd been wrong? "Shift back. Now."

In the back of his head, he could feel Faris's curiosity. The vampire no longer had real ties to Alex, yet this was still something new. Something even he hadn't seen in all his years.

Alex grunted, his long tongue flopping out across his big white canines. "Why?"

"Do it," Liam snapped, using his strength as an Alpha to put more command into his words. Alex bowed his head and his body reversed the process, hair disappearing, body sliding back to a gangly teenage kid. Liam let out a slow breath.

Alex lifted his head, then grabbed his clothes. "Why you gotta be so damn bossy, boss?"

Faris took control, sliding forward with ease. Liam let him, feeling a deep sense of fatigue wash over him. Tired, he was so tired. For a moment, he felt Faris's concern for him.

"He's got to act bossy because he's an alpha, and for some stupid reason he cares for you," Faris said. "Now, let's see what Rylee has up her sleeve."

Alex bounded forward ahead of them, so much of him wolf-like even though no longer trapped in a wolf's form.

Pausing in mid-stride, Faris spoke to Liam. "Wolf, what's going on?"

Faris's words floated to him in a fog. *I feel like I'm slipping away.*

Faris stumbled to a stop. "No, you can't. Not now."

This was what Griffin had been talking about, the Veil being open and Liam's spirit moving on. This was not the time for him to leave and he knew it.

I don't know if I can stop it.

The vampire came to a standstill and they faced one another in a place that didn't truly exist. Liam stared at Faris.

"What are you doing?"

His jaw twitched. "Rylee won't survive without us. Without *both* of us. You know she won't."

"Knowing it and being able to do something about it are two different things." Liam did his best not to completely lose his shit. "The Veil is pulling me, isn't it? Now it's open, and my spirit wants to cross over."

Faris reached out and grabbed his hand. "You can't go. Doran said—" He shook his head and seemed to gather himself. "Doran said we *can* save her. He said she's going to die, prophecy dictates it. But you and I can save her. I don't know how, he just said we had to be there at the end. Both of us."

"I don't want to leave her, Faris," Liam said. "I don't."

"Then we have to bind ourselves together. It's the only way to keep you here. You willing to share her? For good, until this body dies?"

Even though time was slipping by, Liam hesitated. Faris was a master manipulator. More than once he'd seemed to be on Rylee's side, while he plotted his next move and set her up for whatever deeper game he played.

A tug shot through the middle of him, a jerk pulling him from Rylee.

"Do it. Bind us together."

He hoped he wasn't making a mistake.

Faris took his cutlass from his side and sliced through his palm. Blood welled, and even though Liam knew they weren't in the physical world, it still looked and smelled real. He held out his hand. Faris slid the cutlass across his palm. There was no pain at the cut.

They stared at each other. "I love her," Faris said softly. "I would do this for no other."

The vampire's words resonated with truth and Liam accepted there was no ulterior motive in him. Not this time. Faris was doing this for Rylee, to keep her alive.

To keep her safe. It was enough for him to trust the blood sucker.

Liam took the vampire's hand. "Now what?"

"The words to bind are simple. Blood to blood, soul to soul, two as one, neither alone."

He repeated the words and a gong seemed to toll within his chest cavity, resonating with the power of blood and the incantation. Their hands seemed to fuse and for just a split second he saw himself through Faris's eyes.

Blink.

Dark hair, silvery golden eyes, squared jaw, body scarred.

Blink.

Someone who stood in his way, forced him to change plans.

Blink.

An ally in saving the woman they both loved.

Blink.

Shouting in the distance, a voice calling to him, telling him to open his eyes. But how could they be closed when he was blinking? Or was his life flickering in and out of focus? Yes, his life. Did Faris fool him?

"I did not fool you, Wolf. We bound ourselves together." Sounded like Faris's voice, but Liam was in control of the body.

"You fucking well did what?" Rylee yelled above them even as she dropped to her knees and wrapped her arms around his neck.

He sucked in a sharp breath and realized Faris had given him the reins for the moment without asking. He lay on his back staring at the night sky through a swath of Rylee's auburn hair.

"What did he do to you, Liam?"

Putting a hand over hers, he gave her fingers a squeeze. "It's okay. Faris and I came to a perfect understanding."

Faris jumped forward. "More than an understanding. I bound him to me to keep his soul on this side of the Veil. He was being pulled away. I didn't think it prudent given the circumstances."

Rylee let go of him and stepped away. "What do you mean *bound* him?"

Faris gave her a smile. "Liam will be a part of me on a . . . let's say, long-term basis. He won't be crossing the Veil anytime soon. I'd rather share you than lose you, and he agreed."

Her mouth dropped open and then snapped shut with a click. Behind her, the tall elemental, Lark, shook her head slowly. "You two boys are in for a tongue lashing."

Rylee backed away. "I can't believe you did this."

Liam forced Faris back and held a hand out to her. "Rylee, I was slipping away. Faris stopped it and I trust him in this. This time there are no games with him. I should know, I'm in his head."

There was a moment of surprise from Faris and then a wash of gratitude. Not many people had stood up for Faris in his life.

Even his "brothers," created by the same master vampire, who had gone with him to destroy the Emperor and Empress, never stood up for him.

Rylee closed those amazing eyes of hers and bowed her head. "You're telling me I can have you, but only if I have both of you?"

He let out a soft breath. "Until we deal with Orion. Then maybe there will be another solution."

Inside his head, Faris laughed. *There is no way out. We are together in this now.*

Perhaps the conversation would have gone further; more likely it wouldn't have. It was hard to say with the sudden roar from Blaz as he projected his voice to the whole group.

Rylee, we have company and they aren't here for tea and cookies.

3
PAMELA

"**P**amela, go high with Eve. See how bad it is," Rylee shouted. "Charlie, get Doran, tell him to gather everyone who can fight and meet us at the old farmhouse as fast as he fucking can. Don't bring anyone who can't kick ass." She paused and yanked a sheet of paper out of her back pocket, thrusting it at him. "Tell him to follow this to a fucking T or my ass will be fried." Rylee barked out orders and I did as she said, running for Eve.

"You gots it, lassie! I'll tell Doran to bees doing everything on yous paper!" Charlie bolted in front of me toward the backdoor, the paper Rylee had given him clutched in his hand. I saw a few words on it written in big, bold lettering.

Unicorn hair rope. What the hell did she need unicorn hair rope for? My curiosity almost got the better of me and I took a half step to follow Charlie. He leapt through the doorway, twisting the Veil as only a brownie could to travel before I asked him to stop. I caught a flash of the interior of Jack's mansion and then the image was gone along with the brownie.

Rylee's words resonated in my head. The old farmhouse? It was burnt to the ground. Why would she go there? As far as I knew there was nothing left except the barn.

I climbed aboard Eve, and Alex jumped behind me, his arms encircling my waist. "Hang on, Pamie. I'm coming with you."

Eve launched into the air and it didn't take long to see how big the problem was. Blaz was right, no one was coming for tea and cookies. More like with pitchforks and torches.

A mob of humans at least five thousand deep stumbled our way. Like the zombies we'd dealt with in England when I'd first met Rylee. Only these zombies weren't dead.

"Shit," Alex said, his hold on me tightening. "Orion moves fast. We've got to get everyone out of here."

Eve let out a hunting screech, making the hair on the back of my neck stand. "Pamela, can you slow them down without hurting them?"

I held out my hands, shaky and drained after my fight with Orion and all the healing I'd done. "I'll try."

A bolt of lightning arced through the sky at my request and hit the ground at the front of the mob. They sidestepped the hole it made and kept coming. Three more lightning bolts slashed downward with the same result.

"They're mindless. They might as well be zombies," I shouted as my frustration rose.

"Eve," Alex said. "We'd better land. Everyone has to evacuate."

She dropped like a stone and Alex let out a sharp laugh. "I will never get enough of this."

I shook my head. Same old Alex; newer, more human package. Eve landed with a double hop and I jumped off. "Rylee, I think we'd better go. The humans are mindless and they will overrun us if we try to be gentle with them."

"Fucking hell," she snapped.

"Faris, can you open the Veil for us?" I asked.

Faris shook his head. "No. It hurts Liam too much."

What was this? Then why did he jump the Veil to go to Tian Shan and try to save the babies?

The question hit me the same time as the answer did: Marcella, Rylee and Liam's daughter. She was worth whatever cost Liam had to pay.

Rylee didn't question him as she strode toward Blaz. "Liam, you ride with Marco and Berget. Take the heavy curtains. We'll stop when the sun rises and wrap you two into burritos. The rest of you pick a ride; we're out of here."

Even though we moved fast, we were still too slow. The first humans came running around the corner, five or six across, their knives and guns raised. Madness in their eyes flickered with the torchlight. Rylee stepped into them, her swords whirling in the air. "Drive them back. If you have to kill them, do it."

I swallowed hard and raised my hands. Killing supernaturals attacking us was one thing; killing fairly harmless humans was something el—

The sound of a gun retort was followed by a sharp burning in my left forearm. I clamped my hand over it. I peeked under my fingers. Shot? I'd been shot. Not a deep wound; I was lucky the bullet had only skimmed me. The pain and shock snapped me out of my reluctance to hurt anyone. Flicking my hands outward, I sent a roll of pure power into the first wave of humans. It would fling them in all directions, at least fifteen feet back.

Yet even with that, though, there were too many of them. Like roaches swarming an infested house, they just kept coming, climbing over each other faster and faster.

Lark set a quick perimeter, dropping the earth in a huge hollow around us like a moat, which Cactus then filled with fire. A good number of the humans, though, were already on our side of the fiery barrier. Peta shifted to her snow leopard form and kept the humans from getting too close to Lark, her big paws downing them with ease.

I backed up, pulling my short sword and grateful Rylee insisted I learn more than magic when it came to fighting. The first human lunged at me and I didn't bother with a spell. With a swift twist of my wrist, I slashed him across the chest, opening him. He fell to his knees, blinking at me. "Why would you hurt me?"

I stumbled back, horrified. "Pain makes them clear-headed."

"Fuck" was all I heard from Rylee and then nothing more. I turned to see her tackled by eight or nine human men. They piled on her like she had the ball in a rugby game.

Blaz swept his wings forward and then back again, knocking most of the men off. Rylee rolled, and was on her feet in a flash, rubbing at her neck. The men who'd been attacking her lay on the ground, seemingly stunned.

Everyone mount. We have to get out of here. There are too many of these minions of Orion, Blaz snapped, his words hitting us all like a kick in the ass.

Alex ran for Eve, and I followed him. Berget and Liam mounted Marcus with the heavy curtains draped between them. Cactus and Lark with Peta climbed up Blaz behind Rylee and then we were all in the air with a whoosh of wings. Below us, there came a smattering of gunshots and a few cries of pain. I grinned over my shoulder at Alex. "Stupid humans."

He grinned back. "Yeah, and I was one of them."

I blanched and he dropped his forehead to my shoulder, laughing softly, the same way he had hundreds of times before. Same old Alex.

"Rylee," I shouted across the divide between Eve and Blaz, "Where are we going?"

She looked to me and then over her shoulder to the elementals behind her. "That's up to Lark."

Lark gave a nod and lifted her right hand. "Head to the West Coast. You're about to see something not even other supernaturals get to see. I'm taking you to the Rim."

Alex breathed softly behind me, his exhalation ruffling my hair. "The Rim? What's that, do you think?"

"I don't know, but I guess we're about to find out."

Blaz banked hard to the right and we did a one-eighty, heading straight west.

Eve cocked her head and glanced back at us. "Alex, how do you feel now?"

He shrugged and leaned forward. "I don't remember much of my time stuck in between forms, Eve. I have emotions attached to people, but that's about it. I know who my family is." He tightened his hold on me for a brief moment. "That's all that matters, I think."

She bobbed her head and swung closer to Blaz. I wanted to ask Rylee if she felt the same thing I did: escaping the human mob had been too easy.

Like maybe Orion was driving us toward something. I swallowed the fears spooled in me. Whatever we would face, we'd do it together. I placed a hand over Alex's that rested on my stomach. I was with my family again, and we were whole in more ways than one. We'd lost people we loved—Frank's face seemed to float in front of me for a moment—but we were together. And I had to believe that would be enough.

Please, let it be enough.

4
LARK

The air around us was cool, with a hint of the coming dawn. The breeze and the sounds of the world around us were glorious to my freedom-starved body and mind.

Who was I kidding? If the air had been filled with smoke and ash, I would have been as happy.

Behind me, Cactus sat quietly. "Your father isn't going to be happy you were broken out of the oubliette."

That was an understatement. Then again, my father hadn't been happy with me for a very long time. I was getting used to disappointing him.

Peta sniffed, sitting in my lap, curled around herself. Her green eyes all but glowed in the dim light. "Cactus, don't point out the obvious."

It felt as though I'd never gone missing, their banter back to where it left off.

"No, he's not going to be happy. But there is no choice but to go to the Rim and get Jonathan. You know that."

I felt more than saw him nod. Cactus was my oldest friend, the one who knew me the best and loved me despite the dark spots in my life.

And yet, I wished Ash were with me too. I missed him fiercely, as though a piece of me was gone, shattered against the rocks of lost hope. He'd been the one to train me as an Ender and protector of my home; the one to fight at my side as I'd struggled to find my place in the world. I closed my eyes, envisioning his face as I'd done every day I'd sat in the oubliette.

I kept a hand on Peta, letting her calm flow through me. Having her back was at least one wound bandaged. We'd been apart for too many years. A soft purr rumbled through her, as she picked up on the direction of my thoughts.

There was a creak of the leather rigging as Rylee twisted in her seat, and I opened my eyes. The swirling colors of her irises didn't bother me; they weren't that different from my own strangely-colored eyes.

"Jonathan. That's the kid we're going after?"

"Not really a kid. He'd be about sixteen, now, I guess," I said. "He is the reason you and I met. I wonder if Giselle knew we had to meet before this moment, and set it up. The shadow walker that stole Jonathan never really had a great purpose for taking him."

She frowned and I watched her struggle with the new information. "I'd like to say Giselle wouldn't fuck around like that, but when she saw something she thought needed doing, she did it." She said.

"Yes, she was like that." I glanced at Peta, as I debated how much to say about Jonathan. "The automatic writer; he's not going to seem all that important at first. He will be another psychic who can give you a glimpse into your future."

Rylee shook her head. "Not possible. Immune, remember?"

"He will have ways around that," I replied. "The reality is, he already knows he's going to be at the final battle. He saw it as a kid. And while certain players are going to appear more important than him"—I paused, looking for the right words—"He will be able to show you things no one else can."

"A whole new world?" Her eyebrow arched and a smile flitted over her lips.

I stared at her. "I hear the mockery in your voice, Rylee. You forget that every person in your circle has a reason for being here. We are all needed to defeat Orion. One piece missing, no matter how miniscule, could cause our failure and Orion's triumph."

The smile faded, and her eyes swirled faster, the tri-colors blending and diving into one another. She took a slow breath. "Okay, I get it. But there are other things that are fucking dodgy right now, Lark."

"What?"

"There are four horsemen out there: war, famine, pestilence, and death. I don't think that human mob was our real stumbling block, do you?"

Damn, she reminded me of . . . no . . . I wasn't going there. My past memories were all I had trapped in that damn oubliette. And they were raw, like open wounds gouged over and over, never allowed to heal.

I stared into the dark sky ahead of us. "I wouldn't be surprised if we have at least one of them waiting for us along the way. Demons and their goblin-piss surprise attacks. I hate them."

Her eyes flickered. "Have you dealt with many demon attacks before?"

This was where things got sticky. I couldn't tell her everything, not yet, maybe not ever.

Peta gave a slight shake of her head. This was one of those times I was glad Rylee and the other supernaturals couldn't hear my familiar. Only my own kind could. "You can't tell her," Peta said. That's what I was afraid of.

"I've dealt with them enough that I know to be careful and always assume the worst."

Rylee laughed, but it was bitter and cynical. "Like that's any different than the rest of my life."

I wasn't a touchy-feely kind of person, but I could feel her spirit flagging, spiraling downward. Though I didn't know her well, I knew it wasn't like her to mope.

Reaching out, I put a hand on her shoulder and squeezed gently. "Don't think like that, Rylee. That is what Orion wants. He wants you to forget why you're here, why you're so important, and what it is you're saving."

A quick roll of her shoulders removed my hand. "Don't try and soften this, Lark. I fucking well know what I'm going into."

I grabbed her shoulder and half-spun her to face me. "Perhaps I know more than you think, you little fool. If you go into this battle with a hard heart, he will win. Do you understand me? If you go in believing the worst, he will win. If you go in having already given up, he will win."

Her jaw flexed and her eyes narrowed, the three colors swirling faster as her temper rose. "Let go of me, Lark."

"Not until I'm sure you understand."

She shoved my hand off again. "Don't fucking touch me, elemental."

"Then don't be stupid and think you know everything. You don't." I leaned back, glaring at her as she glared right back at me.

Below us the dragon let out a low rumble.

I hate to interrupt, but I need to talk to Rylee.

I let out a breath. Cactus put a hand on either side of my hips. "She'll come around, Lark. She has to."

That was the thing. If Rylee couldn't find it in her to still believe in the impossible, believe we could defeat Orion, we were done before we even stepped foot onto the battlefield.

She had to find that courage again. That strength had brought her this far. Worm shit, why of all times did this have to be the moment she started to doubt herself?

I had less than three days to help her find her heart strength.

Shit on a green stick, this was going to be tough.

5
RYLEE

Take a breath, Rylee. She is trying to help you. Blaz's voice flowed over me and with it a sense of calm. But I didn't want to be calm. I wanted to be angry because the anger helped me block the fear swiftly wrapping around my heart. How the hell Lark had known, I could only guess.

Her connection to Spirit, Rylee; she can sense when you falter. Hell, even I felt it. Why now? What has brought you so low?

I scrubbed a hand over my face, then back around to my neck, rubbing at a bump that had risen there. The men who tackled me at Giselle's place had smashed me good and bruises sprouted all over my back and shoulders. But the piercing stab in the back of my neck really freaked me out. If Blaz hadn't knocked the men off, I would've had my head cut from my shoulders.

I didn't want to speak out loud like normal with Blaz, not with Lark behind me. We might have been cousins, but that didn't mean I was totally comfortable with how easily she read me.

Slowly I formulated my thoughts for Blaz. The enormous loss of supernaturals due to the pox circulating the world, the deaths of Milly and Frank, the way Liam had to bind himself to Faris so he wouldn't leave me again. And above all those things, the fact that Tian Shan was compromised and my daughter was no longer safe.

My heart clenched. That was the crux of it. I couldn't get past the fact she wasn't safe, that she was somewhere in the world and Orion was looking for her. A full body shudder rippled through me. My sweet little girl, hunted by demons.

When Lark put her hand on my shoulder a second time, I didn't shove it off. "Rylee. She is safe with your uncle. He's a demon slayer; he can protect her better than anyone else right now."

"Blaz, you bastard." I hiccupped. He'd ratted me out to her; there was no other way she could have known my thoughts.

You need all of us, and we need you to be open. Let her help you.

"I can't help her, dragon," Lark said. "This is a pain I don't know, and can only guess at. But it can drive you, Rylee, or it can drag you down. You know that. Why don't you Track her?"

I swallowed hard. "Because Orion was tracing me when I Tracked. What if he could somehow walk the process backward and find her?"

Lark sucked in a sharp breath. "Clever girl. I'd bet that's exactly what he's set you up for. So let's throw him off kilter. Track Jonathan. Bring the demons to us and let's take them on my turf." Her voice hardened as she spoke.

I glanced over my shoulder at her. "Your people will be right in the middle then."

"Where they should have been all along," she said. "It's about time they woke up and realized they are a part of this world whether or not they want to be."

Somewhat reluctantly, I sent out a thread, Tracking Jonathan. I knew his name, I remembered what he looked like when he was ten. Freaky little boy he was then, I assumed he'd be the same.

He had dirty blond hair, with a narrow face gaunt with malnourishment, and his eyes wandered in opposite directions. I got a solid ping from him, and in the distance I could feel the weight of eyes on me.

Red eyes flickering like firelight flashed in my mind and then gone. I shuddered and scrubbed at my arms.

"I'm sure Orion is watching," I found myself whispering.

"Good. He'll send one of his generals, I think."

"Good?" I snorted. "Your idea of good is very different than mine. Don't you think it would be better to go in, snag Jonathan, and head back to where the battle is going to happen?"

Lark snorted right back at me. "Wouldn't you rather kill a couple of Orion's generals first? Weed down his supporters and give us a chance to take him out?"

Damn, she had a very good point. I rubbed the back of my neck again, fighting the feelings of despair festering in me.

"Besides, the more attention we keep on us, the safer your daughter will be."

A sudden thought hit me. "Lark, if I die, who will stop Orion? Marcella isn't a Tracker like me." That had been confirmed when she'd been born. My daughter would follow in her father's steps as a Guardian.

"You aren't going to like my answer, Rylee. How about we just focus on you taking Orion out?"

Blaz tipped his head so I could see one eye. *An unanswered question and Rylee go together like oil and water. You might as well tell her, elemental, or you will have no peace.*

She let out a sigh. "Bear with me, this explanation will not be quick."

I nodded and she went on. "Nature abhors imbalance, Rylee. If your sister had never been taken, your Tracker abilities would never have come on line. You would have been 'human' for all intents and purposes.

"Only when Orion opened the Veil and sent his demons through, would your Tracker abilities have come on line. But you would have had no one to train you. No one to help you, and you would be here, right now, likely without a single supernatural friend to stand with you against the demons."

"Fucking hell," I whispered, seeing my life in a different light. "All the shit that happened to me, all the people I met . . . if Berget hadn't been taken, none of that would have happened."

Marco swung closer and Berget stared at me with eyes that were not her own. The vampire Empress spoke through her. "You're welcome, Tracker."

"You knew?" I choked out.

Berget's head nodded. "Everything we did, we did knowing it would push you, that it would force your abilities to open."

Holy fucking hell in a handbasket. My mind reeled as I looked back at the events of my life, seeing the hands of the two master vampires moving things around as if they were chess pieces. "So you were manipulating this from the beginning? This is all you?"

She tipped her head to the side and shrugged. "As much as I was able. I knew you would need a push to become a Tracker. What better way than to take the sister you loved so dearly?"

And there it was, the reason I'd become what I was; the reason I'd lost my sister and began the journey that brought me here. Marco swung farther out again, effectively ending the conversation.

Lark touched my arm, drawing my attention back to her. "Rylee, if you succeed in killing Orion, and sealing the Veil, Marcella will continue on the path she is set on now, to become a guardian like her father."

Berget's words and now Lark's clamored for the front of my brain, but I already knew what was coming, yet I still had to ask. A chill worked its way down my spine. "And if I don't kill him?"

There was a heavy pause in the air and I knew what she'd say, but I waited. Needed to hear the words out loud.

"Then her Tracking abilities will come on line and the task will be laid on her shoulders to defeat the demons and close the Veil."

I spun fully around in my seat to face her. "She's a baby, how can that even be?"

Lark's eyes were sad. "Have you not read the full ceremony? There is no fighting for you, Rylee. Only sacrifice. Your blood is what seals the Veil. Nothing else."

My jaw dropped, I fully admit I hadn't taken into account how literal the prophecies could possibly be. "You mean you'd take her and sacrifice her?"

Lark's eyes flashed. "If you're dead, I will do what I must to make sure this world survives."

"You're a fucking bitch," I snarled at her, my hands automatically going for my weapons. I couldn't help it; she threatened my daughter.

"No, you're the bitch if you don't pull your shit together. Do you see now why it's so important we do this right? We have one shot, Tracker. One shot to save *everyone*."

I lowered my hands from where they'd gripped my swords, her words sinking in. I'd known all along what was required, accepted it, and moved toward it. I'd faced death so many times, it didn't faze me anymore. Not when it came to my own life.

I'd always survived.

I'd always come out on top.

"You're telling me I'm going to die. There's no other way?" The words felt hollow in my mouth, like I wasn't really saying them. My neck throbbed in time with my heartbeat.

Lark closed her eyes and bowed her head again. "That is what the prophecies say, Rylee. The ceremony is there in black and white. There is no way around this. I have been trying to find a way to kill Orion and save you." She lifted her head, her eyes glimmering with unshed tears. "I cannot see a way to do both."

Our conversation was interrupted by Marco swinging close again, his wingtips brushing Blaz's flank. "Sun is rising; we've got to bag these two."

Liam stared at me; I knew it was him by how much silvery gold rimmed Faris's blue eyes. No words passed between us, but I knew he could tell something was wrong by the way he frowned.

The two Harpies and Blaz dropped out of the sky at the next available clear spot, which turned out to be a large boxed store parking lot. As early as it was, there were a few cars scattered here and there. Easily missed by the winged creatures.

Unless said winged creatures were feeling rather destructive. Blaz landed on top of a large burgundy pick-up truck with fancy rims and chrome accents. His claws wrapped around it and he crushed the truck cab like a tin can as he settled on it like a perch.

"Necessary?" I asked as I slid off his back and landed in the lopsided bed of the truck.

Sharpening my claws on the metal. He gave me a wink and I managed a smile. I knew what he was doing. A distraction might have worked for anything else, but not this.

Not a death sentence.

Eve hopped on the tarmac. "I don't like this, it feels so unnatural under my talons."

Alex and Pam still sat astride her back, talking and laughing with her, and I had a brief moment of seeing the future.

Of Alex working with Pamela, and Eve carting them around the country as they . . . did what? There was no way for them to Track children. Pamela turned as if sensing my eyes on her. Her hair blew out around her and I saw her as she would be. A powerful witch with the heart of a lion. She would go after children; she would find a way.

My chest constricted, and I felt like I was saying goodbye. Lark's words hammered home in a way that no other person's could. Every other time someone threatened me, they'd been my enemy trying to kill me.

Lark was my friend, and she was trying to save me.

And even she knew it was impossible. Liam came behind me and I turned into him before he touched me, burying my face against his chest.

"What's wrong?"

"I'm scared, Liam." The words slipped out of me and I couldn't take them back. He wrapped his arms tightly around me.

"It's okay to be scared. This isn't the first time."

"Not like this." I breathed him in, not caring that he and Faris were stuck together. He kissed the top of my head.

"No matter what, we will be okay. You have to believe that."

I wanted to, damn I wanted to more than I could express. To be that girl again who could go in blind to a situation, swinging her swords, and still come out on top. This time, that wasn't going to work. I couldn't stop the doubt any more than I could stop Alex from being a goofball.

Eve let out a raucous squawk. "Rylee, something is coming our way."

Of course there was.

I stepped back from Liam and looked in the direction Eve stared. On the horizon, backlit by the slowly rising sun, a cloud formation swirled toward us. Black-and-gray storm clouds wove in and out of each other, like a wave of water crashing toward us in the sky.

I took another step toward it. "Lark, tell me that belongs to an elemental you know."

She shifted her stance, and her hand went to the spear hanging at her side. "Wish I could. Looks like Orion is not wasting any time trying to finish us off."

"Us? You said I had to be the one to die."

Liam sucked in a sharp breath and I cursed myself. My eyes stayed on Lark. She flicked an eyebrow high. "You think you're the only key to finishing the demons? It'll take both of us, Rylee. If I die, you can't kill Orion any more than I could without you."

"Oh, fuck."

"Yes, that," she said, pulling her spear from her side and sliding the two pieces together. "Of the four horseman, I believe this is Pestilence. Tied to the wind that helps him spread the diseases he carries."

Faris gave a grunt. "Has he not already done that? The whole world has been down with the pox for months."

Lark glared at him. "Only two of us here have true immunity to the diseases Pestilence can spread. Rylee and the dragon. Which means when this demon gets here, he will down the rest of us as fast as possible, leaving her on her own to face him."

"How can you possibly know that?" I asked, even as I weighed her words and saw the validity in them.

"Because it's what *I'd* do. Wipe out the support, and then kill the main objective." Her eyes were hard, and I realized we would learn why she was called "The Destroyer."

Maybe a little unethical of me, but I was kinda excited to see what she could do.

6
RYLEE

Lark set us in formation in a matter of seconds. Pamela and Alex on Eve at the rear; Lark, Peta, and Cactus on Marco on the front line. Blaz and I would circle behind the demon and hit him from the back.

Faris/Liam and Berget were sent into the store to get out of the quickly rising sun.

As I figured, that went over like a ton of shitty bricks.

"I'm not leaving you," Faris snarled, a growl trickling past his lips. Berget smacked him hard, her hand leaving a sharp imprint of her fingers on his cheek, and I had to fight not to smile. I loved her even more when she put him in his place.

"Listen, dumbass. The sun is rising. You have to let her do this on her own. You have to trust that she can survive this," she snapped.

Faris glared at my sister. "It's a demon of the apocalypse she's facing. This is as bad as it gets."

Berget shook her head. "No, it's not. *Orion* is as bad as it gets. When she faces Orion you do whatever you can then. But not now. Right now we need to survive to help her with the battle."

She grabbed his arm and dragged him toward the building sharing the parking lot. I watched them go, wondering if I'd see them again.

I didn't even hug them goodbye or tell Berget that I loved her.

Stop fucking moaning and groaning. This is your life, fucking well deal with it. Blaz's words were a perfect echo of Jack's; so much so, I actually looked around with my second sight to see if Jack's spirit floated close by.

I sucked in a sharp breath and ran for Blaz. "Thanks, I needed that ass kicking."

Yeah, the soft words weren't doing shit. You've got others for that garbage.

My lips twitched as I buckled myself into his harness. He launched into the air, his wings sending litter skittering across the parking lot. I took a deep breath and tried to send the fear away. Blaz's words helped, but I still couldn't shake the dread that clung to my heart—not completely.

Marco waited, his big eyes seeming larger in the early morning light. He clacked his beak a few times as he tread air.

Lark looked at me. "We're drawing his attention. Get your ass in gear and swing behind him. We don't have a lot of time, so don't dawdle."

So much for soft words from others. Blaz and I peeled away to the south and I put a hand on his neck. "There won't be much surprise if we come at him from behind."

What are you thinking?

"Dive bomb him."

That's a one-shot move, Rylee. At least if we miss from behind, gravity isn't working against us.

He winged away fast, and I knew what the demon would see if he looked our way. We were making a run for it, leaving our friends behind.

Something about the setup was wrong, though. "Blaz, go high."

Shit, Rylee, this is not the plan. Lark has it right.

I reached for my crossbow on my back. "Well, she isn't running the show, is she?" I wasn't being petulant. Something felt off about this demon's attack. There was no way to put my finger on it, so I opened myself to Blaz and let him feel what my instincts warned: this was not the way to fight Pestilence. If we did this Lark's way, something very bad would happen.

Blaz grunted as my emotions and thoughts rolled through him.

What do you want to do, then?

"The demon is after me, right?"

Rylee . . . .

"So let's make sure he sees us and comes our way, instead of theirs. Unless, of course, you don't think you can outfly him?"

Don't insult me.

He dipped his wings and within seconds we were turned, heading straight for the rolling black clouds. I couldn't see Eve and Marco, or any of my friends, but a bright light lit the darkness that was the demon, like a nuclear bomb exploding inside of it.

That was either Pamela or Cactus, but I was betting on Pamela. She wouldn't wait, she'd rush in like the headstrong girl she was. Like I encouraged her to be.

"Hurry, Blaz, we have to get to that fucker before he gets to them." Already the wind had gained momentum. I could see the particles of disease on the air spinning outward. Infecting my family with whatever deadly disease he had up his fucking sleeve.

Blaz stretched his neck, flattening his body as his wings picked up speed. Another light lit the clouds, like a storm brewed deep within. For a split second, I thought I saw a figure in the middle of the maelstrom. The demon floated what looked like a hundred feet above the tarmac of the parking lot, hiding within the smoke and mirrors he'd created with the storm. All around him darted tiny lights, like oversized fireflies.

The edge of the clouds reached out to us and I took a deep breath. The scent of road tar filled my nostrils, a scent I hadn't smelled since my first run-in with a demon almost a year ago. It clung to my tongue and coated my throat as I breathed, gagging me.

Mist and shadows wrapped around us and the demon spun slowly, his face a mixture of pleasure and surprise. He was lean and wiry with long hair that curled around his face. Young, was my first thought; he couldn't be much older than me. Or at least, the body he'd stolen wasn't older than me.

All around us lightning danced, and through what I could feel of Blaz, it was his doing; a strength of his we hadn't used often. Able to control the weather, he broke up the storm and sent the clouds at the front of it skittering away.

I unbuckled the harness and stood as I pulled a sword from my back. I pointed it at Pestilence. "You want me? Then you'd better get your ass over here and see if—"

Claws dug into my shoulder, slicing through the leather jacket, and I was yanked upward, clear of Blaz. I swung my sword over my head without looking, cutting the creature's legs off. They fell away from me, the claws releasing in death as a scream rent the air, like the cry of a rabbit being tortured by an overzealous cat.

I fell, blood pouring around me from the creature's now amputated legs. Before I could wonder how high I'd been taken, I hit Blaz's back and rolled, stopping when I came against his spine. "What are they?"

Blaz did not answer me.

Pestilence did.

"My pets? You don't know what they are?" The demon floated slowly toward us, his feet stepping as if he were on the ground, not a hundred feet up. He was dressed in a suit and tie like a high-end businessman, right down to his polished shoes. I found myself staring as he tugged the cufflinks on his shirt.

"I'm going to kill them."

"Ah, but I'm so proud of them. My first of what will be many creations now that I am free of the Veil. Flying monkeys are something humans invented. I wondered if I could actually create them and . . . I could. Lovely, don't you think?"

I glanced where he pointed. Above us were indeed flying monkeys. Though they were like no monkeys I'd ever seen—even discounting the wings. Their bodies were out of proportion, limbs askew, eyes dead. And they were silent; their wings barely moving enough to keep them afloat.

"They are infected with the pox, all of them. Just in case your friends were wondering." He flicked his hand at the monkeys and they plummeted from the sky, heading toward my friends.

My family.

Blaz didn't wait for me to tell him to go after them. He tucked his wings tight and dropped, lightning dancing around us as he tried to take them out. I swung my crossbow around and shot three monkeys, dropping them out of the sky. Three of more than a hundred of the infected little bastards.

Behind us, laughter echoed through the sky. "So predictable."

My heart clenched, but I didn't care that I was predictable. Not in that moment. The monkeys screeched, coming to life as they seemed to understand the dragon behind them was doing serious damage. I swung my crossbow to my back and pulled both swords.

"Grin at them, Blaz."

What the hell—

"Bare your teeth. It's a challenge."

I stood on his back and grinned at the stupid fuckers for all I was worth. "Come on, you little assholes!"

The first monkey who saw me let out an unearthly howl as he arched his back, wings flapping furiously.

Like a rocket, he dropped toward me, his wings not even fluttering for a second as he came with all four clawed feet outstretched.

I swung my sword hard, slicing through his stomach and cutting him completely in half. He fell to either side of me; his death seemed to be a signal to his buddies.

En masse, they attacked.

"Blaz, get Eve and Pamela closer. We need firepower. But not too close! I don't want them infected."

You got it.

The monkeys swarmed, ignoring the dragon, coming straight for me. Fine and dandy as far as I was concerned. The first wave leapt in threes, one from each side and straight on. I kicked out at the one on my left as I slashed my sword to the one on my right.

The one in the middle slammed into me, driving me to Blaz's back. We rolled and another monkey jumped onto my back, grabbed my hair, and yanked me toward him.

In the distance, Pestilence laughed, a deep belly laugh that drove my anger to a peak I didn't know existed. I swung my elbow back, catching the monkey behind me in the face and launching him off. I might have lost hair as I sent him flying, but I didn't slow for a second. Couldn't, not if we were making it through this shit.

I drove my sword through the first monkey, then the second, then the third. Over and over I slashed through Pestilence's creations, taking them apart piece by piece until I was slick with blood and my arms shook with fatigue.

Their teeth found my bare skin, and their claws swiped my face more than once, barely missing my eyes on several occasions.

One grabbed at my legs, tried to yank me off my feet. I stomped at him, then kicked him hard toward Blaz's head. The dragon snapped his mouth over the flying monkey, crushing him and then spitting him out.

They taste like shit.

"Not a surprise," I breathed out as I spun on his back. "They're demon made."

The minutes ticked by, and I wondered at Pestilence and his motivation. Why the fuck hadn't he tried to take me while I was dealing with his flying butt monkeys?

What kind of game was the demon playing?

Only a few left, Rylee. Blaz's words snapped me out of my fog. Sweat slid down my skin, soaking my shirt and jeans as if I showered with my clothes on. I shrugged out of my leather jacket.

"Let's finish this then."

It was only then I realized Pamela and Lark had never arrived.

Motherfucking demon, his monkeys must have broken through to them.

Unless Pestilence had something else up his sleeve. Gods be damned, I hoped that wasn't the case.

7
RYLEE

Blood and gore splattered my white shirt, though Blaz's back had gotten the worst of the mess, and was covered with fur and bits of monkey. The remaining seven bastards flew toward their master.

He gave a slow, haughty clap. "Well done. I see why you've survived this long, Tracker. Orion is afraid of you. Did you know that?"

I struggled to get my breathing under control. "What did you do to my friends?"

I didn't give a flying fuck about Orion. His time would come soon enough.

Pestilence raised an eyebrow at me. "You mean them?" The remaining clouds parted as he pointed. On the tarmac lay Eve and Marco, flat out.

Lark, Cactus, Pamela, and Alex were nowhere to be seen, which gave me a little hope.

I pointed both my swords at Pestilence. "You know, most demons rush me and I kill them. I'm guessing you don't want to play that way."

He smiled at me, his eyes crinkling around the edges.

"Rylee, correct? Perhaps you and I can come to an understanding."

"I'm sorry, do I look like a dumb shit to you?" I wanted to reach for my crossbow. While I could imbue my weapons with my slayer abilities while I held them, the crossbow only gave me a few seconds. But with Pestilence this close, those seconds would be enough. But that would mean putting my swords down and I didn't want to do that, either.

His grin widened, mouth stretching impossibly as his eyes bled from a dark brown to a flickering red. "Perhaps the word *dumb* would be giving you too much credit."

I raised an eyebrow along with the tips of my swords. "Perhaps you'd like to rephrase that?"

He threw back his head and laughed.

I sheathed my swords and grabbed my crossbow, slinging it forward as Pestilence continued to laugh. Jamming a bolt in the channel, I sighted the bow and pulled the trigger.

The bolt flew true, driving through the demon's neck. He stumbled back, the air around him stilling as he fell from the sky like a rock.

Blaz let out a roar that reverberated in my chest.

"Follow him. He's not dead yet," I yelled.

Pestilence's monkeys scattered, running while their master was no longer controlling them. Fuck, they were infected with the pox. "Blaz, drop me and go after them."

Rylee, this world—

"Won't be worth fighting for if they get away and re-infect everyone." For all we knew, Pestilence had a *new* disease residing in his pets. Fucker.

Blaz dropped to the tarmac and I slid from his back. He launched into the sky a heartbeat later. I trusted him to get the job done, to track and wipe them out.

Besides, he couldn't help me with this last bit. Pestilence would only die when I laid my hands on him and drove the demon to the seventh level of the Veil: the deepest level, home to Orion and his demon horde. Or at least, it was until they'd all broken free.

Standing in the parking lot, Pestilence tugged at his cufflinks (apparently even demons had nervous ticks), the wound in his throat already gone and the crossbow bolt on the ground at his feet. "It's a shame, you know, you could have been at the top of the food chain with us. But instead, here you are in the dirt with the rest of the worms." His eyes fluttered to half-mast and a smile slid over his face. "You don't really think you can send me back, do you?"

I slid out of my crossbow and laid it on the ground, then pulled both my swords. "I'm counting on it, actually."

He chuckled. "Ah, the optimism of the walking dead; it knows no bounds."

The wind around me swirled, and I went to a knee, driving one of my swords into the asphalt. If the wind picked up enough, I would need something to hang onto without Blaz around to catch me. "If I'm already dead, Pestilence, then I have nothing to lose, do I?"

His eyes narrowed and his mouth thinned as he stalked toward me. But his body didn't shift as I thought it would.

"What, no monster under your skin?"

"I don't need to be a monster to kill you, Tracker. Do you know what my abilities entail? I'm guessing not since you are standing there like you aren't afraid of me." He circled and I moved with him.

"Enlighten me then. Tell me what you know, oh-demon-of-wisdom." I kept moving with him, my sword I'd driven into the tarmac between us at all times.

"Yes, I think I will *enlighten* you."

I wanted to laugh at him. The classic bad guy monologue? He had to be kidding. Pride had to be on his list of vices.

"The four horsemen are so much more than just War, Famine, Pestilence, and Death. Each has abilities. Many of mine are tied to the element of air. I could suck the wind out of your lungs with a snap of my fingers, if I so chose."

I swallowed hard. "And you don't because I'm such a conversationalist, right?"

"No, I like to feel my victims die, to watch the light go out of their eyes as their hearts struggle to beat one more time. I like to have my hands on them."

I wrinkled my nose. "Rather perverted, don't you think?"

He grinned widely at me. "It's the only way I can catch their souls and eat them."

Oh. Fucking. Hell.

"Yes, I see by your face you finally understand what I am. Why were Pestilence and I attached to one another? A slow death peels the soul from the body and makes it harder to resist me." He snaked out a hand as if to grab me, and I swung my remaining sword as I stepped back.

It sliced off the tip of his middle finger. He snatched his hand back and shook it as if he'd burned it and not had a piece of it removed. "You are going to be so sweet to drink, Tracker. The Blood of the Lost, a vintage I haven't tasted in many, many years. Not since your mother, I believe."

A razor's-edge chill slid down my back and I didn't even think about anything past what I wanted to do to him. Chop him into tiny fucking pieces and have Blaz roast him to a crisp before throwing what was left to the fishes. I leapt forward, swinging with what I knew would look like wild fury. My sword slashed through the air and I missed him over and over again.

On purpose.

Erik's words when I'd trained with him echoed in my head as if he stood at my shoulder and guided me through the exercise.

"Don't let them see how fast you really are; don't let them see the control you have, the ability you have to read them and the situation. Let them think you're out of control. Let them think you are going to be easy. Because they will be anything but, and you need to be ready for the fight of your life."

Pestilence laughed at me, and beckoned me forward. "How in the seventh Veil Orion rose to power is beyond me, if he thinks you're so terrifying." He held his right hand out and a sword appeared in it. Made of a bright white material, it caught the sun and reflected a shimmer of rainbows around us.

I forced myself to pant, sucking air hard, even going so far as to stumble and go to one knee.

If I could get him to come at me, to drive me backward, I'd have him.

Of course, that was when the cavalry arrived and whatever plans I had went to shit.

Alex, in his mixed up werewolf form, ran across the lot from the left, Peta loping beside him albeit a bit wobbly. Lark was behind them and all three were covered in open wounds, pustules that oozed thick green mucus.

"Get away from her," Lark barked out, coughing on the last word.

Pestilence turned to them. "Not dead yet? Let me help you with that, you meddling elemental. I've had enough of you."

He took a step, but the earth below him softened, sucking him into a hole all the way to his neck. Rage lit his features, twisting the handsome face into the monster I knew he was; his mouth opened past the point any human jaw should and three tongues, each one the length of a car, snaked out of him.

"Good job, Lark. Good fucking job." I sidestepped the first tongue, but only just. Saliva flicked out across me, burning through my shirt and pants.

"Shut up, you ungrateful Tracker. If you'd followed the plan, we'd have him by now." Lark dropped to her knees and drove her hands into the pavement, pulling it up and throwing it behind her in chunks. Peta let out a snarl, pressing herself to Lark's leg, and Alex ran to my side.

"I'm with you, Rylee."

I dropped a hand to his head for the briefest of seconds before I had to leap out of the way of the second tongue as it whipped toward us. "If I'd followed the plan, you'd probably be dead along with Eve and Marco."

"Please. You think I can't take care of a demon?"

"I know you can't," I snapped back. I ran toward my sword driven into the ground and went to one knee behind it. Pestilence flicked a tongue at me.

"Alex, stay down," I said as I clung to the handle of my sword. This was going to hurt, no way around it. I took a breath a split second before the thick meaty tongue wrapped around my sword and me. The saliva burned through my clothes and within seconds my skin blistered.

Pestilence pulled me slowly toward him and his gaping mouth. Shivering with pain, I struggled to hold it together. "You're a fucking pussy, pesty boy. Orion sent you because you are the weakest of his generals."

With a roar, he yanked me toward him with a speed I never could have mustered on my own. My body screamed at me to do something to stop the burning, anything to ease the acid eating through me. As Pestilence held me directly over his mouth, Lark yelled at me.

"Tell me you know what you're doing."

"I know"—I yanked my sword upward, slicing through Pestilence's tongue—"what I'm fucking doing." The tongue flew away from me and I dropped, landing with a foot on either side of the demon's head.

I held my sword over my head, poised to drive it straight through him when I saw the laughter in his eyes. "You will never win, Tracker. Even if I die now, you will die later. And I will be free again."

With everything I had, I tapped into all the good in my life, the love I had for my daughter and Liam, for Alex and Pamela, Eve, and maybe even Faris. The emotions flowed through me, calming the rage. In my hands, my sword began to glow, as if lit from within. I didn't think about this new development, couldn't; there was no time.

"Demon, go back to your home."

I drove the sword into his open mouth, only stopping when the hilt was buried in his throat. He convulsed around my blade, his three tongues dancing wildly in the air, like demented cheerleaders for a dying monster.

With a quick twist of the handle, I sliced through him and then pulled my sword out. A waft of rotting meat and sulfur spewed from his mouth, as if a septic main had broken inside him. The green mucus I'd seen on Lark, Peta, and Alex were next, then blood—red and black—flowed like a river around us. I looked down at my arms and legs.

The acid burns were gone, though my clothes were eaten to shit. Alex trotted toward me, the pustules gone and the mucus left on his skin already dried. Lark strode toward me, as though she wasn't covered in left over pox. "Rylee, are you incapable of following anyone else? Should I give up now?"

I glared at her. "Maybe you should remember who broke you out of the fucking oubliette."

Her eyes narrowed and she stepped close to me, using her height to her advantage. Peta shrunk back to her housecat form and leapt onto Lark's shoulders, her green eyes worried.

"Maybe you should remember we're trying to keep you alive," Lark snapped and Peta shook her head.

Well, now was as good a time as any to have this out with her. "Oh, I'm sorry. Did you become a demon slayer in the last ten minutes?"

She shook her head ever so slightly. "We were going to hold him down so you could finish him off, remember?"

"And where were you?"

Her shoulders tightened. "Sick, but we were still fighting for you. Pamela healed Alex and me enough to get our asses here. For you."

"Stop trying to guilt trip me, Lark."

She grabbed my arms, surprising me. With a hard shake, she snapped my head back and forth, and Peta mewed as though that would stop her master. "You little idiot, everything we are doing is to get you to the end in one piece. I don't want this world run by Orion any more than you do, so why won't you damn well let me help?"

I rubbed the back of my neck, feeling the strain of muscles there too. That damn bump from earlier was bigger and I picked at it. A flash of heat shot through me and I snapped my hand away.

A wild rush of anger slid over me as I yanked my two swords out, pointing both at her. "Because you don't know shit, Lark! Who the fuck do you think you are anyway?"

Her eyes widened and she slowly raised her spear as I circled around her. "Rylee, what are you doing? We're on the same damn side."

Swiveling my swords, I loosened my wrists. "Are we? You jumped, distracted me from killing the demon. I don't think we are on the same fucking side." Were we? No, Lark was trying to stop me. Hurt me.

Control me.

Her eyes narrowed. "This doesn't sound like you."

I swung a sword as Alex slid between us, his hands up and his big eyes begging. "Rylee, stop. This is wrong."

With only a hairsbreadth of room, I missed him. But he stayed there on the ground in front of me, unblinking. Trusting I wouldn't hurt him.

The back of my neck tingled and itched, and I put a hand to it, dropping my sword. It hit the ground with a clatter that seemed to break the tension. Alex shimmied forward, and put his face close to mine. "You okay, boss?"

A lump in my throat seemed to freeze my ability to talk, so I just nodded.

"Maybe we should all get inside then," he said, putting a hand to my elbow as if I were a feeble old woman. I jerked away from him.

"Don't" was all I said. They stared at me, their eyes ranging from pity to fear. Neither of those emotions were ones I wanted to deal with; especially not in other people.

Lark turned away first. "Let's get new clothes and get a move on."

I watched her as she strode away, her leather vest and pants eaten through from the flinging acid. Peta dropped from her shoulder and trotted ahead of her, the white tip of her gray tail flicking back and forth rapidly. The shift in Lark's attitude happened so swiftly I struggled to follow.

I had a feeling perhaps Peta influenced it. The cat did seem to know when she was needed.

And it had to be obvious even to the cat that Lark had been egging me on.

Right?

A hair-raising screech turned me around. Eve and Marco were slowly getting up. Whatever Pestilence had done to them had faded. Beside me, Alex shifted—albeit slowly—into his human form. The gangly teenager was buck-naked but didn't seem overly bothered by it.

Pamela, on the other hand, as she walked toward us turned bright red and spun around. "Come on, Lark is right. We need to get clothes."

I snatched up my sword, sheathed both. Limping a little, my right hip sore from something or other during the fight with Pestilence, I headed toward the box store.

"Think they have Twinkies in there? I'm starving." Alex rubbed his hands together and gave me a sideways wink.

"Twinkies, but no rabbits."

He grimaced and shook his head. "I think I'm done with rabbits for a while."

We caught up to Pamela and I slung an arm around her shoulders guiding her so she was on the side opposite of Alex.

He reached around me and tugged her hair. "What's the matter, Pamie?"

"Shut up, Alex." She bit out, her face going even redder, if that were possible. Another time, I would have smiled and laughed. But not now.

From the corner of my eye, I watched him watching her. If it weren't for Frank's death, I knew what would happen.

Alex loved me like an older sister and best friend.

Pamela on the other hand . . . he watched her like a wolf hungry for a meal. Which was not totally surprising. "Pam, go ahead of us. Alex and I need to have a chat."

"We do?" His golden eyes widened and it was then I realized that unlike other shifters I knew—excluding Liam—Alex's eyes didn't revert to their original color. They stayed werewolf gold despite being in human shape. Perhaps leftovers from being a submissive so long . . . .

Pamela hurried ahead of us, her blonde hair swinging loosely down her back. Alex tracked her with his eyes—the same way I knew Liam did me. Yeah, that was not happening anytime soon.

"Uh-huh, you and me need to chat. Might not get another chance to." I stepped in front of him, blocking his path and put a hand on his chest. "Down, boy."

"What? I've been good." His eyes went as wide as I'd ever seen them. A false innocence, if I ever saw it.

My lips twitched despite the morose mood swirling through me. "Look, I get it. I do. Pamela is pretty, smart, a powerhouse of a witch. But she is fifteen and you are what, twenty?"

He at least had the grace to blush. "That obvious?"

"I don't think subtle is in your repertoire, my friend." I smiled to soften what I was going to say. "You need to remember that no matter how grown up she is, she is too young for you, right now. She and Frank were only a year apart. And now he's dead and he was her first love. Be her friend. Be patient."

Cactus strolled by us as he headed toward the store, catching the last bit I said. He burst out laughing. "Be a girl's friend? Goddess, might work eventually. At least, *I'm* hoping."

Alex looked from me to Cactus and let out a low growl. "Don't mock her."

I put a hand on his arm. "Alex. I may not get another chance to say this. Let Pamela have time. If, when she's a few years older, you feel the same way, then you can say something. But not before that. Do you understand?"

He blew out a slow breath. "Yeah, I get it. I'll be her friend."

Cactus patted Alex on the shoulder. "Welcome to the friend club. Membership is free and at least you'll get to hold them while they cry over another man."

Alex grimaced and I shook my head. "Ignore him."

We went into the box store to shop together for the last time.

Although saying we shopped would imply that we paid for our things, which we most certainly did not.

8
PAMELA

I rifled through the clothes on the racks, looking for something . . . or nothing. I wondered where the alarms were; it wasn't like we'd had keys and pass codes to get in. Berget and Faris, or Liam depending on who was in charge, had broken the locks and headed deep into the storeroom.

Berget ghosted to my side as if thinking of her called her to me.

"I saw you looking at the cameras. Faris and I disarmed the whole system when we came in, so we should be good here for a while. All the workers are . . . sleeping now."

"Oh, I . . . I thought we were going to have to rush out."

She nodded. "Yes, like we always do?"

"Yes." I breathed the word, feeling a strange hesitancy in our conversation. We'd talked before, but not alone. Not when Rylee wasn't in the room.

Berget had tried to kill me the first time we'd met, and I wondered sometimes if she still harbored those intentions. I didn't think so, at least I hoped not.

"The blue will look good with your eyes." She pointed at a turquoise button-down shirt.

"It would look good with yours, too," I said softly. A question hovered on my tongue and I took a breath, wondering if I should bother asking.

"Go ahead," the vampire said. "You won't offend me."

"Do you think it is coincidence that you and I look so alike? I mean, what do you think?" I wanted to kick myself, but Berget tapped a hand on the rack of clothes we stood by.

"I doubt anything in this world of ours is coincidence. If you hadn't looked so much like me, maybe Rylee would have let you go into foster care. Or maybe even to the druid who wanted to train you. And without you, she wouldn't have survived this long." Berget cleared her throat. "May I ask you a question?"

I nodded quickly. "Of course."

She seemed to stumble over the words. "Do you think . . . she loves you better than me?"

My eyes sprang open at the mere suggestion. "Are you kidding? You're her sister. She never stopped looking for you."

"And I tried to kill her on several occasions."

"Not your fault." I lifted a hand and carefully put it over hers. "Why would you even think she could love me more?"

Berget's eye's glimmered with tears. "Insecurities run deep, I suppose. I see her with you, and I see the bond you have. I . . . she doesn't turn to me like she turns to you."

I didn't know what to say to that, so I flipped through the clothes. "I think you're right. This blue would look good on both of us." I shoved a shirt at her and then grabbed her hand. "We might not be normal teenagers, but we can act like it for a few minutes, right?"

She laughed softly and grabbed another handful of shirts from the rack. "Okay, let's be teenagers, for now. No spells, no blood, no monsters."

"Definitely that last," I said and caught her eye. We burst into giggles like it was the most natural thing in the world.

Within minutes we were in the fitting room, swapping clothes under the door and leaping out at the same time with the most ridiculous of outfits on. And for those few brief moments, I was just Pamela, hanging out with a girlfriend.

There was nothing to be scared of, no future to wonder about.

No monsters, zombies, demons, or vampires trying to take us out.

And for that moment I forgot I was a witch and we were trying to save the world from being overrun by demons.

9
LARK

I looked at the women's clothes, found a pair of jeans that looked like they would fit, and a dark brown T-shirt. I slid out of my beat up clothes and pulled the human clothing on. My sister Belladonna would have loved to be here, picking outfits, and trying them on. I realized I was doing my best not to think about what had almost happened with Pestilence.

Sitting on top of a pile of cotton T-shirts, Peta stared hard at me.

"You know you were wrong, Lark," she said softly.

I hunched my shoulders a little. "You don't have to rub it in."

"I'm not." She let out a jaw-cracking yawn and then rubbed a paw over her face. "It's my job to help you grow. Admitting you're wrong when you are wrong is a way to do that."

I frowned at her and she grinned back. Dropping my face to hers, she rubbed against me. "And I only do it because I love you."

Scooping her into my arms, I held her to me. "Thanks, cat."

"Anytime, dirt girl. And to soften this, you may have been wrong, but I believe something *is* wrong with Rylee. She is not herself."

"I picked up on that too, but unless she opens herself, we can't help her."

I set her down and my mind immediately went back to the scene in the parking lot.

Rylee had come so close to being killed, and I'd been unable to do anything as my body was wracked with spasms. If Pamela hadn't been there, and hadn't been with it as much as she had, there would have been no way I could have helped Rylee in the end.

Cactus cleared his throat beside me. "You should try the green shirt. It'll look better on you."

"The green shirt is two sizes too small."

"Yes, that's what I said, it will look better on you." He slapped my ass and I glared at him.

"Not now, Cactus. I'm not in the mood."

A low grumbling hiss came from Peta. "Prick, keep your hands to yourself."

"What? You two badass girls kicked that demon into the seventh Veil, everyone is still alive; what more could you want?" He backed away from Peta a bit. He'd learned the hard way not to ignore her.

I finished buttoning the jeans and tugged at the T-shirt. "It didn't go as planned. The whole thing fell to pot as soon as Pestilence arrived. I'm supposed to help Rylee get to the final battle with Orion, but how can I do that if I can't even run a play?"

"What? Have you been watching football?" He smiled at me and I swatted him on the arm.

"Cactus, you know what I mean."

"I don't understand why it's such an issue. When you first started as an Ender, you didn't exactly plan things. You tried, but then you rolled with the punches as things shifted and changed."

How did I explain to him this was different? Lives were on the line, but when I was younger, those lives wouldn't affect the outcome of the whole world.

Rylee's life would. And I was determined to see her through to the end, no matter what.

"You have to let her do her thing, Lark. You have to. No matter how hard it is for you to let go, this isn't your hunt. It's hers. We can only try to manage the fall out, whatever it might be."

Goblin piss and worm shit, he was right, and I felt that from Peta too. She knew it as well as I did. "See if you can find me a belt, would you?"

He leaned in. "Don't I get a kiss for helping you figure out you were wrong?"

I lifted my hand and squeezed his cheeks until his lips puckered. "No. I told you we would have this discussion later."

"It is later," he spit out through puckered lips.

"Not late enough," I murmured as I walked away from him, Peta following me. Rylee was a few aisles over, rifling through the tank tops. "Hey."

She looked at me, her tri-colored eyes swirling. "Hey, nice digs."

I glanced down at myself. "Listen, I shouldn't have tried to take control back there. This is your show, so you lead and I will follow."

Her eyebrows shot up. "Why the sudden change in heart? Admitting you're wrong doesn't seem like something you'd ever do, what with the whole 'I'm an elemental and I'm better than you' shit you've got going on."

I had to bite my tongue not to respond to the dig and remind myself she was not herself in the least. "Oh, Cactus reminded me I was not so unlike your leap-before-you-look style when I was younger. And that I managed to survive my own crazy ideas. Of course, he also pointed out I am support for you in this. I'm one of the keys to the final battle, but right now? This is your show."

She gave a slow nod. "Thanks. You do realize I don't know what the fuck I'm doing, right?"

I rubbed a hand over my face. "Yeah, you aren't the first Tracker I've met. You all tend to be like that from what I understand. It's the Spirit elemental in you, it makes me unpredictable too. Though to a lesser degree." I smiled to soften the words. She laughed and a little of the tension between us dissipated.

"Somehow I doubt that. If we're related, you probably have more than your fair share of a temper too."

Peta snickered softly at my feet. "That's an under-statement."

I ignored my familiar. "Yes, but I've learned to control it." Which I had for the most part. Occasionally, it still flared. My guts twisted with the thought of seeing my family after being locked away for so many years and what that would do to my careful control. Likely break it into a million pieces of pissed off.

The sounds of clothing being pushed aside and a stealthy pair of feet made me step back. Liam stepped out from behind one of the racks. I'd never known him separately from the vampire, but I could only imagine the struggle of choosing between the two men. I snorted softly to myself. Who was I kidding? I was still trying to choose between two men, and was no closer to making a decision after years in banishment and the oubliette to think about it.

I touched Rylee on the arm. "If I can give you a suggestion?"

"If you have to."

"Both of those men are offering you their hearts. Take them. I don't believe love can be wrong, my friend." I stepped back and gave Liam a quick nod before turning my back on them. For whatever time we had here in this quiet pause after the battle, they needed to talk.

I had a feeling we weren't going to get many more of these quiet spells.

"Good advice you gave her," Peta said.

Apparently, I wasn't the only one thinking about the pause in our journey since I found Cactus standing at the rack of belts, his fingers plucking through them like loose harp strings. "I heard what you said to her, about love."

I blew out a breath and picked a belt for myself. "I believe it's true."

"I love you, Lark. You know that."

"And I love you too. But I also love Ash—"

"Don't remind me." He grunted. "I don't know if he and I can share like those two over there."

I looked over my shoulder at the bowed head of Liam and the upturned face of Rylee as they spoke. "They wouldn't be doing things this way if they didn't have to, Cactus. What would you have done if I'd taken the throne? I could have married you and had a man on the side. Loving you both, pretending when I was with one that the other didn't matter, which would be a lie. What would you have me do?"

"I would have you pick me," he said softly, his green eyes as vulnerable as I'd ever seen them. "I would have you tell me you love me best and that he was just a phase."

I blew out a breath and let him tug me to him. His arms wrapped around my body felt so right, so good. And in that moment, I was able to forget I'd been stuffed away like garbage for years. I was able to forget the one other man I loved was missing, and maybe dead.

I was able to forget I was supposed to be the end of the elemental world.

But of all those things, the one I wanted to forget and couldn't, was when the time came, Rylee's life would be in my hands. It would be up to me and my strength whether she lived or died in the battle against Orion.

A shudder slid through me and I clung to Cactus as I hadn't done since we were children hiding in the darkness of the forest on a moonless night. Peta leapt up to my shoulder and butted her head against both of us, purring softly.

"You can do this," he whispered into my hair. "You are the best of our world because you will do what no one else would even dream of. You know, even now the four families of elementals cower in their homes and cover their ears to the death cries of the humans. You will change that, Lark."

I pulled back from him and kissed him softly before letting go completely. "That's what I'm afraid of, Cactus."

10
LIAM

Lark's words hovered in the air between them. He reached out and brushed a strand of Rylee's long hair behind her ear. "Rylee."

"Liam, what if I fall in love with Faris?" she blurted the question, and by the smell of fear on her, he knew it was already happening.

He expected Faris to crow his victory, but again, the vampire surprised him. There was a softening and Faris stepped forward without pushing Liam back.

"I think it will happen, eventually, when there is no longer two, just one." His voice waivered as if both of them spoke at the same time.

Liam swallowed hard, and felt Faris do the same.

Rylee reached up. "I'm not surviving this, so I don't know why I bother to worry about you two."

"Don't be ridiculous. You aren't going to fail; you don't have it in you." He couldn't help but wrap his hands around hers and tug her closer. Her head still fit under his chin, the same as it had in his old body. She wrapped her arms around him and took a deep breath.

"Maybe I won't fail. I have to finish Orion and close the Veil. I believe that much, even if I don't have a gods-be-damned plan. Lark said it and she's right. A sacrifice is expected of me." She looked up at him and her eyes filled with tears. He wiped them away and kissed the trail of tears down her cheeks. Faris held Liam's tongue, keeping them quiet. Liam would have jumped in and tried to fix it right away, but the vampire seemed to know a bit more about women than he initially let on.

And a small piece of Liam was grateful to have the vampire with him, navigating these new waters with Rylee.

She closed her eyes. "I'm not scared to die; that isn't what terrifies me. But leaving Marcella does. She's so little. How will she know how much I love her if I'm not there to tell her? How will she know I would willingly go through everything in my life a hundred times if it would take me to her? The thought of never seeing her again, of not watching her grow up, eats at me like nothing I've ever felt, and I don't think I can do it. I can't leave her. I know I can't."

Her head bowed forward until it touched his chest. What the hell was he supposed to say to that? He blinked several times while trying to formulate the right words, but Faris beat him to it.

"You will never lose her, Rylee. Even if you die, you would never be away from her. She would carry you in her heart, and see you in the mirror every morning the same way I carry my sister. You never truly lose the ones you love, and I believe my sister even now walks with me in my darkest hours."

She let out a sob. "It isn't the same as holding her when she cries out from a nightmare. Or seeing her off to her first day of school. Or watching her go on her first date with the boy down the street."

"No, it's not." He tipped her head up and kissed her, holding her tightly to him as if his love would somehow protect her from her fears, from the path that lay ahead. There was a desperate urgency to the kiss, as if for the first time she let herself feel it. Their mouths were hot against each other, and if they had been alone he knew what would have happened. Even as it was, his hands found their way under her tank top and slid along her skin, feeling the tremble of her muscles as she leaned into him. A groan slipped out of her, a whisper of his name.

Gently he pulled back, keeping his forehead pressed against hers. "No matter what happens, I am with you, Rylee. You are not alone in this, and Marcella will be loved beyond that of any child in this world because of the people who love you, the people you've touched in your life."

She rubbed the back of her neck. Her eyes narrowed and she snapped at him, "Stop trying to soften this shit, Liam."

Kiss her. The thought came over him and he acted on it, pressing his lips to hers. Her eyes softened and she kissed him back, tentatively. A few tears trickled down her cheeks. What the hell was wrong with her? None of this was like her. Tough, yes, that would always be a trait of hers. But not this snapping, lashing out she'd been doing. Something was happening to her.

Slowly, she nodded, and he could almost see the resolve harden in her eyes once more. "Sorry I'm being such a fucking baby."

He cupped her face. "Your eyes are even more beautiful when you cry."

She took his hands and gave them a squeeze before pushing him away. "Get out of here, you two. Round everyone up, we need to move."

The moment was over, but Liam felt the shift in her, as did Faris.

She would love them both.

And they were good with that.

11
RYLEE

Liam strode away as I reached to the back of my neck and the throbbing ache that beat in time with my heart.

I ran my finger over the bump . . . and it moved.

"Fucking hell," I breathed out, horror flickering through me followed swiftly by a thunderous roll of fatigue and a sense of hopelessness so deep I knew I'd never be able to get back out. I might as well lay down and die right there. The fatigue was all bound up with an anger so intense I thought I would burst with wanting to lash out at those around me. They were not the friends I'd thought they were.

The emotional pendulum swung back the other direction.

What was the point in fighting if I was going to die anyway?

Blaz called to me, but I couldn't answer him; I couldn't see past the blackness that had come for me.

The sounds of my friends around me in the store echoed to me as if from a great distance, and I silently said my goodbyes to them, begging them to understand that I was not strong enough.

Hands were touching me, trying to hold me up.

"She's not breathing."

"What is it, what happened to her?"

"I think she's been demon stung; they must have implanted something in her when the humans mobbed us. Cactus, grab my spear, we need the blade if we can find the entrance point."

The world as I knew it faded, and I stood on a white plane of sand, wind whipping around my face and lashing me with my own hair. In front of me stood a man with long black hair streaked with white and silver, his back stooped as if he were about to pick something up off the ground.

I took a step toward him. "Where am I?"

"Desolation, Tracker. You are in desolation."

"And who the hell are you?"

A sigh slipped out of him. "I am the demon who brought you here. My name is Moloch."

My hands went to my swords, but they weren't on my back. "I suggest, Moloch, you send me back. Right fucking now."

He looked up at me from under his long hair, a rather soft smile on his face. His eyes flickered red, but there was no menace in him, which didn't jive for me. Not with a demon. "Tracker, not all demons want Orion to succeed. I am one of those who oppose him, but the only way I could speak to you is if I was a part of your body and brought you to the edge of death. It is how my abilities work."

Swallowing hard, I forced myself to hold my ground as he approached me, limping. "You're the reason I've been so fucking emotional, aren't you?" The rest of his words sunk in. "Wait . . . the edge of death, are you fucking kidding me?"

He shook his head. "The emotions are your own. I only opened the floodgates. When you touched me, on your neck, the venom in me surges. A natural defense I have no control over. I apologize that it caused you grief."

I slapped a hand to the back of my neck. "You're the reason I attacked Lark."

"Yes."

"And the reason I was so afraid."

"Yes. As I said, the venom magnifies that which is already there."

"Then why the hell was I myself sometimes? Why have I not been a fucking lunatic the whole time?" I stared hard at him, but he smiled at me.

"Love. You love those you are with and it is the only true antidote for my venom. It breaks through the poison." He clasped his hands in front of his chest. "As to the edge of death . . . that will not change until I am no longer a part of you. But for now I hold your body in a stasis. You will not die unless I wish it."

I put my hands on my hips, "And you don't wish it because you hate Orion?"

His nose wrinkled up like he'd smelled something bad. "Because the world of demons is not meant to become a part of the human world, or the supernatural, for that matter. We are separate for a purpose." Moloch shook his head slowly. "Orion is a fool. The demon prophecies were written by someone who wanted our two worlds to merge, and so with that goal, she wrote her prophecies. She chose the name 'Orion' because it is a common name in the demon realm."

I raised an eyebrow at him and he laughed.

"Orion is creating these events to follow what is written, because he *believes*. That is the hidden truth of prophecy, Tracker. You can make it happen if you have enough faith. He believes and so, he is changing the world accordingly."

"Prophecies have a funny way of turning out to be truth in my world," I said.

Moloch lifted one hand, a single finger pointing to the sky. "You have your own set of prophecies that say you will defeat him. So perhaps the key is only that your belief must be stronger than his."

Deep words, and ones I wished were true. More likely I needed an army that would be able to wipe the demons out; something I did not have. Unless . . . .

"How many demons support you?" I realized if there were enough demons that would go against Orion, we might actually have a chance against him.

"A few hundred. But we will be there, and we will fight at your side, Tracker." He held out his hand. Slowly, I reached across to him and took his gnarled fingers in my own. Papery dry and soft, his skin felt as though I touched not flesh, but the peeling bark of a tree trunk.

"Moloch, did Orion send you to me?"

A laugh burst out of him as he let my hand go. "Yes, he believes I will bring you to your knees. Which I could." His eyes twinkled at me. "Look for this mark." He turned his head to the side and what looked like a faded scar was imprinted on his right cheek. Two parallel vertical lines with a single slash intersecting them. "This is the mark of those who oppose Orion and his plans."

"Are you going to send me back now?"

"Yes, and I will leave you. And if you don't mind, try to make sure your friends don't kill me in my wormy form. I realize it isn't pretty, but it is my own."

I stepped back from him, then paused. "Wait. I have a question."

He bobbed his head.

This was dicey, asking what I needed to ask, it would tip my hand. But if anyone would know if it were possible, I had a feeling it would be Moloch. It wasn't like I was about to meet another demon I could even partially trust. Still, I didn't want to throw caution to the wind. I revised my question a split second before I spit it out. "Orion bound the witch, Milly, to him fully, didn't he? He could sense her, and she could sense him?"

Moloch gave a start. "Yes, he did. Demons love keeping tabs on their pets to make life the worst hell they could. Does that answer help you?"

I nodded. "Yes, thank you."

The demon in front of me clasped his hands in front of his body, his red eyes boring into mine with an intensity of a razor-sharp blade cutting through me, peeling me open to the world. And then they widened ever so slightly. "Ah, I see what you are about. Dangerous what you would try, but . . . it may work. You are true to your heritage and the strength your people carried. It is an honor to meet you . . . Rylee of the Blood."

A chill swept through me as he gave me a slow, painful bow, and then the wind picked up, slashing my face with sand particles, forcing my eyes closed.

"She's moving."

"Mother goddess, she's breathing! What happened?"

The voices of those I loved most in the world surrounded me as I came back to myself. "I went for a little walk." I croaked out the words as if I truly had been in a desert. "Can I get water?"

"I'm on it, boss." Alex scrambled away, the sound of displays knocked over echoed in the store. Peta lay across my legs in her snow leopard form, her warmth curling through me and her green eyes full of worry. I ran a hand over her head.

"I'm okay."

Liam held me to him, my back to his chest. "Rylee, what in the hell happened?"

I put a hand to my neck and the bump shifted again, and I jerked out of Liam's arms, and out from under Peta, to crawl a few feet away from them.

"Don't touch me and don't touch what's about to come out of my neck," I said. The sound and feel of the back of my neck ripping open sent a gasp through not only me, but everyone else as well.

"Rylee," Lark said softly, "that looks like a lung burrower. What in the name of the mother goddess is it doing *in you*?"

The slithering demon slipped out of me and off the back of my neck to the floor. I turned and looked at it. Black and gray streaked, Moloch's "wormy form" looked like nothing more than an overgrown leech as he slid across the floor at a rapid speed.

Pamela raised her hands, the magic coiling around her fingers.

"Stop! I said don't hurt him."

Liam looked from me to Pam and back again. "And why aren't we hurting the leech thing that just slid out the back of your neck?"

Okay, that sounded more like Faris, but I was splitting hairs. Alex stumbled to his knees in front of me and thrust a water bottle into my hands. I unscrewed it and chugged the entire thing, then handed the empty bottle back to him. "Thanks, buddy."

He gave me a wink. "Anytime, bossy boss."

Lark crouched in front of me. "What was that?"

"That was a demon. He needed to speak to me, and thought that burrowing under my skin, making me an emotional wreck and an asshole all at once, was the best way to get my attention."

She arched an eyebrow at me. "And we didn't kill him because?"

"He's against Orion, and he's going to fight with us at the final battle. Along with a few of his friends."

Lark let out a breath. "You trust him?"

"You saw my heart stop?"

"Yes."

"He could have finished me right there. Orion sent him to do it."

Lark paled, and her eyes widened. "Mother goddess."

"Yeah, my thoughts exactly." I pushed myself to my feet.

I tucked the white tank top into the black stretchy jeans I'd found and proceeded to strap on my weapons one at a time. Double back sheath for my two swords, my whip clipped to my left hip, crossbow slung over my shoulder and adjusted so I could pull my swords, a knife in the sheath at my lower back, a knife strapped to my calf under my right boot, and a quiver of crossbow bolts hanging from my right hip.

Rylee, I'm back. The flying monkeys are all dead, but they seemed to fall apart around the time I reached them. I assume that means Pestilence is taken care of?

Blaz's voice soothed my nerves for a moment and I nodded even though he couldn't see me. He'd feel my intentions. "Yes. Taken care of. One down, three nasty motherfuckers to go."

I looked at those around me and couldn't help the heat in my face. I'd been a complete ass to Lark and Liam, yet I saw no condemnation in either of them.

"Not your fault, Rylee," Lark said as if reading my mind. "You can't always know what's going to happen to you; especially when facing demons and almost certain death." She put one hand on my shoulder and gave it a quick squeeze.

I brushed her hand off and let out slow breath. "Fuck. I'm sorry, Lark. I . . . ."

She snorted and shook her head. "Tracker, you remind me so much of . . . I forget you aren't her. You are stronger than she ever was." She let out a slow sigh and ran a hand over her face. "Forgive me, for thinking you don't know what you're doing. I'm not used to anyone else being able to make things happen. It has always been on my shoulders. It is strange to be asked to trust someone else's judgment. As to the rest, well, it is forgotten already." She turned my hand over so it was palm down and then tapped two of her fingers to it.

"What's that for?"

Her smile slowly lit her face, softening the irritation there only a moment before. "A way of showing respect for someone; you know you are strong enough."

"Thank you." The words flowed off my tongue and it was like she said; the fight between us was forgotten. We were a team and we were going to finish Orion together.

"Let's get this show on the road. We've got a kid to grab, demons to kill, and a fucking world to save," I said.

Liam grinned at me, but in his smile I saw Faris too, and my heart lurched more than a little. Ah, what the hell. I reached for him, grabbed his face, and pulled him too me.

"Welcome back, Adamson."

"We get a minute alone, and I'll show you how glad I am to be back."

Behind us, Lark grunted. "See what I mean, Cactus? Trackers, they're a lot like ogres."

I grinned over my shoulder at her. "I'll take that for a compliment."

She laughed and smiled back at me. "Oh, it was meant to be. Mating and fighting; if there are only two things you're good at in this life, I'd put those at the top of the list too."

Outside, Blaz let out a roar that shook the store.

Incoming humans. Time to leave.

Time to leave, indeed.

12
RYLEE

We bagged Liam and Berget up in the black out curtains and dragged them out of the store as the first cop car showed up.

Marco hopped toward us, his wings fluttering. "Give them to me."

Inside the bag, Faris muttered away. I rolled my eyes. "Quit your bitching or I'll leave you behind." There was no real heat in my words. We all knew I wasn't leaving him. I handed the top of the bag to Marco's outstretched claw. He leapt into the air, dragging the two vampires with him. A sharp slap came from the bag and I bet Berget let Faris have it again.

Even if she hadn't, the thought made me smile.

"Freeze. Put your hands in the air!" The female cop on the left called out to us, dragging my attention back to her. I looked up at Blaz.

"You like smashing cars?"

He spun, flicked his tail high into the air, and then brought it down hard on top of the police cruiser. The glass exploded and the two cops leapt away from their now useless vehicle. They lay on the ground, their hands covering their heads as the rest of us scrambled onto Eve and Blaz.

Lark leapt up onto the dragon's back, using his bent back leg for a launching point, Peta right behind her. Shit, they made it look easy. Cactus followed them, doing the exact same thing. Well hell, if they could do it, so could I.

I ran at Blaz's back leg, jumped and he lowered his knee a fraction of an inch, then helped me with a boost so I was launched onto his back.

"Well done, Rylee." Lark let out a laugh. "But your dragon helped you cheat."

I laughed with her and then, as Blaz lifted and we rose into the sky, I realized how badly my attitude had affected everyone else. How much I'd brought them down.

I buckled myself into his harness. "Blaz, how much of my emotional state from that demon could you sense?"

Almost none. It was as if you were blocking me.

We hovered above the big box store and waited for Eve and Marco to flank us before heading west again.

Swallowing my pride, I opened myself up to Blaz. "You need to be aware of what I have going on."

He sucked in a sharp breath and turned his head to look at me. *Are you sure, Rylee?*

I'd never let him all the way into my head, not to the degree I was offering now. I gave him a tight nod. "Yes, I'm sure. It may be the only way we have a chance to survive. I know what happens if one of us dies."

My father had been a demon slayer, and Ophelia was his dragon. When he was killed, Ophelia lost her mind and became a menace to herself, eventually manipulated by a demon because of that weakness. And if Blaz died?

I couldn't even imagine my life without him, without the constant knowledge that he was—with the exception of Liam—the one I trusted the most with my heart.

A low rumble rolled out of him, and as he turned his head from me, I saw a rainbow glimmered tear slip down his cheek. I looked away, but let him feel the gratitude in my heart for him.

For his friendship and protection.

And for kicking my ass when I needed it.

Blaz roared into the sky as that last thought passed from me to him.

And I feel the same.

We swept westward at a good clip. The miles and the day flew by in a rush that I wasn't sure I liked. Without even doing anything, we were running out of time. Another hour or so, and we'd be able to let Berget and Faris out of the bag again. The sun in front of us slowly set, the sky brilliantly reddening as though a forest fire raged below.

I sensed Jonathan in the distance as I Tracked him to the south. I fed the feel of the boy to Blaz, letting the dragon pick the best route to get to the automatic writer. But I was less concerned about our path and more concerned about Jonathan.

The kid was . . . his threads were, for lack of a better word, weird. He wasn't happy or sad; he wasn't feeling any type of emotion. Not even tired or awake. He existed in a fog that had nothing to do with my ability.

When I'd met him years ago, there had been the same lack of feeling, the same strange apathy that he floated in. He'd been a kid, passed from foster home to foster home because he was such an odd character. Freaking creepy, if I recalled right. I picked up on his creep factor loud and clear again.

A shudder rippled through me. What if the Shadow Walker had kept him, what if that had been his influence instead of Lark's people? How much harder would it have been for us to deal with him then?

It would've been harder to get him to help, of that I was certain.

Around us, the air carried a strange energy, and the hairs on the back of my neck slowly rose. The Harpies started to fall back as a serious headwind slammed into us; the weather shifted so quickly, going from a calm breeze into a serious storm in a matter of minutes. The sky darkened and the clouds opened like someone had slashed a knife through them.

Rain pelted down, hard enough that I was sure there would be bruises, reminding me of London, and the constant wet and gray skies. But this was not London, and I had a feeling it was anything but natural.

Within minutes, we were soaked through, and the rain was not warm. Teeth chattering, I looked over my shoulder at Lark and Cactus. Curled up between them, Peta hid from the rain. "You two can't do anything about this, can you?"

Lark shook her head. "No, and if any Sylphs come, it would be best if we were not seen. But I doubt we'd be able to hide in time, so that's not an option."

Above us a bolt of lightning ripped the sky, searing my eyes. I ducked my head. "Is it a Sylph doing this?" In the back of my head I scrambled for information. A Sylph was an air elemental, and as legendary as Lark was supposed to be.

"I'm quite sure. The four families created a lockdown around Jonathan, from what I understand. They knew I would come for him eventually. He is the first step in me taking back my place in our world." She put a hand on my shoulder. "Look at Pamela."

I whipped my head around to see Pamela standing on Eve's back, Alex steadying her with his hands on the back of her thighs. Her hands were raised above her head and the wind around them stilled, the clouds pushed away. Eve winged closer and the calm encircled us. Pamela's eyes were closed and she dripped with water—or it could have been sweat.

"Pamela, you are a badass," I hollered over to her.

She grinned but kept her eyes closed. "I learned from the best."

Lark shimmied closer to me and whispered into my ear. "I can stop the Sylph, but I need to be on the ground."

"Blaz, you heard the Destroyer. Time to land."

He tucked his wings and dropped like the ten-ton lizard he was. Behind us came the sharp whistle of wind screaming through the Harpies' feathers as they coursed behind the dragon. I leaned over and peered around Blaz's head to see the spot he'd picked to land.

"Blaz, tell me you're joking. Please tell me that isn't Mt. Hood."

The quickest path was to stay north and avoid the higher ranges, then come down the coast line.

Mt. Hood. The sight of the volcano I'd caused to erupt; the place where I'd gained the ogres as allies, then lost them when I confronted their leader, Sas.

The place I'd been when Dox had been killed at my farm. My heart clenched.

So be it.

13
PAMELA

The magic rushed through my veins, more heady even than the cup of wine I'd drank at winter solstice with Rylee. Around me, I could feel the world and every element within it, as though they were a part of me, and with a bare whisper of a thought I could ask them to do my bidding.

That had been the key to unlocking my power, truly unlocking it. Not to demand the magic do my bidding, but to ask it. To make it my partner in all I wished.

What no one had ever told me before was that the magic I carried was a living thing, a creature no different than Blaz, Eve, or even me.

And it was a bit temperamental and didn't like to be shoved around.

Weaving the power through me, I kept the clouds and lightning at bay, redirecting the storm, sending it southeast, away from us.

Something pushed it back, though; another force of magic from what it felt like, though the sensation was there and then gone in a flash.

Alex's hands tightened on me and pulled me down. "Sit, we're landing."

My eyes popped open. "Why did we stop?" All around us was black rock and above us was a mountain with the top blown off. I put a hand to my mouth as I slowly turned to take it in. The charcoal forest, the strange landscape, the mountain, and the crystal clear lake in the distance—this was the place Rylee had been, where she'd made the volcano explode.

Which meant there were ogres nearby; ogres that didn't like us and were probably still being manipulated by Orion.

"Oh shit," I whispered.

Alex squeezed my arms, and then quickly let go so he could slide off Eve's back.

"Don't freak out yet. Maybe it's not all that bad." He pointed at Rylee and Lark, who had their heads bent together. Marco hopped beside us, doing his best to keep Berget and Liam from bouncing on the ground as he landed.

I rolled my eyes. "Alex, this is Rylee we're talking about. How can you say not to freak out?"

Laughing, he winked up at me. "Because I would like to believe we're all getting out of this alive. We'll look back on this someday and tell amazing stories." He paused and turned his head, sniffing loudly. "Do you smell that?'

I swallowed hard. "Please tell me it isn't ogres."

He spun around and looked at me. "How did you know?"

"Call it a bad feeling." I jumped off Eve's back and ran to Rylee, fighting the urge to panic. Ogres were tough, and while my magic was strong, we hadn't been able to fend off the human mob without Rylee getting stuck with a demon. What would happen if it were an ogre mob that came at us?

Blaz's voice whispered across to me. *Easy, Pamela. You are broadcasting your panic.*

I took a slow breath, let it out, and made myself stop hurrying. "Thank you."

You're welcome.

I stopped beside Lark and Rylee. The tall elemental made me feel very small, but her eyes and face were kind. She noticed me first. "What is it, witch?"

"Ogres are coming."

Rylee's jaw tightened. "Better to kill them now than face them later. Seriously, I thought I was done with these assholes."

Lark put a hand on my shoulder. "There is a Sylph coming. They were manipulating the weather around us and are drawing closer. Rylee tells me you took down a Sylph when they tried to stop you from taking me out of the oubliette. Is that right?"

My mouth dried up at the thought of a Sylph and what they could do. I'd been on the receiving end of their power; it was more terrifying than facing Orion as he used Milly's body.

"Yes, that's right," I managed to say.

"Then you, Peta, and I will tackle the Sylph. Rylee and the others will deal with the ogres, yes?" Lark said.

I caught Rylee's eye and she gave me a nod. "Go, clean his clock. Another thirty minutes, and Berget and Faris will be able to help us with the ogres."

Thirty minutes. Did she think it would take that long to deal with the two factions coming at us?

Probably not. But to be safe, perhaps you should stick the vampires farther back from the field of battle.

Blaz's words must have gone to everyone, because Marco flew into the air, his beak moving as he relayed what was going on to Berget and Faris.

Lark led me away from the others. Peta trotted ahead of us, shifting once more into her leopard form. She sniffed the air and then flicked her head to the north, toward the mountain.

"Where are we going?"

"To the base of the mountain. My power and strength lie in the earth, so the more I have it at hand the better."

I kept looking for the Sylph, wondering when he would come flying in. "Do you think the Sylph will attack with you here?"

Lark laughed softly with a bitter note to it. "I'm quite sure if I weren't here, you would have got through fine. I've no doubt they've come to stop me."

"Why?"

She took a deep breath and muttered, "Rylee said you asked a lot of questions."

"How else can I learn?" I snapped at her, embarrassed that Rylee would warn her.

Lark held up both hands. "Easy, little witch. It is only that she wanted me to know that was your way. That you were hungry for the supernatural and all the knowledge you could gain. That is a good thing." She paused and looked to the sky for a moment before answering my original question. "A long time ago, I was set apart by the mother goddess as her chosen one. It means I live outside the rules and stipulations placed on my people, on all elementals, really. It makes me dangerous because I can become the catalyst for change. And change is coming."

I looked at her, then at Rylee. "You two really are related, aren't you?"

Her mouth quirked up. "Yes—"

Lightning struck at our feet, exploding the hardened lava and sending chunks toward us at rapid-fire speed. I was thrown backward, and landed flat on my back, the wind knocked out of me. Rolling to my side, I looked up. Lark stood with her legs spread wide and her hands stretched out to the side. Her feet were sunk into the earth, and it held her tightly as the wind ripped around her, yanking on her. Peta stood in front of her, claws digging into the ground. She snarled at the Sylph above us.

He floated in the air, his long white hair swirling around his body. Like the Sylph I'd faced before, he wore all white, making him seem even paler than he truly was. The mountain shook beneath me, shivering as if it were going to leap up at any moment. I fought for air and gulped down several lungsful, the scent of ozone heavy. He was going to fry her. "Lark!"

"Deflect it, Pamela!"

I struggled to my feet and focused on the clouds above us. The rumble of lightning formed within the clouds. I lifted my hands and the magic poured out of me, sending the clouds flying backward. Lightning shot our way but missed by twenty feet, at least.

I ran to Lark's side and she draped an arm over my shoulder. My feet sank into the ground and held as the earth firmed around them. "Don't hold back. He will kill us if he can."

"I've never let it all out."

She nodded. "Only if you have to. You'll know the moment when it comes, when there is nothing left but to unleash everything in you, every molecule of power you have left to survive."

Although I didn't need to, I held my hands up. The magic paused for a beat of my heart while I directed it to what I wanted. My idea was simple. Grab the Sylph and throw him to the ground so that Lark could cover him with dirt.

Simple.

Right.

The magic shot toward the Sylph and he dodged it, as if he'd seen it coming. But that wasn't possible, was it?

"He can feel it, Pamela. He can feel the vibrations on the air like a snake feels the vibrations of a heartbeat," Lark said. "You'll have to outsmart him."

Rocks shot into the air, flying hard and fast at the Sylph, and he batted them away like they were nothing before they ever reached him.

Changing tactics, I sent fireballs at him, one after another; left hand, right hand, left hand, right hand. Those slowed him down; the first thing that had, and I realized they ate the air. Fire was the key.

"Cactus, where is he?"

"Helping Rylee; we need to do this on our own." She didn't look back for him, though I could see the strain on her face in not doing so. Cactus was her friend, and yet she'd sent him with Rylee. Because Rylee was the one who needed to be protected at all costs.

The Sylph flew toward us and Lark tensed. "He's going to steal our air, Pamela. It's going to be now or never."

I looked back for a split second to my friends, and almost threw up. The ogres had surrounded Rylee, Cactus, and Alex, and Blaz was flat out on the ground. Eve and Marco were above them all and were being kept at bay by several ogres with oversized crossbows. What had happened to Blaz?

"Pamela, focus. We have a job to do. We can help them when we are done." Her voice was sharp and it spun me around. Lark was right. I had to do this on my own. I opened myself up to the magic and beckoned it forward. "Please be enough," I whispered, and then looked at Lark. "I'm going to drop him. Be ready."

She nodded and put a hand on my shoulder. The magic in me leapt at her touch, as if being called by an old friend. Lark gave me a wink. "A power boost, kid. Take him down and show him who's in charge here."

With renewed determination, I lifted my hands, and that's when the Sylph made his move.

The tornado dropped out of the sky and spun toward us, ripping up chunks of hardened lava, any trees that were left, and all the dark gray ash. A maelstrom that would batter our bodies into oblivion if I let it catch us.

"Pamela, whatever you're going to do, do it now. I can't hold us against that," Lark said, with more than a hint of anxiety in her voice. Peta roared her defiance into the wind, but there wasn't much else she could do.

Squinting my eyes against the debris being kicked up, I braced myself. "I can do this. I have to."

Fire danced in front of my hands, growing in size until it blocked our view of the Sylph. Larger and larger, I made a barrier of fire, the tips of the flames turning blue and purple as I expanded it over twenty feet.

My arms shook and legs buckled so I was on my knees in the gray ash, but I didn't stop pushing the size of the wall I was creating. Larger and larger, until I could no longer see anything except red and orange. I was at the brink of my abilities and yet I kept pulling more.

As Lark said, it was all or nothing.

Above us, the Sylph laughed and shook his head. As if we were nothing to him.

"That is the one to attack," I whispered, and my magic heard me. I flicked my fingers, and like a faithful hound, the wall of fire raced away.

"Holy shit on a green stick, what did you do?" Lark gasped and I looked up. The flames were smaller, but they were chasing the Sylph, and gaining on him. He tried to duck down and the fire dropped on him, wrapping him in its embrace. His screams echoed through the sky and the tornado dropped into nothing. The Sylph's body fell and as soon as it hit the earth, Lark was moving, Peta running ahead of her. I paused and looked at where Rylee was fighting.

"Lark, are you good?"

"Go to Rylee. We will finish him."

They ran in one direction and I ran in the other as the sun dipped below the horizon.

My family needed me, and I wasn't about to let them face a herd of wild ogres without me.

14
RYLEE

Behind me the wind howled and the harsh retort of lightning cracking the hardened lava worried me. The sounds begged me to turn around, to run and help Pamela and Lark. Yet I knew their fight was predicated on their abilities with magic.

With the ogres, that wasn't going to be the case.

Alex drifted to my left. "Should I shift?"

"Not yet. Maybe they're coming to make peace because they've seen what a fucktart Orion is."

On my right, Cactus laughed. "Fucktart? I like it. Might even steal it for those moments of sheer desperation I'm sure will come."

I rolled my eyes and reached for my swords, pulling both out of their sheaths. Just because I was hoping they wanted to do peace talks didn't mean I fully trusted them in any way, shape, or form.

Ghosting through the scattered trees, the seven-foot-plus ogres drifted toward us. All the colors were represented: black, red, green, violet, gray, brown, and even a flash of blue skin could be seen here and there. That hurt the most.

Dox's family had been blue and they'd kicked him out for being weak. For showing kindness to others.

Anger flickered along my spine and it took everything I had not to shout at the leader as she strode toward us. Sas, Dox's lover and one of the only violet ogres left to the world.

Her eyes were narrowed, but that wasn't what I focused on. No, her belly swollen with child was what caught my attention. She swayed from side to side like a ship at sea, she was so big. There had to be at least three babies in there. At least.

"Rylee, I'm surprised you would dare set foot in my territory."

"Temporary lapse in judgment. We thought this was a different mountain I'd caused to erupt. My mistake." I grinned at her, though the grin, I knew, was anything but nice.

Her lips compressed and her ogres ranged out behind her. Behind me, Blaz let out a cough, and his voice projected to all of us.

I've not eaten ogre before, Rylee, do you think they taste like beef . . . or chicken?

My eyes widened as the less than subtle insult seemed to hit the ogres as a unit. They lifted their weapons and rushed us with battle cries that drowned even the sound of the rushing wind.

Cactus flicked his hands and fireballs erupted from his fingertips, slamming into those ogres closest to us. "Cooked chicken for you, Blaz."

Beside me, Alex whipped his clothes off and shifted, his body sliding through the change faster than ever. He looked up at me, his tongue flopped out of his mouth sending spit flying. "Geeky werewolf to the rescue."

I took a deep breath and braced myself as the first ogre burst through Cactus's flame throwing. It was a brown ogre, his skin a pale tan, the color of desert sand. His eyes were the same tone, and that's about all I noticed before I was dodging the first swing of the war ax he carried.

The half-moon blade cut the air with a high-pitched whistle, and headed straight for my neck. I dropped to my knees and swung both swords out in front of me, in a crisscross slash. He stumbled back from me, my blade tips catching the edge of his knees and drawing blood.

"I would rather we fought on the same side," I said as I stood and advanced on the brown ogre.

His eyes narrowed. "And I'd rather cut your lying head off and shit down your neck hole."

So much for making nice. He took a second swing with the war ax and I bent backward like a contestant in a limbo contest gone terribly wrong. "Alex, spot me!"

The werewolf got his paws under my back and kept me from falling flat on the ground. Then he pushed me forward as the ogre dealt with the backswing of his big weapon. I shot forward, whipping my sword across in front of me, and taking off the ogre's hand that held his ax. Blood shot out of the stump and I sidestepped it. Though he wasn't dead, he would be soon.

"Alex, you got him?"

"You gots it." He let out a deep snarl and leapt for the ogre, knocking him to the ground. Alex went straight for the jugular, his wicked-long canines crushing the windpipe in a matter of seconds.

But there was no respite for the wicked and I had more ogres to deal with.

Rylee, I cannot do much damage with them so close to you! Blaz said.

"Grab Sas, maybe we can hold her hostage."

I like how you think. He let out a rather evil chuckle and leapt over our heads. But we'd forgotten about the red ogres; the fact that they had magic as strong as any witch. And they knew Blaz's weakness as they knew mine.

From the base of the mountain, two large boulders lifted into the air, a pair of red ogres under them, directing the rocks that had to be at least two tons each.

Time slowed.

In mid-air, the two boulders swung toward Blaz, catching his head between them. As if in slow motion the boulders pressed toward one another, twisting Blaz's head at an unnatural angle. The reverberation of the crunch of bones shot through me as if it were my head being caught in a vice and not his.

Rylee, I am sorry, he whispered to me. Just to me.

"NO!"

Blaz's body was held aloft as the rocks continued to squeeze his head. A final push and they let him go. He slumped downward, blood pouring from his nose and mouth, teeth broken and shattered. Eyes glazing over, the golden light in them dimming at a speed that could only mean one thing—

A scream ripped from me, one not even close to human; primal, feral, a cry that was every bit that of an enraged animal. The ogres closest to me actually stepped back, but that wasn't going to help them.

I dove into the ogres, desperate to get to Blaz, my swords slicing through them as if they were standing still and not trying their best to take me out. Blades caught the edges of my arms; I didn't feel it other than to notice the blood sliding down my skin. Clubs clipped my legs, and though I went to my knees, I fought from there, cutting off legs and driving my weapons through male anatomy.

I forced myself to Track Blaz, forced myself to reach for him.

There was a flicker of life still. We had time if I could get to him.

Please, for all that is holy in the world, let me get to him; let us get Pam to him.

The ogres fell in front of me; Alex and Cactus, and then Pamela, were there with us, Pamela's magic curling around the ogres in ribbons of flame and lightning. The red ogres engaged her, forcing her back a step.

Cactus worked with her, raining fire down on their heads as Alex and I slammed through the ogres, cutting a swath in their numbers. Two blond heads popped up beside us, and distantly I knew that Faris and Berget had joined the fight. The sun must have gone down, but I'd barely noticed.

"Blaz, don't you dare die on me," I screamed at him, desperate to hear his voice again.

Nothing in my head but silence.

Faris and Berget's speed outstripped the ogres and they blasted through their ranks, cutting throats and hamstrings, dropping the remainder of them until there were none left standing except for Sas.

Her eyes were wide and she stepped back, her hands clutching her belly. "You wouldn't dare."

I didn't even look at her. "Pamela, we're losing Blaz!"

I clung to his threads even as they faded, the last of his life gone from him as Pamela laid her hands on his side. "Please, please try," I whispered to her.

Her hands shook as the sobs rippled from her tiny body. "Rylee, he's gone."

I grabbed her hands and put them back on his side. "Try, you have to try. He's not gone."

Letting her go, I backed away. My own Immunity would affect Pamela's ability to use her magic. I clenched my teeth. "Pamela. Please try."

She looked at me over her shoulder, tears streaking down her face. "Rylee," she sobbed my name, "he's gone. I can't . . . I can't bring him back."

I dropped to my knees and tipped my head back to the sky as I screamed, the wail slipping into a sob that shook my entire body. Blaz . . . damn him for leaving me, for leaving me now when I needed him more than ever.

Arms circled around me as my body shook with uncontrollable spasms. The bond between Blaz and me that severed in death left a hole in me like no other. He had been a part of my life for such a short time. And yet it felt like I'd never lived without him.

My hands shook and I didn't even realize I'd dropped my weapons. More arms went around me as I sobbed, unable to feel anything past the loss. Worse than losing Giselle. Worse than losing Dox or even Milly.

Blaz . . . he couldn't be gone. This was a joke; a nightmare I'd open my eyes from and he would be there, inside my head teasing me about my growing feelings for Faris. Kicking my ass when I needed it.

Slowly, I opened my eyes. Blaz was not in front of me, wings poised and waiting for our flight. He was in front of me, his body still. Wings that would never take flight again.

Sas stood to the side of us, Cactus holding her arms behind her back. Liam, Berget, Alex, Pamela, and surprisingly Lark, held onto me. I gently pushed them all back and stood.

Cactus's eyes were wet, but his mouth was a hard line. "Rylee, what do you want to do with her?"

I took a deep shuddering breath. "Whose babies do you carry?"

She shook, her oversized body quivering with what I had no doubt was fear. She was alone, what was left of her people wiped out. "I don't know. Perhaps the triplets. Perhaps Dox's."

Lark stepped forward. "I can tell you."

Sas squirmed, but Cactus held her tightly, his hands lighting up. "I will fry your ass if I have to, ogre."

She stilled and Lark stepped close enough to put a hand on Sas's bulging belly. A few moments passed and she pulled her hand away. "Three children, one blue and two violet. All boys."

So her babies came from both Dox and the triplets. Sas bared her teeth at me. "You are weak, you'd let me live because of Dox. You are a fool."

"How close to term is she?" I asked softly, a deadly, vengeful part of me waking for perhaps the first time in my life. A part I wasn't sure was good or not.

Sas started. "What do you mean?"

Lark looked at me. "Close enough. But what would you do with the babies?"

The reality of what I was saying, or more accurately what I wasn't saying, and what it would mean for her, seemed to hit Sas as Lark and I stared at each other. Sas began to fight in earnest, bucking against Cactus, but he did as he said he would and his hands heated her skin, burning it. Screaming, she went to her knees.

"You can't do this! You're a monster if you take my babies, they're all I have left!" Her sobs didn't touch me, didn't soften me. Liam put a hand on the back of my neck and tugged me to him.

"Don't do this." No, that wasn't Liam, it was Faris. I leaned back into him—just a little.

"Give me one good reason I shouldn't, Faris. They killed Blaz; what right has she to life? To go on as though nothing has changed."

"Of all the people you know, I perhaps understand vengeance the most. My own father killed my sister, turned me into a vampire, and left me to die in the sun. Revenge"—his arms tightened around me—"is not who you are. Justice is."

Justice. But what was just in this case? What could possibly account for Blaz's life?

Lark lifted her one hand and Sas sank to her chin into the earth. "Death is justice, vampire. But I agree, taking the babies first is not the right way. Let her give birth, let her love them and realize the world she would have brought them into." The elemental's eyes hardened. "And then take them."

I stared at her, seeing why she'd earned the nickname 'The Destroyer." I knew what it was to give up a child, to walk away knowing it was best for her. But what if someone had taken Marcella from me? My stomach rolled and I struggled to not let the turmoil show on my face.

"Let her up, Lark."

As quickly as Sas had been pulled down, she was pushed up. I held my sword out and pointed it at her heart, resting the blade on the top of her belly. "For Dox's child, and the triplets, you can live for now. But I assure you, I will come for them. And if I can't," I looked at Lark and she nodded.

"Yes, if you can't come for the babies, I will."

Good enough for me. I turned back to Sas. "The last thing any of those fathers would have wanted would be to have their children raised by a vindictive, manipulative bitch like you." I stepped back and lowered my sword. "When you least expect it, Sas. One of us will come for you."

She stumbled back, spun, and lumbered away from us as fast as she could. I watched her go, the night slowly deepening around us. Faris still stood with me, the only one touching me, the only one feeling the tremors there, just under my skin.

Without Blaz I felt adrift, lost. "He was a part of the prophecies, he was supposed to be the winged one who would carry me into battle," I said. This was part of Orion's plan, to cut me off from those I needed to help me face him down.

Faris put his chin on my shoulder. "I know you don't want to hear this right now, but it has to be said . . . ."

I looked at him, his deep blue eyes rimmed in gold holding more compassion than I'd ever seen from him before, and I was nearly undone. I forced myself to hold it together. Barely.

"Whatever it is, say it. We don't have time for anything else."

He looked where Blaz lay, and I looked with him, my heart breaking all over again when his chest didn't rise. His wings lay still on the ground. Pamela lay against him, still crying her heart out as Berget tried to console her. Alex sat beside her in his wolf form, a high-pitched whine in his throat as tears dripped down his fur.

Faris turned me away from Blaz so I looked only at him through watery eyes.

"There is one other dragon who is Slayer trained. One other who could take you into battle. You know that. We have to find her, which means you will have to Track her."

I squeezed my eyes shut. "Which will take Orion straight to my daughter."

There were no words for the horror that cut through me, for the reality of what I faced. Orion had effectively cornered me, making me decide between my daughter and saving the world.

And I had no idea what I was going to do.

15
RYLEE

Kneeling in front of Blaz's face, I closed my eyes and put my forehead to his. "Wait for me on the other side, my friend." The same words I'd said over Milly's grave. I truly hoped I would not have to say them again in what was left of my life.

The feel of his scales under my skin like every other time I touched him; the sense that at any moment he would leap up and tell me he was fine. I couldn't get over it.

"Rylee, we have to go while the night still holds." Lark crouched beside me. "We can be in the Rim before the morning dawns and heading back immediately."

"I know," I said softly, running my hand over his closed eye. "You can bury him?"

She nodded and I stood. We backed away and with a sweep of Lark's hands, the ground opened up and swallowed my dragon down as if he never were. So fast, it was easy to believe he was somewhere else.

That he wasn't gone.

Yet I knew that wasn't the case at all. I would never see him again.

"Wait, Rylee," Lark said as I moved to turn away, unable to look at the spot where he'd been a second longer.

The ground where he'd been shuddered and green shoots shot upward at a rate that my eyes couldn't follow. One minute the ground was barren and dead, and then it was covered in plants and grass, tree saplings springing up and growing into towering cedars.

Around one of the cedars, a climbing bush wrapped around the trunk, blossoms bursting open and filling the air with their sweet scent. Blue petals flipped open, their softness beckoning. Lark lowered her hands. "With the time constraints, it is all I can do. But I will come back and finish it. After this is all done . . . it is the least I can do."

I stepped forward and plucked a blossom off the growing vine. It was the exact shade of blue that his scales had sported. "This is plenty. He'd have loved to knock it all down."

Alex laughed softly and Liam joined in. I glanced at them. "He was kinda destructive."

Pamela sniffed. "He *was* a dragon."

I nodded and walked toward Eve, pushing my grief away. There was nothing else I could do but bury it as Lark had buried Blaz. We had to move on without him, no matter how much it hurt.

"How many of us can you carry, Eve?"

The Harpy fluffed her wings, her eyes still wet with tears. "A thousand pounds. But I need to carry at least two in my claws. That is where I have the most strength."

Marco bobbed his head. "We can carry you all. It isn't a problem."

Lark snapped her fingers at Peta. "Cat, downsize your furry bottom."

Peta let out a coughing growl and shifted from her leopard form into that of an ordinary gray-and-white housecat. Though I couldn't hear her speak to Lark, I could guess at the conversation based on Lark's expressions.

And based on the stiff-legged stalk of the cat to her mistress.

Eve would carry Pamela and Alex in her talons, and Liam and I would ride astride. Marco would carry Cactus and the blackout curtains in his talons and carry Berget and Lark and Peta on his back.

As we rose into the air above the battle site. I watched as the bodies of the ogres slid under the earth, like a wave washing over them. I thought it was Lark doing it, but she shook her head and pointed to Pamela.

"Pamela." Just her name, and with it a question.

"They were fighting for their lives too, Rylee. No different than us."

I closed my eyes and breathed in the fresh air. She was right. "Stop being so wise when you are so much younger than me."

Liam or Faris, whoever, wrapped his arms around me and held me tightly. A rock of strength, that's what he was. What they both were. And it seemed they knew when to talk, and when not to.

This was one of the latter times.

Blaz's death would haunt me; I knew it already, felt it deeply in my bones like a break that would never truly heal.

But like every other death I'd faced, I couldn't let it slow me down, or take me from the path I was on.

The world depended on me to kick Orion's ass into oblivion.

I stared into the night sky and wondered how many more we would lose along the way.

And if I would crack under the grief.

16
LIAM/FARIS

The trembling in her body eased as she relaxed against him. Inside his head, he looked at Faris. The vampire shrugged. "She needs her peace right now. I've a feeling it's only getting worse from here."

Liam grunted softly. He already knew. Yet, he also knew Rylee better than anyone else and this wasn't her breaking point. Losing Blaz was a blow; there was no doubt. Already he could feel the loss of the big lizard's humor and strength, of his unfailing loyalty to Rylee and her strange pack.

But they would survive, and Rylee would rise above it to continue fighting.

An hour passed and the tops of the redwoods at the northern edge of the forest came into view, peeking through the low-lying clouds.

Marco drew closer to them and Lark gave them a wave. "Expect few to be happy to see me. We'll go to my sister first."

She pointed the way and Marco took the lead. Below them, Alex let out a yip and started howling like a mad man, his exuberance for life overcoming whatever grief he held, at least for the moment. There was the sound of a smack and a soft, "Be quiet, you fool," from Pamela, and he couldn't help chuckling.

Rylee snickered softly.

"They're going to be quite the pair later, aren't they?" he whispered into her ear so Alex wouldn't hear them. But apparently Eve did. Her head whipped around and her beak dropped open.

Rylee put a finger to her lips. Eve grinned and bobbed her head once, understanding clearly.

"Yes, I do think so. He'll help her not be so hard, and she'll keep him from being too wild. Perhaps a little like another couple we know?"

She looked him in the eye and gave him a slow wink. Fatigue lined the three colors, along with a heavy dose of grief, but also something he knew she would need more than anything else.

Belief. There was still hope in her that they could make this happen. That she would come out on top.

Which meant she had something up her sleeve she hadn't told him about. His eyes narrowed sharply. "What are you planning, Rylee?"

Her eyes widened with an effort at looking innocent. Indeed, there was something she was keeping to herself. "Nothing."

"Don't bullshit me, Adamson. I know you. I know that face. That face is trying to keep a secret from me."

She shrugged and turned her back to him. "I'll tell you when I'm damn well good and ready, O'Shea."

Fear for her flickered through him. Rylee's plans were not always known to turn out well, mostly because they weren't plans. Her "plans" were her running by the seat of her pants and leaping before she knew what the hell was going on.

Worse, they all knew what rested on her shoulders. Knowing her the way he did, there was a distinct possibility she was putting herself in more danger than she needed to.

Faris leaned forward inside his head. "Then we have to keep her from doing that. Seduce her, man. We've got the goods to do it: my body and your soul. We'll soften her up and she'll spill her little secret."

His jaw tightened. Seducing her would do nothing for them except to get Faris laid by her. "She'd see through it in an instant."

The vampire didn't seem deterred. "I could bite her. See if I can pick up anything. Though that can lead to other things too." Faris shrugged and then faded a little.

Liam wanted to stuff the vampire further back in his head, but for a second he wondered why. Why would he push a part of himself further back?

Wolf, that is . . . why am I talking to myself?

He hung his head, resting it against Rylee's back as he fought to find himself. Himself.

Liam. Faris. Wolf. Vampire. They blended together inside his head until there was no *other*, no *sharing*.

Just one.

Rylee shifted. "Liam."

He lifted his head. "Is that who I am?"

Her whole body stiffened. "What did you say?"

"I . . . what is my name? I thought I knew a minute ago, but now I'm not sure." He saw her eyes widen and he leaned forward, capturing her lips with his own. This was what he wanted. To feel her skin under his and feel her heartbeat beneath his own.

But hadn't he been with her before?

Love, that was what he wanted. But she loved him, so how could he want her to love him?

The confusion seemed to split his skull, yet with his mouth on hers, tasting her lips and tangling his tongue against hers, there was no wrong place. This was right.

This was home for every part of him.

She pulled away from him. "You feel different."

"Better?" He arched an eyebrow and her lips turned up at the corner.

"Just . . . different. You're both still in there, aren't you?"

"Both? Just me."

She sucked in a sharp breath and ran a hand down the side of his face, and there was a glimmer of tears in those amazing eyes. "Just you."

He smiled again and gave her a wide grin, flashing his fangs. "Just me."

Below them, Eve shuddered. "We're landing soon. Lark called back for us to be ready."

He nodded. "Ready as we'll ever be."

The Harpy began her descent, spiraling out of the sky, through the clouds and the tips of the redwoods.

Wherever they were, no matter the danger, he would protect her. That much he knew without a doubt.

"Rylee, I do have one question," he said as the trees around them thinned and they dropped to the ground.

"What's that?"

"It's rather foolish."

"No such thing as a stupid question, not in our world," she said as she dismounted from the large bird. Eve had dropped Pamela and Alex ahead of them.

He cleared his throat. "What's my name again?"

She spun and stared at him, but that wasn't what caught his attention.

No, it was the oversized black wolf with the white fur zigzagging down his leg that marked a scar. The beast's lips were rippled back over fangs that were at least four-inches long. He knew that wolf, they'd met before, but those memories blurred along with all the others in his head as they slipped away from him.

In a flash, the wolf leapt, knocking him to the ground with a speed he couldn't dodge. A low rumbling growl rippled from the wolf, out of his lips, and felt as though it wormed its way into his own body.

Breaking apart the confusion, dividing what had become one.

And he wasn't sure he liked it.

"No, I don't want to lose my chance for her to love me!" The words ripped out of him.

Faris's words.

Liam was there, inside his head, held back by the vampire's strength. He could do nothing, had no say over the body.

On top of them, Griffin shifted. Fully clothed, the man Liam knew as his grandfather stared down at them.

"Vampire was pulling a fast one on you, kid. Whether you knew it or not, yeah?"

Liam wanted to ask what the hell was happening, but couldn't.

Didn't seem to stop Griffin from answering. "He bound you good; I can see that. Now, the only way to separate is for him to decide to let you go. And that isn't going to happen, is it?"

Rylee came up behind Griffin. "Can you bring Liam forward?"

Faris nodded, but Liam didn't come forward. "Adamson, I'm okay with this. I am, and I need you to believe it and put it from your mind."

Liam struggled against Faris, against the control the vampire had. But it was like wrestling with a mountain. There was nothing he could do.

Rylee stared at him hard, like she was trying to see him. With everything he had, he reached for her with his heart, his spirit. She paused. "Faris, stop fucking with me and let Liam talk or I will stake you right fucking now."

Faris's mouth dropped open. "How did you know?"

"He's the other half of my soul, vampire. And no amount of blending with you can take that away." She stepped closer, and lifted her sword that he'd not even see her draw. "Let him speak, or forever hold your peace."

Faris backed away and Liam waited until he was sure there would be no interference.

Slowly, he stepped forward. "I don't think it was his fault, Rylee."

Inside his head, Faris's shock reverberated through him. *Damn it, wolf, I do not want to like you.*

"What do you mean?"

"I think the binding is doing things he didn't expect. Except for that last bit where he tried to make you believe he was me, there has been no deception."

Can't blame a guy for trying, Faris muttered.

She looked at Griffin. "How long before they totally merge?"

Griffin rolled his shoulders and stood, letting him stand. Liam pushed to his feet, but didn't touch Rylee. He didn't want her to think it was Faris trying to take advantage of her again.

"Griffin, how long?" Rylee bit the question out a second time.

"A day, two at most, yeah?" He shook his head. "Shame, I was hoping the boy would follow in my footsteps."

Rylee nodded, walked toward Liam, and cupped his face in her hands. "No matter what, I love you. If you and Faris truly merge, I will love you. Your soul is mine, to the end. And Faris, if you want me to love you, then stop dicking around. No more games."

Faris was very quiet, retreating to the far recesses of his mind. Which, as far as Liam was concerned, was fine.

She went up on her toes and kissed him softly. There was a moment he felt alone with her and all he wanted was to bury his face against her bare skin and breathe her in.

But the moment passed too quickly and they stepped apart.

"Why is it that we're always in the middle of a crisis again?" he asked softly. "I'm thinking this might be your fault."

She laughed, and though it wasn't a full belly laugh, it was a start.

"Not this time, Wolf. It's all on you."

17
LARK

Rylee let go of her man and looked to me. "Where to?"

This was where things got a bit tricky. "The Rim is what we call our home, where all earth elementals reside. It is hidden from humans and other supernaturals."

"Like with the Veil?" Pamela asked. No surprise there that she asked the question first.

"It doesn't matter, little witch. What matters is that getting you into the Rim may be difficult. My people aren't known for welcoming strangers into their home. Elementals are . . . reluctant to let others know they even exist."

"Are they going to fight us?" Rylee slid her sword back into its sheath. That was something else I had to dig up while we were here.

The sword I'd made for Rylee over ten years ago, right before I'd met her in Las Vegas. Right before I'd been stuffed into the oubliette.

I shook my head to clear my wayward thoughts. "No, but they'll try and block you."

Griffin snorted. "It's why I live as far out in the forest as I do, yeah?"

I pointed at the two Harpies. "You two stay here. Griffin, are you coming with us?"

He grinned, his white teeth catching what little light there was. "Wouldn't miss it for the world, yeah?"

With a nod, I took the lead, and started toward my home, a place I hadn't been in almost thirty years. First I'd been ousted to the desert as banishment for flaunting the rules of my people, and then stuffed into the oubliette for helping Rylee.

A wash of disappointment slid over me. None of the things I'd done were truly wrong, they just were not what my father and his people wanted me to do. Peta's claws dug lightly through the shirt on my shoulder, her mouth right by my ear.

"Easy, Lark. They can't deny you forever. And your sister will help."

That's what I was hoping.

Cactus jogged up to my side. "Are we going to Bella?"

"Yes, that's the plan."

Griffin cleared his throat. "Your sister isn't in the Rim proper-like. She's living in your old place at the very edge with her daughter."

Adjusting my trajectory, I kept walking. Cactus brushed my hand with his and I took his fingers for a moment, squeezing them. Of all the people in my life, he knew how difficult this was for me. To come home and once again be treated like I was useless.

Or worse, a threat.

We stayed to the edge of the Rim, all the way around the perimeter, until we came to my home. The tree was wide at the base and had a pulley system with a simple loop of rope for a foothold that would take me up. The main living quarters were fifty feet above us in the tree and carved into the trunk itself.

I glanced at everyone. "Wait here. I don't want to freak my sister out. Rylee, come with me."

Rylee jogged over to me. "You don't think I would freak her out?"

Bella needed to know this was serious. And if she saw Rylee, there would be no doubt we were fighting the final battle in a matter of days.

"Yes, you probably will, but I think you should come anyway." I reached up and tugged the rope, the pulley system working silently as it sent the foot loop down to us. Stuffing my foot into the loop I held out a hand for Rylee.

I caught her around the waist, winding one hand through the rope as I tugged on a second rope that would release the counter weight with my other hand.

We shot into the air, almost fifty feet before we jerked to a stop. Rylee's arm never tightened on me once. Trust . . . it was a strange thing to have so strongly between us already.

"So this is another cousin of mine then?" she asked.

Reaching out, I grabbed the platform and pulled us to it. "No, you and I are related on my mother's side. I'm the only family you've got. But that won't matter. Bella will recognize you for who you are."

We stepped off the platform and I walked into the hollowed-out tree. The entryway was dark and I called out softly.

"Belladonna."

There was a scuffle of sheets and then a thump of feet running toward us. A lantern flickered on and my older sister held it up. "Mother goddess, Larkspur, I thought you were dead!"

She ran to me, her long dark brown hair curling down her shoulders as artfully as if she'd never slept on it. I caught her in my arms and held her tightly, a shudder going through me. Nearly thirty years away from her, one of my best friends.

Bella let out a sob and pulled back, touching my face as if she couldn't believe I was there. To be honest, I wasn't sure I believed it myself. "You've changed, Lark."

I gave her a half grin. "A little, maybe. The desert will do that to you."

"So many questions; how is it that you aren't dead? Father told everyone you died while helping a Tracker find Jonathan . . . ." She noticed we weren't alone. I moved to the side.

"This is the Tracker I was helping, Bella. And the time has come for the elementals to stand with this world, or watch it go down in demon flames."

She took a deep shuddering breath, then held out her hand to Rylee. "Hello, my name is Belladonna. You must be Elle."

Rylee's whole body jerked as if she'd been shot with the electricity. "What did you call me?"

My throat constricted. "No, this is Rylee, and we're leaving it at that."

Bella looked from me to Rylee and back again, her gray eyes catching the light. "All right, then. What do you need, Lark?"

She was backing me, and a piece of the anger for everything that had been done to me slipped away. "We have to take Jonathan with us. He's going to help Rylee with the demons."

Bella nodded, but her lips were pursed. "I can take you to him, but I don't think he will help. We've never in all the years he's been here been able to convince him to Read for us. He says that payment is required, but no matter what we give him, it isn't good enough. Jewels, money . . . even women." She blushed on that last bit and I didn't blame her. Trying to buy a kid off to help you clean the house was one thing. Trying to buy a kid off to help you understand the future was apparently a hell of a lot harder.

"Mom, what's going on?"

I looked past Bella to a tall woman with long black hair and pale blue eyes. She lifted her hand, all elegance and grace even in that slight movement.

"River, this is your aunt."

The girl let out a soft gasp. "You helped my mother escape the Deep. You helped her keep me safe and protected me against—"

I held up my hand stopping her. "That is not a story for right now. But I promise you when I am done helping Rylee I will come back. We will talk and tell stories of before."

My niece nodded. "A deal then."

Bella reached back and touched her daughter gently on the hand. "Go to bed, I don't want you to be a part of this."

"I'm not a child, mother."

"No, it would be better if you were; then there would be no banishment for you. As an adult, if you were caught even speaking to your aunt, there would be repercussions I'm not sure any of us could save you from."

Rylee shifted on her feet. "I thought you were shitting me about your family."

I shook my head slowly. "No, I am the black sheep, as the humans would say."

Bella grabbed a wrap from the hook on the wall and put it over her shoulders. "Come, let us go get the boy and send him with you. We might be able to make it happen before anyone knows you're even here."

When all three of us were on the ground, Bella gasped and took in the group we'd left behind. "Oh dear. This could be a problem."

Rylee waved at them. "They can wait on the edge. As long as your people aren't going to attack us."

Bella glanced at her. "They won't attack you, Rylee. But they will attack Lark if we run into the wrong people."

I lifted a hand. "Where is Jonathan?"

Rylee pointed before Bella could say, and my blood chilled. "He's that direction, middle of the Rim from what I can tell."

My sister gave me a tight smile and doused her light. "That's correct, he's in the Spiral."

The Spiral was the seat of power for our home, where our father lived with his favored children, and where there would be plenty of guards who would recognize me.

"Worm shit," I whispered.

Bella nodded. "Exactly."

18
RYLEE

Lark's sister had us cover our heads so only our eyes were visible. "It's the best we can do. They would recognize Lark's hair and you don't look like any elemental here with your auburn coloring. Worse, they might take you as a Salamander."

I lifted my eyebrows. "I look like a lizard?"

Pamela tapped my arm. "A Salamander is another name for a fire elemental. Like Cactus, they mostly have red hair."

Lark nodded. "You wouldn't be any more welcome here than me if they thought that, I'm afraid."

With a quick wave, I sent the rest of the crew away. Or tried to.

"Wait for us with Eve and Marco."

Pamela shook her head. "I don't want to be separated from you."

Berget nodded. "Me, too."

Then Alex who crossed his arms over his chest. "Me, three."

Liam's mouth quirked. "I'd say *me four,* but you might hit me."

Lark shrugged. "Your circus, my friend. Your monkeys."

Shit, this was not going as planned, but then, when had any of my salvages? The truth hit me hard. That *was* what I was doing. I wasn't saving a single child or person, but all of them. Orion was the bad guy I was going to save a lot of someones from.

"You can come *if* you all promise to hide if Lark tells you to."

Bella cleared her throat. "We could take them to the Enders Barracks. That way they are close enough to help, but we won't have to take them all the way into the Spiral."

"That's a good plan, but what about the Enders?" Lark said as she finished wrapping her head in the cloth.

Bella looked away. "There are none left. Father disbanded them after you and . . . Ash were killed."

Lark stiffened. "He's not dead any more than I am. They stuck him in an oubliette too, farther away than me."

Bella's eyes softened as though she thought Lark was fooling herself.

This was getting us nowhere. "Fucking hell, we are not doing a therapy session, Lark. Get your head in the game."

If I'd thought she'd stiffened before, it was nothing to the way her back snapped to attention with my words. "Let's go."

"Finally," I muttered. We walked down the center of the Rim. The name of the place was a bit deceiving since there was no real rim, so to speak. The elementals had homes around the edges of a large oval that ran at least three miles in each direction if the clearing I saw was accurate. The homes were quiet and we made it to the Enders barracks without any problem.

Lark pried the double-wide wooden door open with her spear. "The rest of you, wait here."

Peta leapt from her shoulder and shifted into her snow leopard form. Lark shook her head. "No, you are too recognizable. Go to the Traveling room and make sure the armbands are there; guard them. I have a feeling we're going to need them."

Peta let out a long, low snarl but did as she was told, albeit with stiff legs and a hunched back.

Like that, we were down to three and we skirted the edge of a large tree that literally spiraled into the canopy. It looked a hundred feet across, maybe more. The Spiral wasn't made up of a single tree, though, but dozens wrapped around one another in, duh, a huge spiral.

Steps led up to the main doors. Another set of double doors that two guards stood in front of, both wearing clothing similar to what Lark had been wearing when we pulled her out of the oubliette. Brown leather vest and khaki-type pants that were tied around their ankles, boots, and several weapons visible on both of them.

"Let me try and talk us in first," Bella said softly. She stepped in front of us. "Blossom, I need to get herbals from the kitchens."

The woman, I assumed she was Blossom, crossed her arms over her chest and shook her head. "You know the rules. No one in or out of the Spiral during the dark hours."

In my head, Jonathan's threads trembled, a vibration that I'd felt only a few times before. Most recently with Milly and India.

"No time, demons have John!"

Side by side we leapt forward. My swords cleared my sheaths and I was on the guard on the right before he could even draw his weapon. I slammed the butt of my right sword into his temple, dropping him to the ground. Beside me, Lark grabbed the woman, Blossom, by her arms and threw her out of our way.

"Bella, get the others, we need them."

Bella spun and raced away. Lark lifted a foot and kicked the door open. "Lead the way, Rylee."

Locking onto Jonathan's threads I raced toward him. No one got in our way, and I had a feeling I knew why. What would a demon do in a home where everyone was sleeping?

Take them out, of course. The only question was, which demon were we dealing with?

I took a deep breath and reached out to the motherfuckers messing with our world. I Tracked demons and got pings all over the place, the red pulsing energy that was them made my head hurt, there were so many. But it was the one closest to me that I centered on. He was right on top of Jonathan. I ran as fast as I could, but it was like I was on an escalator going backward, like no matter how fast I went, I was going to be late again.

Just like with Blaz.

My jaw tightened. "No, not again." I slid to a stop, feeling Jonathan and the demon he faced right underneath us. "Lark." I pointed down and she gave me a tight nod.

With a flick of her hand the ground below us—no, the tree below us—split open wide as if an axe had been driven into it.

I stepped back and glanced down into a shimmering mass of water.

"Leap before you look," I said and jumped.

I hit the water, shocked when the heat washed over me. Hot springs then, not an underground lake.

For a moment, time stilled and a soft voice whispered over me.

Those who are chosen for greatness rarely want it, Rylee. You are doing well, my child. Very well, indeed, with the burden you have been given. The voice of an entity I'd never met and yet I knew her.

This was the realm of the mother goddess that Lark had spoken of. I felt her approval and power run through me while the hot spring heated my body.

The water broke over my face and I sucked in a deep breath, already forgetting the words, already focusing on the two figures in front of me on the sandy shore.

One was Jonathan, flat on his back and naked as the day he was born. The other was a female demon on top of him. Also naked.

He let out a soft groan. "I thought she liked me."

"I'll bet you did, dumbass," I snapped as I sloshed out of the water. For once, I was glad I wasn't wearing my leather coat. The demon looked up at me. I gave her a wave with my fingers as she snarled. Standing, her body was more than lithe; it was emaciated to the point of her hips and ribs protruding at angles that were anything but healthy.

"Well, hello. I'm guessing you're Famine? Shall I call you Fanny Famine?"

Famine strolled toward me, her hands slipping over her body, touching the bones that jutted from her hips, ribs, and shoulders. "Call me whatever you like."

"All righty then, Fanny it is." I swirled my two swords, loosening my wrists. The slosh of water to my left was the only indicator I had that Lark was out of the water; I didn't dare turn my head to check.

Fanny stared at me, then narrowed her eyes. "You have a mark on you. The mark of the Hoarfrost demon."

I touched my breastbone with the handle of one sword. "That was the first demon I killed, snaggy bitch. And you are about to be yet another in a long list."

Her snarling lips tipped upward. "You should be dead already, but I can remedy that."

She lunged at me, her hands outstretched, going straight toward my chest. I stepped back with one foot to brace myself and drove both swords through her stomach, all the way to the hilt. Her body sagged and I put a hand on her forehead.

"Go back to where you're from, Fanny."

Her head snapped up and she laughed at me. "Not that easy with me, Slayer. Not that easy at all."

Her hands slammed into my chest and threw me back into the water. I sunk to the sandy bottom and then pushed myself up, or at least, I tried to. I heard Lark roar through the water.

"She's tied to the water. Get the hell out, Rylee!"

If only it were that easy. I pushed off the bottom again, my lips just breaking the surface long enough for me to gulp a breath down. Barely.

Motherfucking hell, I was not going to be drowned. But how was I going to get my ass out of this?

19
LARK

Rylee was still under the water. I dropped my spear and rushed the demon. Weapons were obviously not going to work on this bitch. I grabbed her around the throat even as she tried to repeat her move on me that had sent Rylee into the hot spring.

"Keep trying, ugly," I snarled as I dug my thumbs into her windpipe. If I could knock her out maybe—

Both of her feet came up hard and fast, kicking into my stomach as her toes lengthened into six-inch long claws. They slashed at my belly and I fought to dodge each blow even as I clamped harder on her neck.

Her eyes bugged out and her tongue purpled and flapped at me, but I wasn't fooled. It as an act. Her arms flailed at me, clawing at my skin, opening me up. To the left of me, a torchlight flickered.

"Let my friend up," I said as I dragged her toward the open flame.

"Fuck you," she spit out.

Yeah, that was about what I'd expected. I yanked her sideways and stuffed her head into the open flame. Fed by a natural gas pocket, the fire was hot and couldn't be snuffed out.

Fanny—as Rylee had named her—screamed and writhed, her hair catching fire, burning off her head in a flash with the scent of charred skin.

A burst of water and Rylee was slogging back out.

I didn't pull Fanny from the flame, but held her there until Rylee caught up to me, dripping wet and panting. "Bring her out. We need information, and she's fucking well giving it to us."

I pulled Fanny out of the flame, twisted her around, and tied her hands behind her back with my belt. Of course, I made sure to push her head hard into the gritty sand, knowing how it would stick to the burns.

She was a demon, I didn't have to play nice.

Rylee grabbed her and spun her around. Yeah, the sand had ground in good, the charred and sticky skin holding it like glue.

"I'm going to ask you a question. Yes or no. That's all I need."

Fanny laughed, though the sound was strangled. "And pray tell, why would I help you?"

I was impressed that Rylee leaned in as close as she did, putting her nose right to the weeping stump that had been Fanny's nose. "Orion has threatened my daughter, has killed my friends and family. He's taking everything I love from me. You do know he's afraid of me, don't you?"

"He's terrified," she said. "But I'm not."

Rylee smiled and I could see the edge of it, and I was proud of her. She'd grown up a lot, and the look on her face said it all. Fanny would not like what was going to happen to her.

"Do you know I won't be sending you back to the seventh Veil when I break you apart from this body? You will die. Cease to exist. Pfft. Gone."

Fanny shrugged, but I could see the tension in her. I swayed on my feet, feeling the fight in my whole body. I put a hand to my head and went to one knee.

"Rylee, something is wrong." I looked up to see Rylee's eyes widen with horror and Fanny lunge toward her, the burns gone.

"Famine," the demon hissed. "I feed from my victims and their strengths become mine. And you have very strong friends, Rylee."

The ground rumbled and I knew we were in deep shit.

Across from us, Jonathan stumbled to his feet, his hands searching for something. He grabbed a stick and scribbled into the sand as I lay incapacitated, watching Fanny and Rylee dodge each other's blows.

Jonathan looked up, his eyes catching mine. "The only way we all survive is if you kill the demon."

"No fucking shit, Sherlock," Rylee screamed at him as her left foot touched the water.

"You have to pull her guts out, along with her tongue!" the kid yelled, looking at what he had written in the sand. "That's the only way."

Rylee nodded. "One eviscerated demon, coming the fuck up."

My whole body convulsed as the demon pulled on my strength. I fought her, did my best to hold back. If she got a hold of my abilities with Spirit, we were done.

I reached for Spirit and threaded it through my body, using more of it than I'd done in a very long time. It took everything I had left to lift my head. This was a long shot, but I had to try.

"Fanny. Stop."

The demon froze, a shocked look on her face. Spirit roared through me, the strength of it making my words a physical weight that even the demon could not deny.

"What have you done?" she growled at me, shaking as she tried to throw the bonds I'd laid on her.

I wet my lips, tasting the salt of the earth below me. "Give me back my strength." Spirit flooded my words with power and with them, Fanny did as she was told, though she screamed the whole time. She fell to her knees and Rylee didn't waste any time.

With two quick swipes of her sword the demon's belly was open. Rylee booted Famine in the chest, knocking her to her back as I stood and made my way to her side.

Together, we pulled the demon's stomach out, except that it wasn't a stomach like any creature I'd seen. Tiny balls, like glowing orbs, rested within her body cavity.

Rylee pulled one out and looked at it. "Other people's energy." She crushed the ball in her hand and it zipped away while Fanny cried.

With each orb we crushed, her body became frailer until she was a skeleton with a taut covering of skin barely holding it together. Her red eyes flickered dimly. "I hate you, I hate all of you on this side of the Veil."

Rylee leaned over her. "Any last words before I cut out your tongue and throw it in the flames?"

Fanny glared at her. "Your daughter will die in your place and it will be your fault."

With a vicious jab, Rylee drove her sword into the back of the demon's throat and slid her blade across. Half of Fanny's jaw and her tongue flopped out. Rylee picked it up and took it to the brazier, tossing it in.

Fanny writhed at my feet, her eyes wide with shock. "She isn't dead yet."

"I know. I'm going to remedy that." Lifting her sword high above her head she paused at the zenith. The blade began to glow with a pure white light, like with the last horseman, Pestilence. The glowing sword lit up the cavern as if there were no other torches lit. Rylee drove it down with enough force that it buried through Fanny's heart, all the way to the hilt.

With her hands still holding the handle, Rylee whispered softly. "Go to where you belong. Wherever that is." The softness in her voice surprised me.

Peta's voice caught me off guard. "That is the only way to truly end a demon, Lark. They only know hate and death and fear. You must be the antithesis of that. You must kill them with love. You could do it, if you were trained. That is another strength of Spirit."

I turned to see my familiar a few feet away, sitting on her haunches. "So I see you listened as well and stayed where you were told to."

The cat shrugged. Felines, they always did what they wanted, regardless.

"But why is it so hard to kill these demons?" I asked.

Peta let out a soft meow and shifted to her housecat form. "Let Rylee hear me. She needs to understand."

That surprised me; not that Rylee needed to understand, but that Peta would allow her voice to be heard by anyone who wasn't an elemental. I beckoned Rylee.

"Peta wants to talk to us both."

Rylee's eyebrows shot up as the rest of the entourage came running onto the sand. Peta, though, didn't move, her green eyes unblinking as she watched us.

I put a hand on Rylee's shoulder and let a trickle of Spirit run through her, opening her to Peta's voice.

My cat nodded and then began. "The demons you face, they are more dangerous because as long as there is war, famine, death, and pestilence in this world, they have a place to draw power from. It is the only reason you were able to kill the first two; famine and pestilence. They can be isolated. Death and War will wait for you on the battlefield, where each kill that happens, each fight that occurs, will feed them. And in turn, they will feed Orion's strength."

Rylee let out a slow breath. "I think I can stop Orion. But I need to get close to him."

"Wait," I held up a hand. "Peta, since when do you know so much about demons?"

Her eyes were sad. "I was alone a long time, unable to find you, but knowing you were out there. You told me to be ready when you came back. That we would have more strife ahead. I went to every library in the elemental world and learned. Five years in each family and five spent in the human world learning. There was more on demons than I'd like, but I am glad for it now."

I scooped her up and held her tightly to my chest. "You are amazing, my friend."

A slow purr rumbled out of her. "Of course I am. I'm a cat, after all."

Rylee reached out and brushed a hand over Peta's back. "Any ideas on how to get close to Orion, oh mighty cat of knowledge?"

Peta nodded. "Actually, yes. But first thing's first. Lark, your father is awake and I believe he is headed here. Which means we need to go. Right now."

I jumped to my feet, but it was already too late. As I spun, my father waited for me on the steps that led into the hot springs.

"How dare you come back, Larkspur? How dare you steal into my home like a thief in the night?" His words were harsh, but the tone was all disappointment.

Rylee stiffened beside me. "I remember him. He was an asshole then, too. Hasn't changed much."

She was right, he hadn't changed much.

But I had.

20
RYLEE

Lark's father was a dick of epic proportions. Then again, my adopted parents hadn't won any awards for how they'd dealt with me, either.

The king, Basileus, had long gray and brown hair, and except for the slight wrinkles around his eyes, he didn't look all that old. Yet he was close to a thousand—according to Lark.

He had a stocky build with heavy muscles, and his green eyes were, at the moment, hard as flint. But he wasn't the only one who was pissed.

"Maybe if you knew you had a demon in your home, you wouldn't be so quick to dismiss her," I snapped.

Lark put a hand on my arm. "Let me deal with him, Rylee."

His eyebrows shot upward. "This is Rylee, the one you helped in the desert. The one who caused your second time in the oubliette?"

Lark laughed. "Old man, I am *not* the child I was even ten years ago. Your approval means nothing to me anymore. For so long, I thought you were broken, and I could help you heal. And then I realized there was no healing you. The other rulers are right, you are weak."

He sucked in a sharp breath. "How dare you!"

"HOW DARE YOU!" she roared back, and I'll admit, her anger was something I never thought I'd be afraid of. But I stepped back and gave her room.

The earth above and below trembled with her anger. Fucking Destroyer . . . no shit.

She walked toward him, the earth rumbling. "While the world suffers, you stay inside the Rim and hide. But there is nothing you can do to hide from the tidal wave of demons coming, Basileus."

As if using his name was a physical slap, he stumbled back, opened his mouth, and the sounds of screaming erupted above us.

"Bella is up there," Lark whispered, and she was running for the stairs. I was right behind her, my pack with me. Alex shifted in mid-stride, as did Peta. Pamela and Berget ran together, their long hair blowing out behind them. Liam was the fastest, though, leaping up the stairs four and five at a time, passing even Lark. Cactus—where the hell was he?

At the top of the stairs, I saw him, guarding what was supposed to be our exit.

I say supposed to be because as far as I could see, there was no fucking way out. Fanny had apparently brought friends with her for shits and giggles. The inside of the Spiral swarmed with demons—*swarm* being the word of the day. Not a single one was bigger than a small dog and they all had wings. They had picked up Belladonna and held her high above our heads as she shrieked. Cactus was shooting the little bastards with balls of flame. Pamela joined in and the two vampires dove into the melee.

But only I could send them back. "Throw them to me. Everyone throw the little fuckers my way."

Three of them came at once, from Liam, Pamela, and Lark. I dropped my weapons and caught them, holding them tightly as I sent them to the other side of the Veil. A stopgap at best, but it was all I had since the little bastards could crawl right back out whatever hole Orion had opened.

Over and over, biting teeth and slashing claws came at me as my family tossed the demons my way.

I held to my love for my daughter, for Liam, and all the others in my life. In that, this was the easy part. To remember how lucky I was to have so much love, to have all those people with me on this crazy journey.

That was simple.

As I grabbed each demon I whispered the same thing. "Go to where you belong."

I hoped it was farther from us than even the seventh Veil. I really did, but I somehow doubted it.

Sweat and blood slicked my skin, and the scratch and bite marks stung, the tiny open wounds like miniature hot pokers.

The black-and-gray flesh of the demons, their leathery wings and snapping jaws, blurred together until I saw nothing but them.

None of them willingly came at me once they realized who I was. They actively avoided me.

"Flying rat bastards," I yelled as I leapt up to grab one by the foot before it could get farther away. My words were harsh, but my intentions were not. They couldn't be if I was to keep this up.

As quickly as the attack had started, it was over.

I stood with my arms out, aching, waiting.

"They're gone," Pamela whispered, her voice hoarse.

Rubbing my arms, I looked at my bare skin. It looked as though I had red sleeves, and the ache in my muscles picked up in earnest.

"I can heal you," Pam said, coming toward me. I waved her off.

"No, don't waste your energy on me. I'm not badly hurt." I took quick stock of my people before picking up my swords and tucking them in. Everyone was scratched up, bitten and clawed, but there was nothing serious. So what the fuck had the attack been about?

"Where is Jonathan?" I spun as I spit out the question, running down the stairs, fully expecting him to be gone.

And he was . . . almost.

A demon sat on his chest, its teeth latched onto his neck as it chewed into him. I leapt down the last few stairs and across the sand, fully tackling the demon like a linebacker. We rolled across the sand and I whispered for it to go. To return to wherever it was from.

It screeched and then its body dissolved into nothing but a puff of smoke. "PAMELA!" I screamed her name even as I scrambled back to Jonathan. Tracking him, I could feel his threads slipping away, the same as Blaz only hours before.

Pamela skidded to a stop on her knees and slapped her hands on the kid's chest. His whole body jerked upward as she poured her magic into him. Slowly, the skin on his neck stitched back together and his breathing eased as he fell into a drowsy state that wasn't quite sleeping, not quite unconscious.

I dropped my head, my chin touching my chest. "Holy fucking hell, that was close."

A sigh rushed out of Pamela as she slumped beside me. "I've never worked that much magic in my whole life."

I didn't doubt it, and yet I knew worse was coming. But I didn't say that. I didn't have too.

"The final battle is going to be a thousand times harder, isn't it?" she whispered. I reached across to her and took her hand.

"At least."

Her lips tightened, and I was proud of her. Even a few months ago, that comment might have elicited tears, not the hardening of her resolve.

Footsteps echoed into the chamber and with them the sound of raised voices.

"You bring demons into my home and then you expect to me to help you?" Basileus snapped.

Lark's voice was deceptively calm and she spoke as if her father never said a word. "Bella, it's time, I think. You are his heir; I cannot do this."

Watching them, I saw the resemblance between Belladonna and her father, but there was no such connection between Lark and her family. At least, physically. As Bella drew herself straight, she pulled out a necklace from under her nightshirt. A monster-big emerald hung from a silver chain, catching the torchlight and flinging green glimmers over the room. Perhaps it was a mark of the heir to the Terraling's throne. That would make sense.

"Father, I am your heir, am I not?" Bella asked.

The king nodded, a frown on his face. "You are, you know that is only temporary until I decide who would be better suited—"

Bella held a hand out to her father, placing it on his shoulder. "As heir to the throne, I place you under arrest for actively trying to subvert those who would save our world. Ender Lark, please take him to the dungeons."

Lark clamped her hands over her father's and I thought there was going to be another epic showdown. But he deflated under her, like a balloon losing the last of its air.

No more words were spoken as he was carted off to wherever the dungeons were.

Pamela looked at me with wide eyes. "Wow."

Jonathan stirred beneath us. "Wow is not how I feel right now. I was dying. Who brought me back?"

Pamela cleared her throat. "I did."

He sat up and glared at her. "The next time I'm dying, witch, let me die."

Well, wasn't that a pleasant how do you do.

I smacked him in the chest with the flat of my hand hard enough to leave a perfect imprint of my fingers as I drove him back to the sand. "After you do whatever you're supposed to do in this battle, you can dive right in front of a demon and ask them for their personal touch, for all I care. Got it, kid?"

He blinked up at me, his crossed eyes focusing on me. "I remember you, Rylee. You took me from the Shadow Walker."

I nodded. "Yes, with Lark."

He glared at me. "Why is everyone so intent on keeping me alive, when all I want to do is die?"

"Like I said"—I crouched beside him—"once you help me, you do whatever the fuck you want."

"But I can only help if you have the right payment," he said softly and I felt it there, within the threads of his life as I Tracked him.

The same madness that had taken Giselle's mind was eating away at his.

And he knew it.

21
RYLEE

Lark was back in a few minutes, her face deeply troubled, if the look in her eyes meant anything.

"Lark, what's wrong?"

"I'm not sure, but the air feels strange on my skin and the scent of demons is still very strong. Too strong. We need to go."

I grabbed Jonathan's hand and jerked him to his feet. Pamela turned away, a red haze on her cheeks. No time for niceties. "Let's get him pants and get the fuck out of here then."

Belladonna pulled her wrap from her shoulders and handed it to Lark. "Here. It isn't pants, but it will cover him."

Lark snagged the material and wrapped it around Jonathan's waist in a few quick loops, tying it off at his hip.

Lark's sister laughed. "I see you haven't lost your flair for dressing people."

"Bella," Lark said, "we have to rally everyone. Every family, every elemental has to be at this battle, or we don't stand a chance. They were the only supernaturals not affected by the pox."

Bella took a deep breath and nodded. "You know I stand with you, Lark. No matter how bad it gets, or what we must face."

Lark snapped her fingers in the air. "Time to go." She jogged up the stairs and we all followed. I brought up the rear with Jonathan in front of me. As I passed Bella, she touched my arm and I paused.

She opened her mouth and then shook her head. Tears glittered at the edges of her gray eyes. All the unspoken words were there. Be careful. Save the world. But louder than both of those was the simple *don't let my sister die.*

I nodded, but could say nothing. This was war, and Lark was one of our generals. Which would make her a target. Still, I would do what I could to keep her alive. As I would for all of my family.

We wove up and through the Spiral while the air around us crackled with tension. Lark was right, the scent of demon was far too strong for this to be the end of the invasion here. Orion knew I was here. What would I do if I were in his place?

"I'd send more than one general," I breathed the words out a split second before the Spiral exploded in a burst of flames around us. We all hit the ground, the heat blasting like it was pushed by a storm.

"On your bellies, keep moving," Lark yelled and we followed as she took us to a side hallway with no flames. Once more on our feet, we ran, trusting Lark to get us the hell out of there.

"Which demon is connected to fire?"

Peta glanced back at me, her voice as clear as any others. "War."

Lark slammed to a stop in front of a dead end. "I'm going to open this up; it will take us directly into the Enders Barracks. From there, go to the lowest level. Bella, go with them, show them the bands and how to use them."

Bella nodded. "Be careful, Lark. I've lost you once, I don't want to lose you again."

Lark touched her sister's head gently. "I'm not going anywhere. I've too much trouble to stir up."

She put her hand on the wall and the tree split open, not unlike what had happened in the floor of the Spiral.

"Pamela," Lark called to her. "I need your help."

Pamela paused and looked at me. I nodded at her, though it tore at my guts. "Go, kick ass. Show them what you can do, witch."

Her lips twitched and she clapped her hands together, a sharp rumble of thunder echoing outside. "Consider it done."

Cactus, and of course Peta, stayed with Lark as well. They would hold the demons off long enough for us to get out of here. Once more, we were separated.

The rest of us leapt through into the darkness that was the Barracks. I looked back to see Lark for a split second before the tree closed.

There was one torch flickering against the wall showing me a training area, old, rusting weapons on the walls and what was left of several rotting leather uniforms.

"There aren't enough armbands for everyone. You have to decide who will go with you, Rylee, and who will stay behind. There is only the ability to move four of you," Belladonna said as she led the way across the floor.

I goggled at her. "Stay behind?"

"I'm sorry," she said, "It is the only way."

Leaving any one of my family behind was unthinkable. Pamela staying with Lark was different. I knew Lark would protect her as much as Pam would protect Lark.

Alex touched my arm, turning me to him. "I can fly back with Eve and Marco. We don't have to worry about the sun coming up if you take the vamps with you."

My heart clenched at the thought of Alex not being with me. But he was right, he was the obvious choice. I grabbed him in a hug, holding him tightly. "Don't take any chances. Go straight to the farmhouse."

He hugged me back, his gangly arms surprisingly strong. "Yuppy doody, boss."

I swatted him on the back and let go before tears could start. Bella pointed at the hallway at the far end of the room as she grabbed the torch from the wall. "The stairs lead down to the Traveling room. We have two armbands. One of you will wear a band, the other will hang onto that person."

"How does this work?" Berget asked. "Is this like jumping the Veil?"

An explosion outside of the barracks shook the whole place, and dust fell around our ears. Bella waved a hand as if it were nothing. "No, not like that. With the Veil, your soul is at risk if you are not a necromancer. They are the only ones who can jump without damaging themselves."

I glared at Liam, but meant at Faris. "This was what you meant when you said it would hurt Liam? That it would eat his soul if you jumped us?"

He turned to me and I knew I was looking at Liam still. "Yes, that's why he wouldn't do it. He knows you, Rylee. I hate to admit it, but he does. You would never forgive him if he'd broken my soul in trying to get us here."

Bella tsked softly and another explosion shook the structure. I Tracked Pamela and Lark.

They were both pissed as cats stuffed into a toilet and swirlied. But the power running through them both . . . it was beyond wild, beyond anything I'd ever felt.

Pamela was the strongest witch the world had ever seen, and that included Milly, who'd been able to do things like jumping the Veil and breaking bonds with demons.

Yet Lark was making Pamela look like a human next to the power she was running. I wasn't sure the explosions were related to the demons attacking.

The earth rolled beneath or feet and Bella ran ahead of us. "Hurry, we're almost there."

She ran for a wide set of doors, shoving them open. Despite the need to hurry, I couldn't help but stop and stare at what we stumbled into. The room was round, as if we were standing inside a globe looking out at all the countries and oceans of the world.

Bella touched the globe with both hands and *pulled* it toward her, enhancing the picture until it was clear, as if I stood in front of the scene. "Rylee, you know where you're going?"

I nodded, and reached for the globe tightening the view, zooming in, until it showed the barn on my farm, and the burnt-out shell that had been my home. "Here, this is where we're going."

Another monster rumble sent us all to our knees. Bella gasped. "I have to help them. This is how the armbands work. You put it on," she shoved a smooth wooden band onto my upper arm. "With this hand," she tapped the one with the band on it. "You touch the spot you want to go. With the other hand, twist the band clockwise. Counterclockwise will bring you back here."

She looked at us one last time as she stood in the doorway. "Good luck."

Alex didn't hesitate, just waved and followed her up the stairs. As if he were going on a date or to a party, not into a war zone. But that was Alex.

"Berget, you first," I said. "Take Jonathan with you and hunker down in the barn."

She slipped the band on and touched a spot of ground on the globe directly on the west side of the barn. Where the morning sun hadn't touched yet. Jonathan wrapped his fingers around the belt at her waist.

"A piece of advice?" he said.

"What is it?"

"Whatever you do, don't let go."

Berget touched the map and twisted her armband at the same time. A blast of wind roared through the room and their bodies were sucked into the globe with a pop of air and a burst of light.

"Fuck me," I whispered.

Liam grunted. "You have to admit, that is far more impressive than jumping the Veil."

I looked at the map, and though I knew what I had to do, I didn't think Liam was going to like it.

"We're not going to the farmhouse, are we?"

Damn, was I that easy to read? "No, we aren't."

"Marcella?"

Gods, I wanted to go after our daughter, but not yet. I swallowed hard. "No."

"Then who?"

"Orion."

22
LIAM

He wasn't sure he'd heard her right. Because there was no way she'd said they were dropping into Orion's lap.

"No, no, no." He held up his hands and a demon flew into the room. He grabbed it and held it out for her as if it hadn't interrupted him. She cupped the demon's head and whispered to it, and it dissolved.

"Yes. I need to see him, to get close enough to touch him." She looked him straight in the eye. "I have to bind him to me, Liam. It's the only way I will ever beat him."

"Bind him to you? Are you out of your mind?" he roared as she touched the armband.

"You can either come with me, or I can leave you behind to fly home with Alex," she snapped. The fear in her voice calmed him. She wasn't being wildly reckless.

"You actually have a plan, don't you?"

Her eyebrows rose. "Is that so hard to believe?"

"Of you, yes." He grabbed the waistband of her jeans and let out a breath. "Where you go, I go. That's the deal. But how are you going to convince Orion to touch you?"

She adjusted the globe until it hovered over Washington, DC. "He's in the White House, with the president." With a flick of her fingers, the view shifted from the steps of the White House to the Oval Office. "I need you to bite me, and then invoke the bite to make me fast enough if he decides he doesn't want to go along with my plan."

With a flip of her hair, she bared her neck to me. "Do it, please."

Invoking the bite . . . it would temporarily give her the speed and strength of the vampire. A bonus for those willing to share blood with a vampire, but it was also one more tie to Faris.

Inside his head, the vampire laughed. *I think we are far beyond those worries, aren't we?*

Faris was right. Liam bent to her neck and brushed his lips against her soft skin, placing a kiss where his teeth would go. He slowly punctured the skin, allowing his fangs to carefully slide in. The moan that slipped from her nearly undid him. Holding her tightly, his body pressed against hers, the surge of emotions and blood enough to send his libido into overdrive. Her fingers tangled in his hair. "Don't stop."

Around them, the world shook on its foundations, and all he could think about was how good it would feel to rip her clothes off and take her right there on the floor. To remind them both how very alive they were.

With a great effort, he pulled back from her and licked the two pinpricks where his fangs punctured. Faris said nothing.

"The Oval Office," he said carefully. "That will be loaded with security, guns, men, and probably the president."

"You bar the doors, I'll do the rest," she whispered.

Liam's gut clenched. He knew what the security would be like, and while bullets wouldn't kill him, they would kill Rylee. "Are you absolutely certain that's where he is?" He made himself let go of her, at least for the moment.

She snorted and gave him a look that told him everything he needed to know. Her eyes only swirled that fast with the three colors when she was Tracking. "I think I should know."

He put his other hand on her waist and closed his eyes. "Can't blame me for trying to talk you out of this."

There was the sound of the rushing wind, a flash of light, and he opened his eyes. The Oval Office looked like the movies portrayed it, with a large desk and white, rounded walls.

Except that most movies didn't have a demon sitting on the edge of the desk with one leg bent, and the other on the floor, his mouth hanging open in shock.

"Surprise," Rylee said. Liam let go of her and ran to the doors, locking them down. They only needed Orion. No one else; certainly not the president's men.

The demon was put together like a body builder, his shoulders and neck stacked so high with muscle that it looked as though he had no neck. A bald shining head and red glowing eyes the color of fresh blood topped off the image.

He gathered himself together quickly, standing and folding his arms over his chest. "Rylee, how lovely of you to drop in. What can I do you for?"

It was only then that Liam realized the demon was not alone in the Oval Office. The president sat behind him tapping furiously at whatever panic button he had. "Mr. President, we're only here for Orion. Not you," Liam said.

That didn't seem to calm the leader of the free world, not one bit.

Rylee held her hands up. "I want to talk about a truce. Terms that we could both live with, demon."

Orion's eyes widened. "Why?"

"You threatened my daughter. I take that fucking seriously. If I can keep her safe, even if it means the world goes to shit in a poorly woven handbasket, then I'll do it."

It took everything Liam had to keep his mouth shut, to not grab her and shake her. She had a plan and whatever it was, he would trust her.

No matter how damn crazy it sounded.

"Ah, a mother's love. A powerful motivator. What do you have in mind?"

She held out her hand. "A simple truce. You stop killing my family and the supernaturals, the elementals too. And we will stay out of your way."

Orion stared at her hand as if she held a serpent out to him with fangs bared. "A simple truce?"

She nodded, her hand not wavering for a second.

Orion lifted his eyes to her, then back to her hand, then back up to her eyes. Liam tensed as the sound of fists and guns pounding on the door behind him took up a rather desperate tempo.

"Oh, pretty Tracker. An offer like that before you were trained as a Slayer . . . that would have been an offer I would take. But now"—he spread his hands wide—"I think not."

She lowered her hand. "That's too bad."

Liam had to fight not to tense, he knew her too well to think she would give up. Not when they were directly in front of Orion.

I've invoked the bite. Faris whispered to him from the recesses of his mind.

With a burst of speed that was inhumanly fast, Rylee leapt at Orion. The demon backpedaled right over the president's desk and into his lap. "I'll kill him." He held the president up with one hand and Rylee shrugged.

"Go for it. That's why we have a vice president."

Orion threw the limp president away from him and Rylee was on the demon in a flash. He tried to jump the Veil but she grabbed his left hand and dug her nails into him.

The Veil opened up in a slash and Orion pulled her through, closing it behind them.

Liam stared at the spot where they'd been, unable to believe what had happened.

Are you really that surprised? This is Rylee, after all, when have her plans gone right?

Though Faris had a point, Liam didn't want to hear it. The door behind them shattered and the tips of guns stuck through the door. "Faris, right now my bigger concern is getting us the hell out of here."

The window. It's still dark on this side of the building.

That, it was. He bolted across the room and hit the window as the men burst into the room. The window shattered and he fell from the sky, landing with a soft thud in the green grass below. He didn't wait to see if the president's men were going to shoot at him, he was certain of it.

Rylee had the armband, so at least she could go back to the Rim if she needed to escape Orion.

Out of the frying pan and into the fire, trading one demon for a horde of demons. The problem was, he couldn't decide which was worse.

23
RYLEE

Orion screamed at me as we slipped through the Veil. Liam was going to be pissed as hell that I'd left him behind. Again.

There were flashes of color: metal gray, murky water, an American flag, the words SS BOSTON in broken spray paint on the wall. We hit the deck of the ship hard and water splashed up around us, but I didn't let go of the big bastard. My brain struggled to make sense of where we were. Because the only ship I'd been on that looked like this was supposed to be at the bottom of the harbor in Boston.

Orion tried to fling me off, snarling as his face twisted into a rictus mask. I swung my legs around in a wide circle, and slammed into something hard and cold. The crack of my shin bone being smashed into whatever unbending material I hit seemed to please Orion.

"Let me go, Tracker, and I'll make your death quick."

"Fuck you, asswipe." I dug my nails in harder, and took a breath. This was going to be my one shot at binding him to me.

"Don't you dare," he hissed, his eyes glowing even as he scrambled backward from me. His free hand pulled back and then slammed into my face.

The words slid from my lips. "I bind thee to me. My death will be yours, and your death shall free your soul. Demon to Slayer, these two souls are now twinned."

Around us, the roar of voices emerged, along with a brilliant flash of orange light. Sparkles floated down around us like fireflies that had lost their wings. I let go of Orion, and searched for his threads inside me.

Except they weren't threads like I was Tracking someone. No, they were the emotions and sensations like I'd gotten from Blaz. Like a distant conversation I was always a part of, even if I wasn't welcome to the party.

Orion stared at me. "No, this cannot be."

On my knees I grinned up at him, and slowly flipped him off. "Game. Set. Match, you big dumb bastard."

He couldn't kill me, unless he wanted to die right there on the ship's deck. "You couldn't have, it's not possible . . . ." He shook his head and stepped back, breathing hard. I stood gingerly and dusted my pants off.

"You are going to lose this game," I said.

Without warning, he lunged at me, his fingers going around my neck. "I will kill you; the binding doesn't affect me."

I closed my eyes. I would not fight him. If he killed me, we would both die. I felt it in my bones, all the way to my cracked shin that throbbed in time with my heartbeat.

This would save the world and there would be no need for anyone else to suffer.

Orion's fingers tightened. "I am not bound by you, Slayer."

I didn't open my eyes. "I love them enough to die for them."

My heart thumped harder as he squeezed, slowing my blood flow. It took everything in me not to fight him, to hold still and let it happen. This was what I'd banked on. Orion's arrogance that he would be different than the other demons. That somehow he would be safe from a Slayer's binding.

There was a moment of disconnect as my heart stuttered and death crept along my legs, working her way up my body. But it wasn't death's voice I heard; it was Giselle's.

Leaping before you look again, eh, my girl? Rylee, you may kill Orion, but what about the Veil? It is wide open for the demons to pour through. If you die, then it will be on Marcella to close the Veil, and by the time she is of an age to do that, the world will have been devoured.

Fuck.

My eyes snapped open and with the last of my strength I kicked out with both feet, catching Orion in the belly and knocking him away from me. The world was spinning, but I could clearly see I wasn't the only one suffering.

Orion lay flat on his back, breathing hard. I struggled to my feet, swaying. "What was that about the binding not working?"

His red eyes looked straight into mine. He took a few more deep breaths before he sat up. "Why did you stop me?"

I shook my head. "Why were you willing to die with me?" The answer flowed from him to me in a series of images and thoughts.

Orion truly thought he was the savior of his people, and he would do anything to keep the Veil open for them. Even if that meant dying with me.

I didn't want to see him as anything other than an asshole demon bent on destroying the world. He shook his head slowly, as if trying to clear his thoughts.

He stumbled to his feet and I backed up—limping—and pressed myself against a wall. "You are willing to die for your people."

"And you are willing to die to save the world from us."

An impasse. I put a hand to the cold metal behind me. Rust flakes came off against my skin and I truly looked around.

Orion *had* resurrected the ship we'd sunk in the shipyard in Boston.

"I thought it a fitting place to hide my people. A ship that no longer exists in human records."

He circled me and I looked up, knowing what I'd see. Tiers of levels above us were filled with glowing red eyes as a veritable horde of demons stared down at me.

I didn't dare touch the armband out of reassurance. I had a way out of this mess. Time to get as many answers as I could.

"Your ogres are dead." I reached for my swords and pulled them out of their sheaths.

Orion laughed. "They were cannon fodder. Useless." I thought of Blaz, inadvertently giving him the news that my dragon was dead. Orion's eyes widened as he picked up on it. "Apparently not so useless. I may have to reward that last female for killing your set of wings."

I slid around the edge of the ship, doing my best not to limp.

Orion's eyes narrowed. "Do you really think you can escape? Your death is assured. I will not stop my people from killing you. It may slow them down not to have me lead, but it will not keep them out of this world. They have been denied too long." A bead of sweat rolled down his bald head. Fear fed through our bond. He was uncertain of the outcome if we both died. But I wasn't.

Giselle was right. There had to be the final ceremony to close the Veil and it was my blood that would do it. I'd hoped by binding Orion, I could escape that ceremony. Do things my way.

End things my way.

Orion let out a roar as my thoughts slid into his and I sheathed my swords then grabbed the armband, turning it counterclockwise. The world dropped away from me and within the space of two heartbeats, I was back in the Rim, deep in the Enders Barracks.

Smoke filled the room, sticking to my lungs, bringing me to my knees. Choking, I crawled to the center of the globe, and pulled my farmhouse close to me. My hand hovered over it as my mind raced. The smoke curled around me, making the image in front of me flicker in and out of view and slowing me down from making a sudden choice.

I needed Ophelia to ride with me into battle. I could Track her and be at her side in a matter of seconds. There was no way Orion could beat me to her. With the distance between us, Orion's thoughts and emotions were dim and I could pick up no distinct words. Which meant he could pick up none of mine.

"Please let this be the right thing to do," I whispered as I Tracked the red female dragon. The dragon of my father.

Her threads beat strong and healthy, and she wasn't moving, which was all the better. I moved the globe quickly, repositioning it as I scrambled to get to her before Orion did.

Because I could already feel him moving in that direction, using the Veil.

"You aren't going to beat me there, motherfucker." I put my finger on the tip of the mountain Ophelia rested on and twisted the armband.

No, Orion wasn't going to beat me there.

Not this time.

24
ALEX

I buried my hands deep into Eve's feathers, hanging onto her as we swept through the sky. The wind ruffled my hair and I breathed it in.

To have my mind back, to have woken up from the dream of being trapped as a submissive, was hard to believe.

"Eve, how long before we make it to the farmhouse do you think?"

She clacked her beak three times. "A day if we push hard."

A day. That would give them plenty of time to do what I was considering. I swallowed hard, the submissive part of me all but whimpering with the thoughts rushing through my mind. I pushed back that part of me. Right now, Rylee needed me to be stronger. The loss of Blaz was too much, and she needed all the support we could give her.

"We need to make a couple of stops when we hit Bismarck."

Eve looked at me over her shoulder. "Why?"

Clearing my throat first, the words still sounded funny to me without any 'yuppy doody' attached. "I think we can bring more help for Rylee."

Bobbing her head, Eve squawked her agreement. "Good idea, Alex. What about the wolves along the way? We could stop and ask them to help."

The idea of talking to other wolves, really, and shifters for that matter, twisted my guts. But for Rylee, I would do it. I straightened my back.

"Yes. If you see any sign of wolves, take us down."

Without another word, she tucked her wings into her body and dropped out of the sky. "Then here's your first chance."

Seconds later, we landed and I slid off Eve's back. Marco gave me an encouraging bob of his head. Right. I could do this. I wiped my hands on my shirt, but they sweated right back up again.

We were in a valley with the sun rising over the horizon. Day two in the countdown to the final battle.

"How close are they, Eve?" I asked, slowly stripping out of my clothes.

"Hiding around the copse of trees." She flicked her beak at a cluster of evergreens.

Here and there, I could see the glimmer of watching eyes. Asking my body to shift was easy, though I was sure it was nowhere near as smooth as Liam's shifts. Within seconds, I was on all fours and trotting forward. I sat about twenty feet from Eve and Marco, tipped my head back and howled.

Silence met my call.

A growl slipped out of me. I was not going to let them act like I was a submissive and ignore me.

I howled again, this time longer, deeper, and with as much authority as I could muster. Dropping my chin, I had to fight not to scramble backward. A male alpha the color of autumn leaves and easily as big as Liam stood in front of me. His pale amber eyes bored into mine.

I swallowed hard and shifted right in front of him. "I was a submissive, but I learned to be strong enough to shift."

He shifted and slowly stood. His hair was the color of maple leaves in the fall and it brushed the tops of his shoulders. "We've heard of you. The Tracker did this?"

Maybe this wouldn't be as hard as I thought. "Yes."

Breathing in slowly, he held the air before releasing it. "Why would you call on us? Do you wish to become part of our pack? Not all my members would agree to have you join us."

"No"—I shook my head—"I'm a part of a pack."

"Then why are you here?" He didn't seem angry, just confused. I stood a little straighter, trying not to laugh at the ridiculousness of having a serious conversation while standing buck naked with a guy who was also buck naked. And acting like the whole situation was normal. My lips twitched.

"The world is being threatened by demons. The Tracker is the only one who can stop them, but she needs all the help she can get," I said. "You and your pack could make the difference between success and failure. And I tell you now, you do not want her to fail."

He seemed to consider my words. "You want us to risk our lives for someone not a part of our pack?"

I barked out a laugh. "The world will die if she fails. The demons will rule us. So you can either fight for her, help her succeed, and possibly die in the battle.

Or you can hide here like a bunch of untested poodles needing to go to their groomer and surely be killed as soon as the demons take over."

His eyes glittered dangerously and I knew I'd gone too far. But I would not back down. A snarl ripped out of him and he launched himself at me, shifting in the air.

I spun and shifted, kicking the dirt out behind me with my clawed back feet. I met him head on, clawing and biting, going for his throat.

He was bigger and stronger, but I held my ground, even when he cut my leg open.

Even when the fear bit at me as hard as his teeth.

Eve screeched, but Marco yelled at her. "Stay out of it, Eve!"

Marco understood. I had to do this.

I had to prove I truly wasn't submissive, if not to the other wolves, than at least to myself.

Growling, I grabbed the auburn-haired wolf and flipped him over onto his back, scrabbling against the ground for better purchase to pin him. I had more flexibility than him in my mixed-up form, an advantage I used fully. He flipped out from under me and side-stepped, panting as he caught his breath. Slowly, he nodded. He tipped his head back and let out a howl that echoed in the air.

Calling his pack to him.

Calling them to help us.

I turned and looked at Eve, my right eye already swelling closed. I gave her a thumbs up.

She snorted and ruffled her wings. "Boys, I will never understand them."

Laughter spilled out of me. "Probably not."

Did I care that I'd been beaten up? No, not really. The wolves were already gathering, getting ready to follow us. I couldn't ask for more than that.

I only hoped we could convince more than a single pack to step up.

25
LARK

Pamela was on her knees beside me, panting for breath. I wasn't in much better shape, but we'd held the demons back, and except for a few burning trees, we'd done well. Thick smoke curled between the redwoods, wrapping through the crowd like a creeping, climbing fog. The Enders barracks was still burning, but it wouldn't take much to tamp it down, so for the moment we'd let it go. For now, the demons were gone. That was all that mattered.

Beside me, Peta was bloodied, her white coat spotted with red. My familiar let out a cough. "Demons taste horrible, Lark. I hope you know how much I care for you to sink my teeth into those things."

A small smiled tugged at my lips and I dropped a hand to her head. "I know, my friend. I know."

Around us, my people stood, their hands raised and shaking with fatigue as if expecting another attack. They'd done well, repelling the invaders to the point no one else was lost.

War had given up not long after Rylee left. He was here for her, and no other reason. That had been the only reason we'd survived, and I knew it.

Bella was on my right, the emerald stone still glowing with power.

"Are they really gone, Lark?" Pamela whispered up at me.

"For now."

Around us, the murmurs started.

"What do you mean for now, are they coming back?"

"No, they only wanted the Tracker. She's gone, we're safe."

I spun and faced them. "You are *not* safe. Those demons will come back, it is only a matter of time."

My people—Terralings—stared at me as if I'd sprouted a redwood from the top of my head.

Bella gave me a nod, then turned to face her people at my side. "Larkspur is right. The demons will be back. Unless we stop them." She paused, letting her words sink in. "We have a choice. We can stay here and hide in the Rim as we always have and pray to the mother goddess that the Tracker is strong enough on her own to stop the demons. Or we can help her, and be assured we have done all we can to take this threat not only from our world, but the world as a whole."

The arguments broke out in earnest then. Voices raised in anger and fear as people realized what they were being asked to do.

"The mother goddess wouldn't like us to fight."

"We are supposed to be neutral."

"Larkspur is anathema. Why are we even entertaining her and her friends?"

That last stung, but it shouldn't have. Not after all these years. Bella let out a breath.

"I will go wherever Larkspur leads. I name her as my heir to the throne."

Oh shit, I hadn't expected that. I stared hard at her as did everyone else.

Our people shuffled their feet. I stepped forward, and bowed my head for a moment, breathing in the Rim, letting my home sink into my bones for the first time in almost thirty years.

"Mother goddess, help me find the words."

I am with you, child.

"Terralings," I said their name softly, yet still gained their attention. "We are the children of the earth and the wards of all living things, more so than any other elemental family. Our blood runs in the veins of this world, and those that live off it. We have every right— no, *responsibility*—to fight for those in our family who are threatened with harm and destruction." I walked toward Blossom, my old friend and the last of the Enders trained. "My friend, would you fight for your brother if he were pitted against a superior force?"

Her eyes slid sideways to look at her younger brother. "I would fight to my last breath for him."

I stepped past her, deeper into the crowd. "And you, Hyacinth, I know you are a gentle soul, you bound up my wounds more than once. Would you stand between your daughter and her enemies? Fight for her life with your own?"

Hyacinth nodded quickly. "There is no doubt. She is my world."

Through the crowd I moved, asking the same question over and over. They all answered the same. They would fight for those they loved. I came to Niah, the old story teller and sometimes fortune teller when the mood struck. She had no family, so to speak.

"Niah. Would you fight for those who are here, those who call themselves Terralings?"

She stood straight, her eyes meeting mine. "I would fight for them even though our blood is not the same. We are family."

"Pamela." I called to the young witch. She walked toward me, perhaps feeling the weight of the moment hovering over our heads. I put a hand on her shoulder. "A witch, who fought at our side, and carries our blood in her veins. Is she family?"

Niah smiled and reached out for Pamela, drawing her into a hug. "She is. I see in her my long-passed daughter's eyes."

Around us, the Terralings slowly reached out to Pamela, touching her. Acknowledging her as one of their own. I knew what they would sense. With the amount of power in the earth flowing through her, it was hard to believe she wasn't a full elemental. The best part, though, was that she had strength in all five elements. Enough that any elemental would see her for what she was.

A child of all five families.

My heart beat faster. *Please let this be enough.*

I held my hands up, palms facing outward. "I will face the demons without you, if I must. To defend my family. Pamela. Rylee. I will do all I can to protect this world we call our own and all who reside in it. We are their tutelaries. And I, for one, will no longer look the other way." I turned to Griffin, who stood on the edge of the group. "And you, Great Wolf, will you stand with us? With your grandson and his mate?"

Griffin shifted into his wolf form, threw back his head and howled into the night air. He leapt forward, stopping in front of me, bending one front leg so he could bow. He almost ruined it with the big wink he gave me from the dirt.

Peta moved up with me, pressing her body against my legs. "I am with you, Lark."

Pamela put a hand on my back. "I am with you, Lark."

Bella went to one knee in front of me beside Griffin. "I am with you, Lark."

I looked out at my family and slowly, one by one they dropped to their knees.

"I am with you, Larkspur."

"I am with you."

"I will stand and face them."

My eyes burned with tears. Years of emotion that had not flowed since my first banishment. I walked amongst them—my people—touching each one until the last. Until Niah. I went to my knees in front of her.

She wrapped her arms around me, holding me close and whispering in my ear. "Your mother is so proud, Lark. You are going to change this world. Not destroy it, but remake it into something better, stronger."

I pulled back from her. "I hope you're right."

She smiled at me. "Have I been wrong yet?"

The laugh that escaped me was only a little bitter. "A time or two."

Niah held up one finger. "But not this time, child, not this time."

I truly hoped she was right. May the mother goddess have mercy on us all. If I was wrong and this wasn't the right thing to do, I would be condemning my family to utter destruction.

Standing, I held a hand out to Pamela, but spoke to my sister. "Belladonna, take them to the ceremonial grounds near the badlands." We locked eyes. She knew the place I spoke of, we'd been there together once before. Right before I'd been banished the first time. She drew in a slow breath and nodded. I went on for the benefit of the others. "That is where the final battle will take place. Wait for me there before going into the fight, no matter how bad it looks."

"Where are you going?" Bella asked, and I felt the worry of my people as keenly as a sharp knife against my skin.

I gave her a half-smile, took her hand, and squeezed it.

"I am calling in the favors owed to me. It will not only be the Terralings who stand with Rylee and this world. Not if I have anything to say about it."

26
RYLEE

The cold snapped through me like a bitch slap from hell. I tried to take a deep breath, but my lungs seemed to freeze, and I knew I didn't have long to find Ophelia. I stumbled through the snow, following the dragon's threads. Even though she was only a few feet in front of me, I couldn't see her. She lifted her head, her body completely covered by a thick layer of snow and ice. Her violet eyes blinked at me and her voice cascaded through my body.

Rylee? Her head lifted sharply and she looked past me. Looking for Blaz. I reached her side, my whole body shaking as hypothermia hit me as hard as if I were still affected by the Hoarfrost demon's sting. My hand went automatically to the black snowflake on my chest, tracing the pattern. "Ophelia. I need you to make a fire."

Here, come closer. She snaked her head around me and pulled me into the curve of her neck. A deep rumble echoed through her body and a few seconds later the scaled skin under me heated. I clung to her, sheltered from the wind by her body, and I burst into tears. "Blaz is dead, Ophelia."

A low-pitched keening slid out of her. *I felt him die. I knew he was gone, but Erik didn't believe me. It is why I sent him and the children away.*

I blinked up at her. "What do you mean?"

Ophelia's deep violet eyes shed tears that froze as they fell through the air. *I knew you would need me to fly you into the final battle. And I knew if you came for me, the children would be in danger. I couldn't have that.*

Pressing my forehead against her neck, I breathed in the scent that was uniquely dragon; wind swept skies with a touch of ozone, and with Ophelia, an underlying layer of meadow flowers. "Thank you."

There are not only your children to think of, Rylee. I laid my eggs days ago. My head jerked up without meaning to.

"Blaz and you?"

Yes. He knew; he knew I was carrying a small clutch.

The cold had receded enough that I could think clearly. "Ophelia, we have to go. We have to get back to the farmhouse. But I will freeze my ass, most literally, off if we travel without anything . . . ."

She clawed at the ground in front of her and dug out a long, heavy flying coat. *I made Erik give me his for you.*

There were holes in the top of the coat. "You yanked it off him?"

He didn't believe me when I said Blaz was gone. It is the curse of being called mad, Rylee. No one believes you. Especially after what happened with the demon. She looked away and I put a hand on her.

That had been hard, for her to realize she'd been duped because she so badly wanted to bond with another Slayer. A demon had convinced her he was a Slayer and she was his dragon. Her grief over losing my father had left her open to manipulation and she'd fallen for the ruse, which had almost cost us dearly.

Around us, the direction of the wind shifted, and with it came the sound of howling that was anything but natural. I Tracked demons as a whole, gasping at what I felt. I grabbed the coat and pulled it on. "We've got to get up in the air, 'Phelia. We've got incoming nasty fuckers."

She shifted her weight and the remaining snow slid off her body. Using the rigging attached to her, I climbed up and strapped myself in as the gusts picked up, as if the very elements were against us.

As soon as I was buckled in, she threw herself sideways and we dropped into open air. We'd been on the edge of a high cliff deep in the Brooks Mountain Range in northern Alaska. She tucked her wings tightly to her body and we shot toward the ground at a speed I'd never felt with Blaz.

Male dragons are known for their strength and power with the elements. Females are known for their speed and maneuverability. You know that. I do not understand your surprise.

I did know that, we'd worked together for months training, both Blaz and I. But I'd never ridden Ophelia during those months. She gave a hard bank to the right, flipped sideways and slid between a narrow gap in the mountains.

"So you can outrun these bastards?"

I do not know; how many are there?

I Tracked the demons again. "I'm guessing, but at least thirty." The impressions I picked up were odd, though, thirty that kept blending and twisting into more, and then less. How the fuck was that even possible?

"They're doing something weird."

If we were bound together, I could read them through you.

If we were bound, her life would be tied to mine; but there was a problem. One dragon, one Slayer. That was it, no second chances. "That's not possible, though. Erik said so."

She let out a long snort that curled flames back over her neck. *Erik does not know everything. Your father trained him, and while he taught him all he could, Erik did not like learning from his brother. His pride kept him from truly understanding. The question is, would you even want that with me?*

Carefully, I Tracked Ophelia. I wanted her emotions more than anything, to know what she was truly feeling.

She was scared that she wasn't good enough for me, but inside that fear was a kernel of hope.

I put my hands on her hide. "Okay, I'm going to try and bind us together."

Her thoughts whispered back to me, and I understood the fear in her. *I will not survive another rider's death, Rylee. Promise me you won't die.*

I sucked in a breath and lied. "I promise, I won't die. The plan is for all of us to get out alive."

Then do it. We are stronger together than apart. Blaz wouldn't mind. He loved us both.

I pressed my hands hard against her. "That he did. But he doesn't have a say in this, does he?"

Ophelia laughed, the echo of it rumbling back to me. *No, I suppose he doesn't.*

The thing was, I didn't know what had bound me and Blaz together. We'd flown together after fighting, and when we'd landed, we were bound.

Highest heights and lowest valleys, Rylee. That is what we must do. And you must allow yourself to enjoy it.

She tipped her body and began to climb into the ether reaches. We passed the last mountaintop and I swayed in my rigging as the air thinned and I struggled to breathe. "Too high," I whispered, hoping she could hear me.

One more stroke of her wings and then she tucked them to her sides and rolled in the air. We seemed to pause for a breath, as if gravity had somehow failed.

The free fall was like nothing I'd ever experienced with Blaz, and I realized something.

He'd always held a little back.

I think he was afraid to lose you, always knowing what you would be asked to do.

"That bastard." Easier to be mad at him than to remember the pain of losing him.

The mountaintops raced toward us and with them, the first of the demons. I stared hard at them, trying to make out what form they'd taken. Flying monkeys again? Harpies? Dragons?

None of those shapes.

They looked like people, with wings and long tails tipped at the end with an arrowhead. "Fallen angels?"

That is very, very bad.

Of course it was.

Ophelia plummeted toward them, and as we drew closer, they tipped their faces up to us. Pre-requisite glowing red eyes, of course, but other than that, there was nothing. No nose, no mouth, not even ears. They were completely naked but there weren't any distinguishing features that would mark them as male or female. As in no breasts, no twig and berries.

We blasted through their ranks, sending them spraying to all sides as if a wave of air had hit them. As we continued our free fall, I stared back up at them. "They're regrouping, tell me what's so bad about them."

They are literally *the fallen ones. They were good once, even fought against the demons. But somewhere along the way they lost themselves to the darkness. Their touch can paralyze, and then they will take their time raping you with their hands and then tearing your guts out of you. Not necessarily in that order.*

The wind screamed around us and I kept my eyes on the fallen ones. I didn't need to look at the ground; I knew Ophelia would deal with the fall.

And like that, the bond snapped open between us.

Her emotions and fears, her worries and strengths flowed into me, and mine flowed into hers.

It is predicated on trust, Rylee. But I could not tell you that. It can be harder to bind yourself to a dragon the second time. I was . . . concerned.

"Didn't want to tell me that, either, huh?"

She laughed and all of a sudden, she changed the angle of her wings and we skimmed the ground. The plant life around us whooshed outward with our passing. The scrub grasses of the arctic were brown with only hints of color here and there. "Better to land and fight?"

No. Now you will see what a fully trained dragon can do for you, Rylee. Blaz was good, better than any other dragon could have been for the minimal time we had to train. She paused and tipped her head so I could see her violet eye all but sparkling at me. *But I am better than him, by a very large margin.*

"Humble too," I said, trying not to laugh. Gods save me from dragons and their pride.

Ophelia let out a roar and did a somersault in the air, flipping us to face the fallen ones. They hovered at a distance of a hundred feet or so. Each held a flaming sword to go with their flaming red eyes.

"Lovely. So best practice, don't let them touch me. How the hell am I supposed to send them back then?"

You need to be faster with your sending. No more long words. A simple command. "Go" will suffice.

I let out a breath and nodded. "Then let's kick demon ass, lady bird."

Ophelia reared back and shot a blast of flame toward the fallen ones. They scattered, and before the flame died, she shot toward those closest to us. I was thrown back in the harness, shocked at her instant velocity.

We raced toward the demons and they swept in at us, swords pointed straight at Ophelia. How the hell was she going to avoid this?

My heart was in my throat as the seconds ticked slower and everything moved as if trapped in the thick ice of the high mountain. Ophelia back winged, essentially slamming on the air brakes right in the middle of the fallen ones while simultaneously rolling in the air, her tail lashing out. They had no choice but to fall back or be sliced by the tip of her tail. I clamped my mouth shut against the quick rise of nausea.

"Holy shit."

I've bought you time.

I was already out of the harness, and stood on her back. "Come on, feather heads, let's do this."

Four fallen ones darted toward me at the same time, one from each direction. Below me Ophelia rumbled and shot flames at those encroaching on her space.

Their wings cannot stand the flames. It is their weakness.

"Damn, I wish Pamela was here." I leapt at the demon closest to me. The glowing red eyes were all I saw as I slammed into it. "Go."

The fallen one reared its head back in a silent scream, its body arching, bowing backward until its head touched its ankles and it cracked in half. A sharp burst of light and an explosion of air sent me tumbling onto Ophelia's back. Nothing was left of the fallen one except for a few feathers fluttering through the air. Not that the show deterred its buddies.

One grabbed me from behind, hands icy and burning at the same time. The armband from the Rim broke under its grip, shattering into tiny frozen pieces. But I didn't slow my sending. "Go!"

Good, you are getting faster.

More blasts of flame lit the sky as Ophelia twisted and rolled beneath me. But our connection allowed me to move with her, timing each step with her moves.

The fallen ones shifted their attention from her and they swept upward, out of the range of her flames.

I've downed perhaps ten.

There was a split second where I thought we were going to make it unscathed. The morning light opened up around us and my first thought was the nasty winged fuckers would take off.

But of course, they weren't vampires. They shifted their formation and came at me en masse, hands outstretched. Sheer numbers alone, I couldn't possibly send them all back through the Veil at once.

You can and you must! Ophelia yelled at me, and I didn't hesitate—couldn't hesitate—as the demons reached for my body.

"GO!" Over and over I yelled the word while clammy hands grasped at me, touched my face, grasped my hand, pulled at my legs. Go. The word was so simple and yet, it held the command I needed. Slowly, they exploded around me, bending back, their wings bursting apart at the seams as their bodies were sucked back through the Veil. They were gone and we survived another round of Orion's attacks.

But the damage had been done.

A slow, icy paralysis slid through me and I fell to Ophelia's back, flat on my face.

My mind refused to believe I couldn't move, and panic reared its head as I demanded my muscles to respond.

Be easy, Rylee. All is not lost.

"How can you say that? I can't fucking well move!" Even my jaw was freezing up, my words ending in a slurred and broken clip that didn't sound like anything I was actually trying to say. I felt as though the Hoarfrost demon had found me, again, a thousand times over.

Trust me, this will help. She rolled, dropping me off her back and into the open air. With a sinuous twist of her body, she caught me in her claws, holding me gently. What did she think would help?

The ice forming on my spine was making my teeth ache. My muscles were so stiff, I wondered if it was similar to having rigor mortis while your heart still beat. If that was even a possibility.

Trust me, this will help. She repeated as she threw me into the air, right in front of her. The rumble of fire in her belly was the only warning I got as Ophelia opened her mouth and dragon fire surrounded me.

27
LIAM/FARIS

He was only a few hours from DC, but there was no choice; he had to get away from the sun. He'd done well, managing to travel as far as he had in the time allotted. The suburbs he'd entered would have to do to hunker down for the day. The morning was still early enough that very few people were awake.

Sliding through an unlocked basement window, he dropped to the ground. The interior was dim, but not enough to keep the sunlight out. A door on the far side of the room beckoned and he jogged toward it. The knob turned smoothly in his hand and he stepped through into a fog of pot smoke and the distinct smell of an unwashed male body.

Holding his breath he shut the door behind him and made his way toward the closet on the right. The kid on the bed rolled, let out a fart, and then scratched his ass.

Faris grimaced at the back of his head. *Disgusting human.* Liam snorted, but kept his words to himself. No need to wake the kid up.

You need to feed.

He shook his head. Not a chance in hell he was taking blood from that kid.

Fair enough, but if you feed, we could jump the Veil.

Liam shut the closet door and slid to his butt. Scrubbing a hand over his face, he considered their options. At this speed, there was no way they'd make it back to North Dakota by the next morning. Even if they managed to hotwire a car, he didn't think they'd make it.

"How bad will it be? How much of my soul will jumping take?" he asked softly. The black interior of the closet made it easy to feel as if he were talking to someone beside him, instead of inside him.

Faris gave a proverbial shrug. *I don't know. You saw Milly, she looked fairly intact and she had been jumping the Veil for a long time; even though I didn't know it. Well before anyone of us ever met her. She hid her abilities well.*

Liam grimaced. Using Milly for an example didn't really set his mind at ease. She'd betrayed Rylee on more than one occasion, though she had always tried to make it right. And in the end, she'd done the right thing. But had any of that been tied to jumping the Veil and having her soul used up, or was it all Orion's influence?

He knew he didn't have a choice, not if he wanted to be there in time to stand with Rylee against Orion.

"Let's do this."

Faris gave a nod of approval as Liam stepped into the kid's room. There was no choice, he was going to have to drink from the pot-smoking teenager and hope whatever was in his system was already through.

Three quick steps and he knelt beside the bed before he could talk himself out of what he was doing. The kid rolled toward him, muttered something about making a score, and Liam snaked his head toward the bare neck presented. His fangs popped through the skin, and the kid gave a little start.

"Not so hard, baby, you know that's not how I like it."

With his eyes squeezed shut, Liam had to fight to keep his mouth on the kid's neck and keep drinking him down. In the back of his head, Faris laughed. *You see, it's not always glamorous to be a vampire.* He paused, as if thinking. *That should be enough, Wolf.*

Wolf, was he even that anymore? He pulled back from the kid and wiped his hand over his mouth. There was a lingering taste of drugs on the back of his tongue. Faris giggled. *I think the good stuff went right to me.*

Shit. A high vampire in his head? Wonderful, fucking wonderful.

On the bed, the kid moaned and grabbed at himself. "Come on, baby, finish it off."

Liam stepped back and Faris laughed even harder. *Yes, do finish him off so I can tell Rylee all about it. Cheater, cheater, pot kid eater.*

Rolling his eyes, he looked at the wall and the poster plastered to it. Rock bands, and a giant pot leaf in a myriad of colors were the main choices. "Faris, jump us to the barn on Rylee's property."

Only if you let me kiss her. By myself. No meddling from you. There was still an edge of giddiness to the vampire's voice, but he was serious.

"As long as she knows it's you and wants to, then fine." It sure as hell wasn't up to him who Rylee kissed. The part of him that was wolf disagreed, but there was no time for semantics. Rylee was his mate, but she was also a woman who could make fire-hardened steel look soft. And if she wanted to kiss Faris . . . he couldn't really get pissy about it since he shared the vampire's body.

Faris didn't step forward, but he showed Liam how to open the Veil. With the latent necromancer abilities flowing through Faris's veins, he was able to touch the layer of the Veil between the human world and the supernatural. Like touching cellophane stretched tightly on leftovers. Drawing his fingers together, he pulled it away while he thought of the barn and . . . there it was. Dim and shadowy, the interior of the barn beckoning him; North Dakota still held onto the night for an hour or so. Without a glance at the kid, he stepped through and let the Veil shut behind him.

"You bastard! You said you wouldn't jump the Veil, that it would hurt Liam!" Berget's voice caught him off guard and he swung around to face her. He held up his hands.

"I was in DC, Berget. I had to get back here and there was no other way."

"Liam?"

He nodded. "Faris has been taking a vacation. He showed up long enough to give me directions."

Berget let out a sigh and shook her head. "No one else is here, Liam. Shouldn't Doran and the rest from England be here by now?"

He looked around the barn, seeing only the automatic writer Jonathan asleep in the hay. "Rylee sent Charlie to get them. You think something went wrong?"

"Orion knows who's a part of Rylee's team. He's going to try and stop us all. Like he tried to kill Jonathan."

Liam ran his hands through his hair and began to pace. He could jump the Veil, though eventually it would cost him pieces of his soul. What would it matter if Rylee and everyone else were dead?

Nothing. Nothing would matter then.

"Don't tell Rylee." He held his hand up and twisted the Veil so he could look into Jack's mansion. He'd opened the Veil at the front door, so they could look into the main hall. Berget touched him on the shoulder.

"Hold it open; I'll step through and see—"

"Faris! Keep it open. Don't let go!" Doran's voice shouted in the distance. The pounding of hooves almost made him close the Veil regardless of the daywalker's words.

Berget fell backward as unicorns burst through the opening, followed by Doran, Will and his leopard shifters, Deanna, India, the spirit seeker who was barely out of childhood, Charlie with a half-dozen other brownies, and Mer the green ogre. The two shamans they'd sent to London stepped through as well: Louisa and Crystal.

"Close it, man! Close it the fuck down."

He let the Veil snap shut, cutting off the sound of howling renting the air. Jonathan sat up in the hay.

"Demons."

Berget went to him, cooing softly in the way of a vampire hypnotizing its prey. "No, go back to sleep. Those are nightmares, Johnny."

He flopped back, a murmur on his lips. "I wish they were nightmares."

Didn't they all?

Around them, the unicorns settled into the hay, their glimmering horns picking up the light. Liam counted a dozen and that included little Calliope, though she was different than the last time he'd seen her. Her nub of a horn was no longer a nub but an actual horn that protruded two feet off her forehead and had a wicked gleaming point. Her eyes turned toward him and she bobbed her head.

Thank you, Wolf. You have our gratitude, yet again.

Will and Deanna gave him a nod and went with their group to the back of the barn, near Jonathan. They sprawled out, and it hit Liam that they hadn't run from something. They had been battling for their lives when he'd opened the Veil.

Doran slapped his hand on Liam's back. "Good man. They almost had us at the end there."

Faris laughed softly, but didn't try to push forward.

"It's not Faris running things right now," Liam said.

Doran's turn to laugh. "I know. I am a shaman still, remember?"

"What was chasing you?"

"Demons, of course, but they'd taken up in residence amongst a few of the remaining vampires, werewolves, and Harpies that were still sick. Which cut our numbers down yet again. We lost at least half of our people in that fight before you opened the Veil."

Liam shook his head. No one was safe from Orion and his lackeys.

"Now what?" he asked Doran, hoping the shaman had some brilliant insight as to what the next step was. How to prepare for the coming battle, what weapons they would need, or who they had to bring in.

Doran's green eyes were serious. "Now, we wait for Rylee and pray to the gods she arrives before Orion."

Closing his eyes, he tried not to worry that Rylee wouldn't make it in time. But the woman had her own way of doing things, and it was rarely the way he would see them done.

And showing up late to her own party?

That had Rylee written all over it.

28
RYLEE

Ophelia's fire engulfed me and I didn't get my mouth shut in time. The flames raced down my throat, into my belly and lungs as if I'd invited them in. The heat was intense, but it didn't hurt as it raced along my nerve endings, synapses, and bones, burning out any trace of the paralysis.

The flames died down and Ophelia caught me, tossing me onto her back. *There, better now?*

"Shit, a little warning would have been nice." I tied myself into the harness, sweat sliding down my skin under the long coat.

But you trust me.

"That I do. But a warning would have been nice too."

Ophelia was already winging south toward the farm. We were a long way away though, and I was hesitant to believe we would make it. Until I looked at the ground. The view flashed by, easily five or six times faster than when I'd ridden Blaz.

Shit, we were going to make it with plenty of time.

That made me nervous. Through the bond to Orion, he pick up on my unease, while I felt his frustration.

Something hadn't gone his way and I didn't think it was the fallen ones' destruction that bothered him.

Something happened, something he'd been banking on. As much as he was able, he tried to pull his thoughts away from me. He was on the East Coast still and there was a flash of irritation that I was still watching him. That made me grin.

What does he think, that you won't spy on him now that you have that connection? What a moron.

I laughed and pressed my hands against her. "Any ideas as to what he might be up to? You can feel his bond through me, right?"

Yes, I feel him. A gust of wind swept in from behind us, pushing us even faster. *But there is too much distance to pick up a true direction of his thoughts.*

That was the problem. I didn't want to be closer to Orion. No, it wasn't worth it, of course. We'd be close enough, soon enough. Far sooner than I wanted.

I curled down against Ophelia's back. "I'm going to try and sleep. Wake me if anything seems off, anything at all."

Of course, I am not Blaz. I will not keep you from what is your calling.

No, she wasn't Blaz, but that was okay. Her strength echoed through me in a different way. Perhaps . . . perhaps I'd had to lose him so Ophelia could truly bond with me. Maybe this was fate playing out. Not that it made his loss easier.

Strapped to her back, I shimmied until I could lay myself somewhat flat. Exhaustion hit me hard despite the wind racing around me. I was warm inside Erik's coat, and with my face buried in it, I smelled him and remembered I was not alone. I had family in him, Lark, and my pack of misfits. A smile flitted over my lips as I sagged into the restraints holding me to Ophelia's back.

Sleep swept over me and I drifted into strange dreams of death, fighting, and blood. But the last dream made my breath come in gasps.

Erik held Marcella. They were at a home I recognized, a home I didn't think he even knew about. My adoptive mother held her hands out. "This is Rylee's child? You look like Rylee's father. I met him once, though I don't think I am supposed to remember that. Things are fuzzy now and again. How did you find me?"

No, no, no. Erik, don't give her the baby! I wanted to scream at him that she wasn't what she seemed. But he handed the baby over without hesitation.

"I checked in on Rylee once, when she was little." He shook his head, seemingly lost in a memory for a split second before he went on. "Rylee would want you to know your grandbaby, I think. And this is a good place to hunker down for a few days. If you don't mind." Behind him, Coyote held Zane on his hip. Little Z with his green eyes just like his mother. Milly's features were plainly stamped on the little boy's lips and cheeks, and his sweet temperament was obviously still there by the way he curled into Coyote, resting his head on the Guardian's shoulder.

My heart ached to hold him and my Marcella, to breathe in their innocence and believe the world was right for a moment. The image swung to my adoptive mother as she jiggled Marcella. "Such a beautiful child. Thank God she didn't get her mother's hair."

Erik stiffened and held his hands out as if he saw what I did. "Give her back."

"No, not yet. I want to hold her tight."

She lifted her eyes and I saw it then. Not a flicker of red like I'd been suspecting, but a flicker of madness. She'd lost her mind somewhere between losing her daughters, her husband, and then seeing the supernatural come to life. "I want to hold her forever. I can raise her, she can be my new daughter, the one who loves me the best."

Erik reached for Marcella as she began to cry, fat tears rolling down her sweet soft cheeks. He caught my mother by her arm and stopped her from running. His knuckles turned white as he pressed. "Let her go, or I'll break your arm."

She let out a sob and thrust the baby at him. A wave of relief flowed through me. I had no doubt what I was seeing was real.

The door behind them burst open and a bevy of trolls burst through. Their skin hung loosely on their bodies as they grabbed at the babies. Coyote fought with one arm, while he clung to Zane with the other, but the trolls circled him and snatched the green-eyed boy from his arms. He snarled and kept fighting, but despite the fact he was a Guardian, he was still outnumbered.

The trolls poured in like a nest of oversized ants, piling on top of him and weighing him down with sheer numbers. Seeing past the seething bodies was difficult. An arm was flung out of the pile of bodies, and then Coyote's head.

They'd ripped his head off as he tried to protect Zane.

I wanted to close my eyes, but I couldn't. There was no way to escape what was happening.

No. This was not real. It couldn't be. Ophelia felt on my horror and tried to soothe me even while I slept, but I pushed her away. I had to see what happened. I had to see if they got away with . . . .

Erik went down under fists and boots, his body encircling Marcella. There was screaming from my mother that was silenced with a meaty thud, the babies were crying at the top of their lungs and then the trolls stepped back from Erik. He was curled around Marcella, but his chest didn't rise and fall, and the wounds in his back were too many. Marcella still cried under him and by the angle of his knees I knew he was not laying on her but instead holding himself up. Even in death he was protecting her.

Protecting me.

A sob ripped from me, not another family member gone. My chest constricted as I fought to stay in the dream, vision, whatever it was, as long as I could. I couldn't take my eyes away from Erik's hunched body or Zane's little face scrunched in fury.

The door swung open again and a large, bald man stepped into the room. Orion looked right at me, his red eyes glittering. He had done this . . . of course he had.

"You may hold the world in your hands, Tracker. But I have your daughter. What is she worth to you?"

The vision—because I knew without a doubt it was no dream—scattered. I woke screaming, jerking at the rigging that held me to Ophelia's back. Her roar echoed my panic and pain, and she dropped from the sky. We were somewhere over the northern prairies from the open fields I could see.

I'd slept through the day and the night was upon us again.

"Go, we have to go to them!" I clawed at the leather holding me down with a frantic fury I couldn't contain, but it made me sloppy.

Rylee, we can't. There is no time to rescue your daughter. We have to complete the ceremony and pray that it is enough to save not only the world, but Marcella and Zane too.

The pain ripping through me was unbearable. I couldn't think past it, couldn't think beyond the fact that Orion had my little girl. He had Zane. He'd killed Erik and Coyote as if they were nothing.

Orion could possess either one of the babies if he so chose, and I would be forced to kill them. A howl ripped out of me that was picked up by a pack of wolves below us; their mournful cries echoing my pain back to me.

This was not happening; it couldn't be.

Yet I knew without a shadow of a doubt it *was* happening, and that no matter how much I wanted to rush off and save them, Ophelia was right. It was time to finish things and pray it would be enough to save them.

Sobbing, I leaned over my dragon's back and clung to her. "Hurry, Ophelia, please hurry."

Her wings picked up in tempo, and within seconds we were skimming the skies, flying faster than ever before. I felt the strain on her, and knew she was pushing herself beyond her limits for me. Knew that it could come back to haunt us later, but I struggled to care. All I knew was I had to get to the ceremonial grounds and make this happen.

One way or another, I would end Orion's life, save my baby girl and Zane, and put this whole fucking debacle behind us. I had to.

There was no other way.

29
PAMELA

There was no way we were going to make it back to Rylee in time to be a part of the last battle. We were *still* at the Rim as Lark searched for something. I'd followed her into the Enders Barracks and watched as she tore apart a small room. "Goose shit, where the hell did he put it?"

"What are you looking for?" I dared to ask.

She stopped and put her hands on her hips. "A sword. I made a sword for Rylee."

I frowned. "But she has swords, two actually. Shouldn't we be going?"

It had been almost an hour since she'd told the elementals she was going to get help. An hour felt like forever when I knew we were down to less than a day before Orion brought his hordes against us, and if we failed, the world.

"I know we need to get going, but the sword is for the ceremony. It's what will make the cuts."

"The cuts?"

Lark didn't look at me, but her shoulder's tightened imperceptibly. "Cuts into Rylee to drain her blood. Without it, the ceremony won't be complete. So yes, before you ask, we *have* to find it."

I swallowed with difficulty. Lark backed out of the room while shaking her head.

"I think Ash hid it, but where?"

"Did he leave you a hint?" I suggested, wanting nothing more than to hurry this up, but also recognizing the importance of a ceremonial weapon.

She put both hands to her face and rubbed the heels of them into her eyes. "Yes, I think so. Always go back to the beginning. That's what he told me the last time I saw him. The *beginning*." Her voice softened on the last word and then she was sprinting past me.

I tried to keep up with her as she ran through the main part of the barracks and into the forest. A flash of long blonde hair was all I saw between the trunks of the redwoods and then she was gone.

"She'll be back, so don't you be fussing yourself, yeah?"

I looked at Griffin, seeing again his strong resemblance to Liam. Or at least, the resemblance to the way Liam *had* looked. The dark hair and eyes, his build, the shape of his jaw, but more than that, the way he moved. Predatory and smooth, like he was never in a hurry, but could be in a split second if he chose.

"Griffin, can I ask you a question?" I felt I couldn't blurt out whatever I wanted to. Like maybe it would be rude.

He held out his hand in front of him and waved it across. "Ask away, little witch. We are practically family, yeah?" He winked at me and I wasn't quite sure if he was referring to the fact that I was a part of Rylee and Liam's adoptive family, or something else.

I had a feeling it was something else.

"You seem to know a lot about the supernatural and elemental worlds."

His eyes twinkled with barely disguised humor. "That, I do."

I paused thinking of how to word my question right. "How exactly do they intersect?"

He crossed his arms over his chest. "That's a big question."

I noticed he didn't use his usual *yeah* at the end, which made me think he was really considering answering me. A flush of excitement rushed through my body at the thought of learning something new. I smiled tentatively. "I keep hearing bits and pieces. Like Rylee has elemental blood or I have elemental blood. But I want to understand how this works. Since I have to wait here for Lark, and I can do nothing else, perhaps this will help me understand things better."

Griffin crouched and drew in the dirt with a finger. Five circles came first and he attached each of them together with a single line to make one rough larger circle. "There are five elemental families: earth, wind, air, fire, and spirit. Lark is of the first family, earth. But her mother was of the fifth family, spirit. So she is a half-breed. The side of her that is spirit is dangerous, and when used improperly, chips away at her soul, eating it piece by piece. Which is why she don't use it much, yeah?"

I nodded, soaking every word up. "She could control people with Spirit, couldn't she?"

Griffin nodded. "You saw her control that demon at the underground beach to keep it from hurting Rylee, didn't you?"

"Yes, and I wondered why she hadn't done it before, with any other of the things we've faced."

"It is a last resort. She can't use it freely; it is too powerful and destructive to her. So only when there is no other choice does she dip into that side of her heritage." He cleared his throat and started drawing again. From the five circles he drew lines outward. "This is where you won't be able to find any books that teach you this bit, yeah?"

I leaned forward, watching eagerly.

"The entire supernatural world is derived from the five elemental families in one way or another. Always with a bloodline crossed with the humans, of course. The humans were the melting pot for the elementals and all their offspring.

"From the elementals of the earth, you get werewolves, brownies, leprechauns, and necromancers. From the elementals of the air, you get Harpies, my namesake the griffins, fairy folk, and psychics.

"From the elementals of fire, you get witches, automatic writers, Readers, and fire drakes. From the water elementals, you get mermaids, naiads, and sirens. And from the Spirit elementals, you get only one offshoot: Trackers.

"Of course, the list isn't inclusive, there are many, many more creations, but they all are derived from the elementals somewhere in their family branches."

I opened my mouth to question him more but he held up his hand. "I ain't done yet, yeah?"

He branched off more circles from the second set he'd drawn. "Some of those creations were powerful enough to make species of their own. Like the necromancers learning to make zombies and vampires, or the witches learning to make trolls and goblins. Now there are a few creatures outside of the elemental world in terms of creation. Unicorns, dragons, the Kracken, and firewyrms come to mind. A few others, but they don't matter much at the moment."

His hands hovered over the original five circles. "Now, here is where the story gets interesting. The first four families of elementals got jealous of the fifth-born because of their ability to control others." He put his palm over the fifth circle and slowly rubbed it out.

"They took out their own siblings, cousins, and family because of fear, and the bloodline thinned, leaving only a few still in hiding. Those few kept moving, never finding a home. They married, had children, and all were caught and killed, yeah?"

My throat tightened and I struggled to swallow. "Just killed? For no reason?"

Griffin leaned closer to me, his dark eyes filling the sphere of what I could see. "For what they could do, little witch. For their strength."

Heart beating wildly, I stared hard at him. "And how do I fit in here?"

He flashed a smile and pulled back. "You, you're a blend of all five families, with a bit of everyone residing within your blood. It's why you can heal, why you can use the elements with such ease. You'll never be an elemental in truth, but you *are* strong like them."

A dash of fear zipped through me. "But . . . then a part of me is still human?" I wasn't sure if that was good or not. To me, humans were weak. They were blind and most times foolish in their choices. An easy example was how willing they'd been to believe Orion and his games.

Griffin nodded. "That's what dilutes the power and makes you stronger than the other witches, but not so strong that the elementals here want to wipe you out. It's a bad trait of theirs, killing what they can't control. It's why Lark has had such a difficult time in her life."

"Fear. They kill what they fear," I said, looking at the ground. Peta sat at my feet, looking up at me. I reached for her and she leapt upward.

Burying my face into her thick fur, I was no longer sure I wanted to know more about the elemental world. If they killed what they feared and I was stronger than some of them . . . I looked up in time to see Griffin nod.

"That's right, little witch. You should be afraid. You should be, yeah?"

Yeah, indeed.

30
LARK

I ran through the Rim and deep into the redwood forest. The northern edge was where my story truly began.

A place where I'd lost my family, my memories, and my childhood in a single fell swoop. The place that only two other people knew had any meaning to me, and Cactus sure as hell didn't know about the sword for Rylee.

My father had taken it from me, saying it wasn't needed. I had no doubt Ash would have recognized the sword as something I made, and if he'd seen it, he would have done his best to take it from my father.

Which would explain why Ash was also banished or more likely in an oubliette.

Ash would've defied my father and buried the weapon in the woods. A part of me wasn't surprised. Ash always *had* kept a step ahead of me. Even though I didn't realize it until after I'd been banished.

The clearing opened in front of me and my feet stumbled, despite trying to move faster. It seemed that my body remembered the place too.

"You know, I'm surprised you'd come back here."

I dropped to a crouch as I spun around, swinging my spear out in a wide arc. The figure who'd spoken drifted through the forest toward me, hidden underneath a solid black cloak. Not one of his features visible, but I wasn't surprised. We'd met more than once, and the bastard always seemed to be around when things went wrong.

"What are you doing here, Blackbird?"

He laughed softly. "Not what you think. The sword is deep within the ground and encased with several spells. Your friend, Ash, did that to protect it from me."

Ash's name on his lips was like a blow unto itself. I clenched the haft of my spear tighter and started toward him. "We end this now, Blackbird. You're the reason Ash and I were banished."

"Ha! You did that on your own; you didn't need my help. But I think you need it now, little Larkspur of the Rim. Half-breed princess. Ender. Destroyer." My many names rolled off his lips with an intimacy I didn't appreciate. He moved with me, keeping always the same distance between us.

He was the only elemental I'd ever met who was able to contain not one or even two elements like I did, but all five. All five elements, and he was powerful with every one of them.

In the past, I would have told him to go to hell . . . but I'd had time to mellow in the oubliette. He would make a strong ally, if I could figure out what he was up to. "Why do I need your help, exactly?"

"Because the demon hordes will wipe out this world if we don't all step up and take our place in the battle."

His words were deadly serious, and they chilled me through and through. He said what I already knew, but still, it was hard to hear the truth from him after all the lies he'd spewed.

"You're offering to fight against them?"

His head bobbed. "Yes. But I want Rylee's sword when it's over."

I thought about the sword. I'd made it, and with the making of it had unintentionally imbued it with a few abilities I shouldn't have. In particular, the ability to open and close the Veil like a key.

"I can't make that deal. You'll have to ask her."

"She'll be dead, we both know that." He came to a stop over a patch of wildflowers. A softly bobbing cluster of white and blue petals: larkspur, my namesake.

Blackbird folded his arms over his chest. "Aww, how sweet, he planted your flower for you."

"How do I know you will keep your word and help?"

Blackbird held a hand out. "A simple handshake. When this is done, we will go back to being enemies."

I reached out and took his hand, clamping down hard as I wove Spirit over his fingers.

"Say it then, make a vow."

He tried to pull away from me, and while he was stronger in the elements, he was not physically stronger than me. A sigh slipped out of him. "I swear to help you in the fight against the demons, Larkspur."

It would have to be enough. I let him go and dropped to one knee.

My jaw tightened as I put a hand to the earth, feeling the sword encased in cement about thirty feet down. Like its own miniature oubliette.

There were spells around it for sure, but beside me, Blackbird did his thing, breaking them up. A spell for every element and he disabled them. Which left me wondering why he'd waited on me.

I closed my eyes and worked the earth around the sword, bringing it up with a speed that rumbled the ground.

"Impressive," Blackbird muttered.

"You couldn't manage it?"

"I could. But you and I are probably the only two who could, except for perhaps Basileus." His words were light, but there was a hesitancy in his voice that gave light to his lie. There was something he wasn't telling me.

I didn't say anything more. He might be working with me for the moment, but I had no doubt we'd be on opposing sides soon enough.

The cement box spit up out of the ground, and with it came something I didn't expect.

The reason Blackbird had waited on me.

Sandlings. Creatures made from the earth, like animated golems, that were quite literally un-killable because they weren't truly alive. They looked human, moved like humans, but were faster and stronger. They had teeth made of sharpened stones and their hands were tipped with nails made of old bone filed to points. Normally they were used for training in the Enders Barracks.

But this was not the first time I'd encountered them in a situation that was most definitely not training.

Blackbird took a step back. "You think your friend set this up?"

"No." I breathed out, counting the Sandlings as they continued to emerge from the ground. More and more, until the ranks filled the clearing.

"You think they want to be friends?"

I stared at Blackbird. "This is not the time for jokes, you idiot. Even you can't kill them."

Whoever made the Sandlings had to un-make them; that was the only way.

Which meant we were screwed.

"Keep them off me!" I bent and put my hands to the cement box, knowing that whatever kickback it had wouldn't be aimed at me. The power of the earth roared through me and into the cement. I broke the molecules apart, tearing the stone away to reveal the prize I sought.

Around me, Blackbird whirled, his cloak swirling around his legs as he protected my back. Fire and ice, earth and wind, ripped through the clearing, blowing the Sandlings to their knees. But they slid into the earth only to reemerge a few feet behind Blackbird.

For a breath of a moment I stared at the sword laying on the dirt in front of me. A katana, made with hundreds of folds of steel to create a hardened and yet flexible blade. The edge was tipped in silver, and the handle was a perfect fit for Rylee's hand. Three diamonds were inset in the handle and a large chunk of blue amber finished the touch at the end of it. I picked it up and cut through the Sandling closest to me. The blade whooshed through him, sparking against the rough material the Sandling was made up of.

But even with the sword, the creature reformed at my feet, clawing itself out of the ground.

"Larkspur, while this had been fun, it truly is time for me to go. I will be there, on the battlefield. That is all I can tell you."

Blackbird lifted a hand to me and then shot into the air as a violent snap of wind lifted him out of harm's way.

"Coward!" The world went silent and I stared at the Sandlings. They stared back at me for a heartbeat, and then they ran at me.

I spun and bolted from the clearing, the sound of crashing underbrush behind me. Pumping my arms and legs, I called the power of the earth to me, sending it out behind me in a wave. The earthquake rippled backward, the strength of it shaking the foundation of the trees around us, sending leaves and branches flying to the ground.

That move would buy me time, but not a lot. To my left, a Sandling sprung out of the ground, reaching for my legs even as I leapt away. Its hand caught my ankle and yanked me out of mid-leap.

I hit the ground hard, knocking the wind out of me, but still, I kept moving. Hands came out of the ground like a freak-show zombie cache gone wrong. I plunged my hands into the earth and loosened it up, turning the area all around me into quicksand. The Sandlings struggled, giving me time to stand. Each step I took, I firmed the ground under my feet until I was farther away.

But again, they dissolved and reformed near me.

"Mother goddess, this isn't funny anymore." I ran for the Rim, knowing the only chance I had was to get as far away as possible. I was fairly certain I knew who'd left the Sandling trap for me.

Cassava. That scheming bitch was still at it; and this had her name written all over it. My stepmother would never rest until she had her hands on at least one throne within the elemental world, and she didn't give a flying rat's ass who she hurt in the process.

I burst into the Rim, but didn't slow. "Peta, Cactus, Pam, Griffin. To me, now!"

Pamela spun around, Peta in her arms. Griffin grabbed her and dragged her toward me. "Where the hell is Cactus?"

He came running around the corner, Sandlings hot on his trail. He had blood running down one side of his face and he wasn't moving as fast as he should have been. "Lark, we're surrounded."

"Where is Bella and the rest of the family?" I barked out as I backed toward Pamela, Griffin, and Peta. The Sandlings kept their movements slow as they stalked our way. Like they knew they had us.

Which, if it weren't for the sword in my hands, they would have.

"Already gone. Everyone's on their way to the meeting grounds outside the farm."

A breath of relief flowed from me. That was at least going right.

I held the sword above my head and made a perfect slash downward until the tip of the sword was buried into the ground, whispering the Latin to go with the invocation. "*Velata facie terroris*. Take us to The Pit."

The Veil ripped open in front of us, shimmering for a moment before revealing the interior of the Pit. Home of the fire elementals and Queen Fiametta.

I only hope she remembered she owed me her life.

I took a deep breath and stepped through the opened Veil. Somehow, I doubted it was going to be as easy as I was hoping.

31
ALEX

Every stop we made, more wolves joined us. They saw me shift, they'd heard how I had been submissive and now wasn't, and that it was Rylee's love that helped me make the change. We'd gathered at least two hundred werewolves, and a few other shifters along the way.

Unlike some of the other supernaturals, they'd stayed out of the cities as the pox hit and had kept their people safe.

More than all that, though, was the number of submissives that came along with the packs. Apparently, not all the packs killed their weaker members.

What I didn't tell them was that Pamela was a big part of me being able to shift. Maybe the only part when it came right down to it.

"Why aren't you telling them about Pamela?" Eve asked as we dipped through a cloud bank, staying low enough so the ever-growing wolf pack was able to keep us within sight.

"Because what if it was just me? We don't know if she can heal the rest of them, Eve." I rubbed a hand over my head and scratched behind one ear. "I mean, maybe it's because she cares for me."

"You mean because she loves you." Eve grinned back at me, and I couldn't help the heat in my cheeks.

"Not like that."

"You want to *kiss* her."

"Evie!" I couldn't help the choked laughter that escaped me.

Marco laughed with me, his wingtips touching Eve's. "Stop teasing him, Eve. His face looks like a tomato about to burst."

I shook my head, still smiling. "Is it that obvious?"

"No," Eve chuckled. "I only know because Rylee and Liam were discussing you. I will make sure you don't let our Pamela know you love her until it is time." She clacked her beak at me and I held up my hands.

"I'm not arguing with a protective Harpy."

"Smart man, don't ever argue with a Harpy," Marco said softly. Eve snapped her beak at him and he settled a few more feet between us.

Eve shook her head and neck, ruffling her feathers. "I think you would match her well, Alex. And I think she loves you already, but she doesn't know it."

That's what I was hoping. As much as I loved Rylee, and she was a part of my life and would be forever . . . it wasn't what I felt for Pamela.

She was stronger than she realized with so much heart . . . and fire . . . and those blue eyes that made me forget that I was supposed to wait for her to get a little older.

"Look at him, he's thinking about her right now," Marco crowed, and Eve screeched, laughing.

I shook my head, grinning. "Yeah, so what?"

They laughed, but there was no malice to it. The wind blew around us, picking up as the currents swirled and I realized how close we were to Bismarck.

"Eve, what about the half-breed trolls?" I had to rack my brain for the name of the female who'd helped us take out Ingers and the black coven when they'd tried to get the army involved in wiping out the supernatural world.

"Tara," Eve squawked.

"Do you think we could find her, and convince her to help?"

Marco shook his head, his eyes narrowing slightly. "You think they won't be dead? They were susceptible to the pox too, Alex."

I chewed at my bottom lip thinking. "But the trolls were working for Orion all along, right?"

They nodded in unison.

"So wouldn't he have put something into play to keep the trolls from picking up the pox?" Even as I said the words I knew I was wrong. In London, right as Rylee had returned to us from Tian Shan and leaving her daughter behind, there had been a troll infected with the pox.

"Good thinking, but how do we find them?"

Already I knew it was a long shot, but we had a little time. A few more on our side might make the difference.

"We've got a wolf pack of two hundred. You don't think they could sniff out a few trolls?" I grinned, already seeing the chaos in my mind of wolves all over downtown Bismarck, freaking out the general populace.

I all but vibrated in my seat.

I couldn't wait.

Without another word, Eve and Marco dropped out of the sky so I could speak to the wolf packs about the plan.

Being wolves and loving a little chaos themselves, they agreed.

This was about to get fun.

32
RYLEE

Ophelia flew hard all night long. There were demons here and there, and they came at us fast and without warning. But we destroyed them as if they were flies and gnats. Like they were nothing.

I Tracked Marcella and Zane constantly, feeling their uncertainty. The trickles of fear that flared up here and there. But no pain, they weren't being hurt. And they were themselves, there was no possession happening. Yet.

That was about all I had to keep myself going; knowing for the moment, they were alive and as well as they could be while in Orion's "care."

As the sun climbed in the east, we neared my old farm. Or what was left of it.

Rylee, I have to ask. How do you know this is the place the final battle is to happen? Even your father never figured that out. Even Jack wasn't sure, I think.

"The books of prophecy, or one in particular, I should say." I frowned into the bright sunlight. "The book of the Blood of the Lost was very straightforward, there was no double entendre to the words. It said, 'The Blood of the Lost shall be spilled on the steps of her home, and therein will the world see not all is forsaken, but as it should be.'"

But your home, it could be anywhere you've lived, couldn't it?

"Not in this case." We flew over the farm in a big sweep, the cornfields bending under the downdraft of her wings. "Stay up for a minute. What do you see where the house burnt down?"

Ophelia back winged, and tread the air with ease. *The remnants of your home, the charred out timbers.*

"And under that?"

She strained her neck forward and then shook herself. *A ceremonial slab. That is where your blood will be spilt.*

I nodded, a sense of relief flowing through me. "So you see, this is the right place. I think I knew it all along, which is why I was drawn to it. Why so many fights happened right here. This land . . . I've been fighting for it all along." And the loss of my home made sense now. Without being burned to ash, we'd have had a bitch of a time getting to the slab.

Ophelia spiraled to the ground, landing beside the barn.

I will clear the rest of the timbers so the pathway is clear. How soon before the ceremony starts?

"That will depend, I guess." I slid from her back and dropped to my feet. "There is more than one factor involved here."

The barn door creaked open and I was relieved Doran stepped out. He swept me into a hug, holding me tightly. "We'll get her back, don't doubt it for an instant. That girl has too much ahead of her to have it any other way."

I squeezed him as hard as I could. "I want to believe that."

A loud racket of wood cracking turned us both to where Ophelia was tearing the remains of the farmhouse down and away from the ceremonial slab with no little amount of glee on her face. "Dragons and their love of demolition. Never gets old for them," I said.

Doran gave me another squeeze. "I'm going to set things up for you. To a fucking T as per your paperwork you sent." He let go of my arms and pulled from his back pocket a tattered piece of paper with my handwriting on one side. It was only then I noticed the braided rope looped around his neck and over his shoulders. Unicorn hair. I stroked a hand down it.

"Let's hope it holds. The book of the Blood of the Lost said it would," I whispered.

"Believe it, Rylee. You can do this. Now go and get the job done."

His words helped me center myself. The long road was almost finished; a little further and everyone would be safe.

Will stuck his head out of the barn. "Rylee, I'm sorry, but the crazy boy wants to talk to you."

"Factor number one in dealing with this shit," I muttered under my breath.

Lark said Jonathan was a key in deciding my fate. But I'd heard those words before about other people. Alex was also supposed to be a key in the final battle.

So was Pamela, and of course Lark. Hell, Liam wasn't even supposed to be at the battle, though I supposed since his physical body wasn't there that was perhaps still holding true.

But since none of them were here, I was about to see how big a factor Jonathan was going to play. Trusting Lark was easy and she said he was important.

That was good enough for me. I walked into the barn, the sunrays coming through a couple slats, highlighting dust motes in the air. A deep breath and my lungs filled with the scent of hay and old leather. Jonathan sat up at the back of the barn with Deanna beside him.

"Jonathan, you have to help us. The world is depending on it." She was cajoling him, holding his hand in hers. He snatched his fingers away like she'd pinched him.

"No. I have to have proper payment. That's how this works." His eyes met mine. "Tracker. You understand, don't you? I can't just help you; there has to be appropriate payment or this won't work."

Deanna let out a deep sigh and glanced at me before looking at him again. "Can you tell me what the payment is? Then we can get it for you."

He shook his head violently and I wondered if that was why his eyes were all screwball. Too much head shaking for the freaky-assed kid.

"No, no, that's not how this works. If you deserve to be Read, then you have to have the payment. You have to understand what it is I want. I can't tell you."

I crossed my arms, thinking about what Belladonna had said. That they'd given him money, jewels, and precious gifts in an effort to get him to write the future for certain things. The elementals had gone so far as to send beautiful women to his bed; none of which was the correct payment. At least in his mind. Which meant it would be something so out there that we likely wouldn't be able to figure it out.

"Let me think a minute." Fuckity, fuck, fuck. What the hell did he want? What would a boy his age want for payment?

Each minute that ticked by was one closer to facing Orion. Although it was early morning, by the time the sun set we would be battling for the world. "Fuck." I paced through the barn. There was something in the back of my mind, from what seemed so long ago it could have been another lifetime.

My feet came to a halt in front of Jonathan as the possibility solidified in my mind. Could it be that simple? That easy? "If I get you two pieces of payment, will you Read for me two futures?"

He nodded. "Do you think you know what the payment is?"

"Believe it or not, I think I do." I turned to leave when a hand shot out of the shadows and pulled me in. Liam.

"I really wish you'd stop leaving me behind, Rylee." His lips were against mine as he spoke, and in the darkness I didn't feel or see anything but him. And for a split second I was sad. Faris . . . I didn't love him like I loved Liam. No one could ever come close to that.

But . . . he spoke to a darker part of me. A part that maybe, if I were honest with myself, even Liam didn't quite understand. The part that could kill without remorse, and could stand in the darkness without fear. A part that perhaps liked that darkness more than the light on certain days.

I kissed him, thinking all those things as he snaked his arms around me. Our mouths and tongues tangled in a heated kiss that was bittersweet because I was about to do exactly what he'd said and leave him behind again. "I have to go."

"I know. I'll be here." The words were weighted with more than their straightforward meaning. Liam would always be there for me. Of that, I had no doubt.

I stepped back and ran for the barn door. We didn't have long, and I had to get to Bismarck for Jonathan's payment. I went to Doran first. "You got any human cash on you?'

His green eyes widened. "What will you give me for it?"

"I already owe you a kiss? Isn't that enough?"

He grinned at me, wide enough for his fangs to hang out. At times like this, I still wondered how he'd become the leader of the vampire nation, and I helped him do it. He pulled out a wad of hundred dollar bills. "This enough?"

I flipped through them and nodded. "Yes, thanks."

"That kiss is coming, Rylee. I feel it in my bones," he called after me as I ran toward Ophelia resting in the cornfield.

"My friend, we've got to fly a little more, can you do it?"

Even as I asked, her fatigue washed through me.

Not if you want me to fly tonight with you in the battle. I need to rest, Rylee.

Something butted me from behind. I turned to see Calliope, the young leader of the Tamoskin Unicorn Crush. She was the most unusual of colors, all white except for a black mane and tail, and black stockings up her legs; a stunning coat with a personality to match. And now a horn that was no longer a nub, but a deadly weapon two feet long.

Even though she was barely out of being a foal, she led their herd.

Her thoughts drifted over mine, not unlike the way Ophelia spoke, only much softer. *One of us could take you. We are faster than those human vehicles, even though we could not match the dragon for speed.*

Looking past her, I was shocked to only see a dozen unicorns. All that were left after the pox swept through. Another piece of my heart chipped away. The unicorns were one of the few pristine spots in our world, and I loved every moment I had with them. So many were gone, and I felt their loss as keenly as if I knew them each personally.

"Thank you." I swept a hand down her neck, the soft fur still very much that of a baby.

Tiomon, please take her. You are the swiftest of us all.

A petite bay mare trotted forward. Her black stockings rode up over her knees and her black mane and tail hung low. The golden horn jutted out of a tiny white mark on her forehead. *It would honor me.* She bent a knee, and dropped her head. An invitation to mount. I leapt onto her back and checked my weapons. Why did I think I was going to need them?

Call it a hunch.

Or maybe call it my life.

"Tiomon, are you ready?"

Her laughter sparkled through my mind. *Tracker, I am always ready. The question is, are you?*

"Oh, probably not, but I'm kinda used to that."

Again, she laughed, and I tangled my hands into her long black mane, weaving the silky strands through my fingers. Her energy flowed along my skin, and with it, the smell of hot sand and exotic wildflowers. A flash of an oasis in the desert rolled through me. Home. That was her home, so far from here, across the world, and yet she'd come.

Hang on, Tracker. We are going to fly on the back of the wind.

Tiomon leapt forward and I thought maybe she was shitting me about the wind thing.

Her hooves made no sound as she skimmed the earth. I dared a look down only to see a blur of legs and ground. "Tiomon, I need to go into the heart of the city. You sure that's going to work?"

She flicked her head once, her horn catching the light and reflecting it around us.

Watch me, Tracker, watch me.

33
RYLEE

Tiomon skidded to a stop where I directed, her hooves sparking along the pavement. What would have taken three hours to drive, she'd done in about an hour. I slid off her back, my legs trembling from gripping her sides so tightly. Sweat slicked her body, but she pranced on the spot, flipping her head up and down several times.

You are a good rider, Rylee. I think I would like to run with you again after the battle is over. She blew a big gust of air through her nostrils as if clearing her lungs. I patted her on the hip.

"Thanks. Let's make that a plan, Tiomon."

She flicked her head up and down again, her mane floating through the air as her horn caught the light. All around us, humans walked, shopped, and drove. And they didn't even look our way.

There was a freaking unicorn standing in front of them and they didn't even see her. A little girl stepped out of the shop I'd come to and looked right at Tiomon. Her blue eyes welled up and she whispered a single word, "Unicorn."

I crouched to her and nodded. "She is that, indeed. Don't ever forget it, kid. You're one of the lucky few."

The little girl reached up and Tiomon dropped her head to nuzzle her hand. I left them. I had things to do.

The shop in front of me was one I'd visited more than once.

Hannigan's Shenanigans. A toy store extraordinaire. Swallowing hard past the memories the store brought up, I pushed the door open and stepped inside. I swept through the front part of the building, ignoring the looks I got. While Tiomon was invisible to the human world, I, with my bristling weapons, most certainly was not.

The clerk was one I'd dealt with before. Melanie, if I remembered right.

"Melanie, I'll be in and out in a flash." I held both my hands up over my head as I strode to the back of the store. The stuffed animal section. I scanned the wall, wondering which two to pick.

While it seemed a silly thing, I knew there was a reason for everything that fucking well happened. Even this.

I reached up and brushed my hand against a fluffy brown bear that was at least three feet tall. The fur tickled my hand and I grabbed it. That was one. But the other? A large stuffed eagle hung to the left of me. Its eyes were glass, and seemed to be looking at me. I didn't hesitate, but grabbed it and yanked it down. Both had long strings still attached to them. At least I would be able to tie them on for the ride back.

"No, you can't have that one, its display only," Melanie said, as she tried to take the eagle from me. I clamped down on it and looked her straight in the eye.

"Melanie, do not fuck with me. I'm taking these two stuffed animals, and I can either pay for them or walk out without paying. Which do you want?"

Her eyes widened and she swallowed hard. "I could call the police."

"Over a stuffed animal?" I reached into my pocket and pulled out the bills Doran had given me. "This should cover it, yes?"

"You're the one trying to stop Orion from helping us. I saw you on the TV," she spluttered.

Definitely time to leave. I strode from the room while Melanie yelled behind me.

"We have to stop her; she'd going to hurt Orion!"

What I found, though, when I stepped out of the shop was not at all what I'd expected.

The humans could see Tiomon as clearly as I could apparently. She looked at me.

How is this possible?

Tying the two stuffed animals to my back, I shook my head. "I don't know, but we have to get the fuck out of here—" Perhaps Orion had inadvertently opened humans' eyes.

As soon as the thought rolled through me, I knew it was true. Those who had the pox had been touched by the supernatural. And now they could see it.

Several sets of hands grabbed me and yanked me away from Tiomon. "Stay away from her, you filthy demon!"

I was thrown backward, the stuffed animals cushioning my fall. A ring of humans circled me, and for the first time, I was afraid of them. Sure, they had no supernatural powers, they couldn't heal fast, and they would fall back from my sword like children.

But there were so many of them that even I knew they would eventually overwhelm me. A boot slammed onto the ground beside my head, barely missing me. I rolled and pulled a sword at the same time. The blade caught the string attaching the stuffed eagle to me. Fuck it, I only needed the one.

I whirled my sword around my head and the mob backed up a few steps, though the growing murmur sent chills down my spine. Searching the faces around me, I tried to find one with a semblance of reason. "I am not your enemy," I said, holding my sword at eye level as I slowly walked toward Tiomon.

"Get her!"

Fucking hell. I jumped forward, and the three women in front of me scattered like chickens, squawking that I'd attacked them. Tiomon leapt toward me and I pulled myself onto her back. Or at least, I tried to.

Hands yanked at me, pulling my hair, legs and arms in all directions. "Let me the fuck go!"

"Hang onto her, Orion said he would deal with her himself."

Rylee, we must get you out of here. No matter the cost. Tiomon's voice was full of sorrow as she spun and reared up on her hind legs. The golden horn on her head glittered in the light, and she let out a battle cry that made the hair on the back of my neck rise.

Plunging downward, she drove her horn through two of the humans who held me at the same time, skewering them clean through. Lightning fast, her hooves shot out, breaking bones and sending bodies flying until I was free of the hands that held me.

Scrambling upward, I was on her back in a flash. She spun half a circle and stopped.

The little girl who'd first noticed her lay on the ground, trampled by the mob. Her mother held her, rocking and crying. But all that had gone unseen in the push to take me down for Orion.

Ah! My heart is breaking, Rylee. This is why we don't let the humans see us. Tiomon shook her head and trotted forward, slowly lowering her muzzle until it brushed against the girl's hair. She blew out a quick breath and the girl stirred, taking a deep breath. "Momma? I dreamed a saw a unicorn and she was so beautiful I cried."

Tiomon backed away, reared up, and we were off and running. Behind us the crowd screamed, but as Tiomon said, there would be no catching her. She was far too fast.

I held tightly to her; we'd gotten what we came for. I only hoped it would be the payment he wanted. Burying my face into Tiomon's neck, I let the rhythm of her body roll through me. There was no sound to her steps, but there was still a motion that felt like it fit in with the beat of my heart.

Slayer, it is because there are only a few creatures who could ride with you into battle against the demons. Dragons are one. Unicorns are the other.

"What are you saying?"

I will remain after the battle. I believe I am meant to stay with you. But for another rider. One that is very young yet.

Her words hit me like a bolt out of the blue. "You mean Marcella, don't you?"

Yes. She will be a Slayer too; it is in her blood. And I already feel drawn to her through you. So I will stay and watch over her from a distance. When she is ready, I will let her ride me.

"You're going to make her work for your bond, aren't you?"

We are not like dragons. We do not crave a rider, and yet when the time comes, we will not deny it.

"Does that mean you can tell she will survive?" That had been the reason for the second stuffed animal. A Reading for Marcella.

She went silent as we skimmed along, the minutes ticking by. *I cannot see the future, Rylee. But I know I must stay here with you. Perhaps it isn't for her . . . there is another child, one that will need a companion as well. A companion who would understand him completely.*

Now she spoke of Zane. I tightened my grip on her mane and forced myself not to ask any more questions.

Sliding to a stop in front of the barn, a billow of dust rose around us, obscuring my vision for a moment. I all but fell off Tiomon's back, my muscles aching and legs wobbly while I got them under me again. "Thank you."

It was my honor, Rylee. As it will be to go into battle with you against the horde.

She turned and trotted away, to where the rest of the herd waited, as though she hadn't run several hundred miles in a matter of hours.

I strode to the barn, untying the stuffed bear from my back. Stepping from the bright light to the dim interior of the barn, I took a moment to let my eyes adjust. Doran sat on one side of Jonathan and Deanna on the other. Will was nowhere to be seen, and from the dark part of the barn I caught a glimmer of two blonde heads: Berget and Liam.

Holding the bear out in front of me, I headed straight to Jonathan. "Will this do as payment for Reading me?"

Jonathan tipped his head to the side and Deanna choked out a laugh. "Rylee, you went all the way to town and got a stuffed animal?"

I didn't look at her, but kept my eyes on the kid. He reached for the bear and I let him have it. Curling his arms around the stuffed animal, he buried his face in the fur and drew in a slow breath. "It smells like the wind."

"Well, the wind certainly whipped through the fur." I squatted in front of him. "Will the payment suffice?"

He grinned at me. "Only if you tell me how you knew what I wanted."

Doran grunted. "Yeah, I'd like to know that too."

A half-grin tugged at my lips. "My mentor, Giselle, was a Reader. Whenever I asked her to read my palms, I brought her a gift. She loved the stuffed animals when I first moved in with her. It seemed natural to bring them to her as a thank you, since she wouldn't accept money or any other gifts."

Doran laughed and shook his head. "Damn."

Jonathan leaned toward me. "I can't truly read you with your Immunity intact, you know that, don't you?"

This was where things got tricky. "Yes, I know."

His strange eyes darted around the room. "They will have to protect you, the demons will come when they sense your Immunity slip away."

Cold chills rippled through me. "But you will show me what I need to see?"

He grabbed a book covered in scales I hadn't noticed and a thick piece of charcoal, scribbling with a mad fervor that shook his whole body. "Two paths, with no right choice, only the choice you must make."

"Oh, well, that's fucking simple." I snorted.

He bobbed his head, still scribbling away. "That's what I always say."

Doran stood. "I'm getting the other shamans. They can help set up a circle of protection."

I sat and crossed my legs under me. "Jonathan, how long will it take?"

"Don't know, never do." His eyes were moving in completely different directions as he drew strange symbols in the book. I leaned forward.

"Not yet, Rylee. When the time is here, you will put your hand on the book and I will work around it."

"Then what are you doing right now?"

"Reading those around me. The threads are wild with danger and death," he whispered. The only sound was that of the charcoal scratching on the thick paper in front of him. I looked at Deanna and she stared back at me.

"I don't want Will to die," she said, her voice pitched low. "He can bring our people back from the brink at home. He has the charisma to do it."

"I can't promise anyone their life in this, Deanna, you know that. Hell, I can't even promise my own life."

She closed her eyes. "I have seen his death, Rylee. I will do what I can to stop it, and if you can . . . please, if you can and I am already taken down, will you try?"

Fucking promises and all tied to me. For the first time, I knew I couldn't even pretend.

"No. I won't. I have one job here, Deanna. You *know* that. How can you even ask me to set his life above mine right now?" Gods above, I sounded like a bitch, and I was from time to time, but right then I knew I was right.

Jonathan leaned toward me. "She isn't feeling herself, I think."

"What the fuck do you mean?" I stared at him, when I should have been looking at her.

Deanna launched herself at me, a copper blade in her hands and her eyes a distinct shade of red. The blade slammed into my stomach hard and she jerked it out for a second strike as I rolled her under me.

"Fuck you, Orion," I screamed as I wrapped one hand around her throat and the other around her hand with the knife. I didn't even have to say the word "go," the demon was thrown out of her with a mere thought from me. For a second, Deanna was back in her body.

"I'm sorry, Rylee. So sorry. Tell my brother . . . ." her body went limp and her eyes flickered closed.

"I will," I pushed her off and tried to sit up. The pain through my stomach slammed into me as I clenched my muscles.

"Rylee, get over here, let me take a look at you," Liam called to me from the darkness. Berget added her pleas to his.

"Rylee, it's bad. I can smell the blood."

"How long until sundown?" I didn't look at them.

"A few hours," Berget said. "You can't mean to go into the battle wounded? Oh my god, that's exactly what you're planning to do. Why would you do that?" She was crying, and the sound gutted me as surely as Deanna's knife had.

I twisted to glare at them both and had to bite back the groan that rose to my lips. "And who would heal me? There is no one here. And nothing either of you could do."

Berget held her hands out. "That's not true, the shamans—"

The door banged open and Doran strode in followed by Louisa and Crystal. They were the last two female shamans, the rest had all been killed by their own Guardians as they'd been possessed by demons.

"The shamans have to hold down the protective circle, and if they heal Rylee then they will not have the strength. It is up to you, Tracker." Doran was being particularly formal and I knew why.

This was it. The final battle was hours away and the tension rose around us like an electrical storm on the horizon.

"Do the circle, I will wait for Pamela." I bit the words out and scooted closer to Jonathan. Doran held the door open and in trotted the remaining unicorns, Mer the ogre, Charlie and a few brownies, and a couple other supernaturals I hadn't met, but I was guessing were members of Will's Destruction. Will, of course, was already in the barn. But what shocked the shit out of me was that India was there, walking alongside Calliope.

"No, India, you're too damn young!" She wasn't even ten years old. She *could not be* in this battle against the demons.

Her hazel eyes met mine. "This is my world too, Rylee." Her hand clutched Calliope's thin mane and I realized another bond had been formed. For better or worse, we were going into battle with children.

That was it . . . that was my entire army to battle Orion and the demons. A weird sense of relief flowed over me. There was no way I was going to make it out of this alive and the finality of that understanding brought with it a strange sense of peace.

Liam let out a snort and began to pace. "Rylee, don't. You aren't going to die and you sure as hell don't need to speed the process up."

I turned my back on him, though it hurt both my body and heart to do it. "I know what I'm doing and this is the last time I'm asking you to trust me."

Jonathan reached for my hand and I gave it to him, dripping in blood from gripping my stomach. "Pull back your Immunity, Rylee of the Blood, and I will show you the two paths that will be your choice."

I did as he asked, peeling my Immunity away from my hand first, then up my arm and over my shoulders and head. Like pulling off a long sleeved shirt, I mentally tugged at it until my entire upper body was without protection. Through gritted teeth I spoke. "Is that far enough?"

"Farther would be better."

Fucking hell. Sweating, my head aching and my guts on fire from the knife I pushed my Immunity farther down until it pooled at my feet. With a soft pop it slid off me and I gasped. "What the fuck happened?"

Jonathan looked straight at me. "You can't have your Immunity going into this battle, Rylee of the

Blood. You must give up all your weapons to face Orion. Even those that are an innate part of you."

Holy fucking hell. I couldn't stop the shivering that took over my body; part fear, and part shock. Doran let out a low growl and from the shadows Liam echoed the sound. I knew without a doubt that if the sun hadn't been high, Liam would have tackled Jonathan to the floor and strangled him.

Jonathan reached out and took my right hand, covered in my own blood and pressed it into the book on a blank page.

He began to write around my fingers, and outside the barn, a single howl erupted through the air.

Doran looked at me, his green eyes determined before he turned away. "They're here. Do what you must, Rylee. We will protect you."

I took a breath to answer him, and the world was sucked away and I stood at the juncture of two paths, Jonathan beside me.

"We will walk them, and you will decide which one you want to follow."

Right, like it was going to be that fucking easy.

Somehow, I doubted it.

34
PAMELA

Lark took us deep into the heart of the mountain, where the air was so hot it felt as though it burned the back of my throat. Keeping up to her long-legged stride was hard, and I was constantly jogging to keep up. Peta ran ahead of us, seeming to lead the way.

"Why is Peta in front?" I asked.

"Because she lived here a long time. It's a labyrinth down here, Pamela. Don't forget that if you ever come on your own." Lark glanced at me, then back at Griffin. I followed her gaze. He strolled as though on an outing at a park. His hands touched the sides of the tunnel we hurried through, lingering here and there on a gem or jewel that was embedded.

Cactus was on the other side of Lark, but he was quiet and his eyes seemed troubled. Why did I think that didn't bode well?

Torchlight lit our path, but still the place felt dark and dank to me. Even with the heat. I swiped my hand across my forehead, but the sweat had already dried. Like a sauna that was so hot, I couldn't even get relief from my own sweat.

We burst out of the tunnel and a large ornate door stood closed in front of us. Made of solid gold, there was a glittering bejeweled dragon etched across the doors. With gems for eyes, the dragon looked life-like enough that I wondered if it was a supernatural I hadn't heard of before, but it was like no dragon I'd ever met.

"Firewyrm," Griffin said softly in my ear, answering my question before I asked.

Lark firmed her back and placed her hands on the doors. "Stick close, the queen can be . . . prickly."

Cactus let out a quiet snort. "That's an understatement."

Lark glared at him, then turned and shoved the doors open. We went through, side by side. A woman sat lounging on an ornate dais raised a few feet above the ground at the far end of the room. Her hair was blood red and her eyes were as blue as mine. A thin circlet of gold wove through her hair and held the long strands back from her face. She was a beauty, of that much I was sure. But I somehow doubted that would make her any easier to deal with.

The queen was not dressed in a gown as I would have thought. No, she was dressed in black leather from her head to her toes, like Magma, the fire elemental I'd faced when we were freeing Lark from the oubliette. The black leather matched the large jungle cat at her side.

A slow smile slid over her face. "Larkspur. It has been a long time, my friend."

Perhaps this wouldn't be so bad after all.

Lark bowed from the waist and I mimicked her. "Queen Fiametta, I will not take much of your time."

"Nonsense, we must eat and recall the stories when you were here last—"

"We cannot. The demons come for this world, and I am here to ask you to stand with us against them." Lark spoke swiftly, and the fervor in her voice made me want to leap up and tell her that I stood with her again. Griffin put a hand on my shoulder and whispered in my ear.

"Not yet, little witch."

Fiametta let out a sigh. "Larkspur, there are always going to be threats to this world. Elementals ride the waves of fate like boats bobbing on the ocean."

My whole frame shook and I couldn't help myself. I shook Griffin off. "If the world falls, you will be next. Orion won't stop with wiping out the supernaturals."

The queen's eyes slid to mine and I held her gaze. "What have you brought me, Larkspur?"

"A child whose blood is evidence that all families have blended."

Fiametta stood and walked down the dais, stopping in front of me. Her hand cupped my face, turning it upward. "I see the fire in her. She is the one who killed Magma, isn't she?"

My whole body clenched with a sudden spurt of fear. What would they do to me? I'd almost forgotten the battle for Lark's freedom and the elementals I'd faced.

"Yes, I am," I whispered. "And I would do it again if it meant freeing Lark."

The world seemed to narrow around us and behind me Cactus groaned softly. Fiametta's eyes never left mine.

"How is it that you inspire such loyalty, Larkspur?"

I straightened my back. "Because she fights for what she believes in; like any true leader should."

Fiametta's smile was slow, like a cat seeing something it wanted to pounce on. I crossed my arms over my chest and held her gaze.

The queen spoke to Lark, but her eyes never left mine. "I offered you my help, Larkspur. Not the world. Not the Tracker. And not even for this girl here would I step outside of the Pit." Fiametta waved a hand at me, fire blooming over her fingertips.

Lark took a step toward the queen. "We saved you, Fiametta."

The queen's gaze sharpened along with her tongue. "And I would not throw that gift away for a battle that is not ours. You know that, Larkspur. You know this is not our battle."

A change slipped over Lark, one so subtle I wasn't sure at first what I was seeing. She turned and addressed the crowd that had gathered so quietly I hadn't noticed them.

"The Terralings, my people, go to fight at the side of the supernaturals for the safety of this world. As elementals, do we not owe it to the world we sustain to protect it? Do you think the demons will stop with taking the humans down? How long before they turn their greedy eyes to us? How long before they decide to rape our women, and destroy our sanctuaries? To steal our magic and subvert the elements themselves to their whims?"

A low murmur rumbled through the crowd. A tall man stepped forward, his body encased in the same black leather as the queen's. His hair was cut short, pale blond with hints of red slipping through it.

"Lark, I will stand with you against this threat. You saved our boy, and our family. I owe you my life."

He dropped to one knee and Lark went to him, touching him on the shoulder. "Do not kneel to me, Brand. I am not your queen, nor do I want to be."

Griffin leaned down beside me. "Show them what you can do with their element, little witch. Convince them you are one of their own."

A few others stepped forward and spoke for Lark as I considered what I could possibly do to convince these elementals I was truly of their blood. I stepped forward, and at the same time, called the fire to my skin. It danced over me as I'd seen it dance over Fiametta until it lit me like a torch.

The weight of the queen's eyes were the heaviest, but all of them were watching me. "I am of your blood, your queen has pronounced it. Yet I am the weakest of you, am I not?"

There was a low murmur of assent. The magic trembled over me. "And I will go into battle, and you will hide here and wait for the weakest of your own kind to keep you safe. You *are* cowards."

I let the magic go and slumped to my knees. Griffin caught me before I could hit the ground. "Well done, yeah? How did you know that pride is their downfall?"

My body shook from the exertion it took to control that much fire. "I didn't. I only said what I knew would push me to do something."

He chuckled softly. "It's not a guarantee, but I think you've given it the best you can, yeah?"

I smiled up at him, the edges of my mouth trembling with fatigue. "Yeah."

35
LARK

We left the Pit, with only a few assurances of help. Brand and his family would be at the battle. At least that was something, I had to believe it.

That was it. Even the firewyrms were reluctant to commit, despite my cajoling. The fact was they'd barely stuck their noses out of the tunnel that would have taken us to their nests. Ungrateful bastards.

Frustration and fear nipped at me. I could *feel* the seconds ticking by, drawing us closer to the time I was to stand with Rylee and help her with the ceremony.

Unable to face another failure, I took us to the Deep. Queen Finley welcomed me with open arms. Her blue hair fell to her waist in long curling waves that brushed against her soft curves. She'd matured into a beautiful woman, with a confidence and grace that I knew she'd earned.

"Lark, I know what is coming," she breathed into my ear as she hugged me. "My Seers have told me we must fight for our lives or risk living under the boots of the demons. We will be there. Even now, I have sent my best to gather at the place you have spoken of."

I pulled back from her. "You always were wiser than your years, Finley."

She waved a hand at me, bracelets tinkling against her ivory skin. "I have sent an emissary to the Eyrie."

"What's that?" Pamela asked.

"Not a what. A where. The Sylphs reside in the Eyrie. And they don't like me much," I said softly. My last visit there had been catastrophic to say the least.

Finley nodded. "I remember. Which is why I sent a note to the queen, asking her to help on my behalf. She did promise to fight at my side if the time ever came."

I swallowed hard. "Then we have done all we can. We must hurry."

Pamela looked around us with more than a little awe. "I would like to come back here one day."

Finley looked at her and then did a double take. "She carries our element."

"She carries all five."

The young queen gasped and took a step back. "Is she Requiem's child?"

"No, no. She is a blend of the five elemental bloodlines. Though she is the strongest witch ever born to this world; not an elemental in truth." Finley slowly relaxed and I understood all too well her fear.

Requiem was a monster from her past. I didn't blame her for fearing his shade still. "Finley, I can take us all there in a matter of seconds."

She looked at me, and my hand on the weapon at my side. "Been making things you aren't supposed to again?"

Hell, had everyone heard of my indiscretions? Likely, since that was something my father was wont to do; announce how very far his half-breed daughter had fallen.

"Something like that."

Pulling the katana from its sheath at my hip, I slashed it through the air to the left of me, whispering the words, "*Velata facie terroris.* Take us to Rylee."

The cut in the air shimmered and split open wide, but there was nothing on the other side. No world, no farm.

I let out a sharp breath. "Pamela."

"What does this mean?"

"It means she isn't on this plane of existence. Right now, she is somewhere within the seven Veils."

Pamela grabbed my hand. "But what does it mean?"

"That right now we can't use her as a pinpoint."

'Then use Alex. He's on his way there with Eve and Marco," she said.

"They are flying, Pamela. We can't jump through to them." But Belladonna should already be waiting for us at the designated waypoint. With a flick of my wrist, I brought the blade through the air again. "*Velata facie terroris.* Take us to Belladonna."

This time, the cut opened up in the middle of a cornfield, the long waving stalks lolling back and forth in the breeze. Finley and the other Undines went through first. The young queen went right to my sister and embraced her as though they were long lost friends, even though I knew they hadn't seen each other in many years.

I did a head count of the Undine's who came through. A little over three hundred. Added to the two hundred of my family that gave us a tiny army.

But I knew without a shadow of a doubt that if Fiametta and the queen of the Sylphs didn't agree to fight at our sides, we were done for.

My heart clenched. To have come so far and to fail yet again . . . it was as though I heard the laughter of all those who'd told me I was not strong enough; that I was a useless half-breed with nothing to her name but a vague connection to royalty.

"Lark?" Bella called to me and I opened my mouth to answer her only I was unable to speak. The sight behind my sister stilled my tongue.

The sun was at the edge of the horizon, but that was not the image that froze my blood.

No, it was the black wave of demons pouring out toward us. Slashes in the Veil opened at a speed I couldn't count, both on the ground and in the air. Thousands of openings, and out of each, thousands of demons leapt into our world.

A fierce anger ripped up through me, my connection to the earth opening fully. I was the Destroyer.

Time to do what I was created for.

"We have to keep them busy, long enough that Rylee has the time she needs. Fight with all you have!" I shouted to those assembled.

The Terralings and Undines spread out in a line. Five hundred against millions of demons.

Pamela put herself right beside me, her face tight with anger. "I'm not letting them get through."

Ahh, to be so young. To believe one could conquer a horde with a faith so fierce that it shone. To think I'd been that young once was hard to recall.

I sent a wave of power through the earth. The ground heaved and rolled at the height of a redwood. It slammed into the first line of demons, sending them flying backwards, breaking them in half, tearing limbs from their bodies. A cheer went up around me and the other elementals joined in.

Cactus worked with Brand and his family, lighting fire to the corn and Pamela pushed the flames with her connection to the air. She caught it up into a tornado of fire and sent it spinning toward the demons. The smell of burning tar ignited the air as she cut a swath through them.

I ran forward, pulling my spear free. Whirling it around my head, I cut through the demon closest to me. His eyes widened and his mouth opened in shock, as his body began to dissolve. "You are not the Slayer; you can't kill me."

"Watch me," I spit out as I whipped my spear around, clearing a circle around me the full length of the shaft. Everywhere the blade touched the demons evaporated.

Rylee was the Blood of the Lost, a Slayer in truth. But the makeup of her blood and mine was the same.

And while I did not have the blood needed to close the Veil and defeat Orion on my own, I did have the blood needed to destroy demons.

I closed ranks with a big boy, a creature that towered over me. His body was serpentine, lithe, and lightning fast. He snaked his head toward me, his mouth open and fangs dripping with venom. I got my spear up in time to deflect the bite, but the momentum drove me to my knees. I found myself looking right into the demon's mouth as he tried to clamp down on me.

Both hands on my spear, I held it against him. I softened the earth under his feet, and sank him to his neck in a split second. Yanking my spear from his teeth, I spun it around and drove it deep into his mouth. The demon dissolved and I was grabbed from behind. The force of the grip crushed me to the point where my ribs creaked from the pressure. A blast of water slammed into us both, sending us flying.

"Sorry, couldn't direct it better," came a voice that I thought might have been Finley. In a puddle of mud, I spun on my knees, and dispatched the lobster clawed demon that had me in its pincers.

Around me, earth exploded, fire spun through the ranks, and deep lakes sprung up. The water swallowed the demons whole, dragging them down, but the lakes were quickly filled with writhing pissed off demons.

"Lark! I need more space for the water!" Finley cried out.

"Bella!" I ran for where I'd seen her last. "We need to work with the Undines!"

I whipped around two demons, taking their heads in violent slash. Where the hell was Bella?

River—my niece—was there, fighting for all she was worth as she spun her two elements together. Earth and water. I reached her side and dropped to one knee. To do what I was going to attempt, I needed to have my hands in the ground.

"Watch my back."

"Always," came Bella's voice behind me.

Driving my hands into the earth I opened myself to the power that resided in me, delving deep into it as I hadn't for years. Fear chased the power and I pushed it away. If I burned out, then so be it.

Around me the battle raged, and the demons were not being held back in any sense of the word. We were surrounded.

"Mother goddess, help me," I whispered.

The voice that spoke softly to me was not the mother goddess I knew. *Destroyer. Do what you must to cleanse my land.*

Power like nothing I'd ever felt slammed into me, a virtual avalanche of strength I couldn't possibly contain. I let it go, pushing it deep into the earth and opening a crack. Tectonic plates shifted and the world around us groaned as I did the impossible. I knew it was impossible. I knew I shouldn't be able to do what I was doing, and yet I still moved the ground with a strength that seemed unending.

With a groaning scream, the earth opened in front of me, the crack running deep enough that there would be no bottom. The elementals around me didn't pause, didn't hesitate. They pushed the demons toward the crack, driving them with all their strength, sweeping them away like the filth they were. Waves of water and earth crashed into the demons until only a few were left, stragglers that ran from us.

Breathing hard, I realized I still held the power that had been offered to me and was still using it to sweep the demons away. The edge of the massive crack through the earth crumbled and a pair of clawed hands reached up the edge.

"No, that isn't happening," I hissed. I drove my hands back into the ground and pulled with all I had. Closing a fissure of that size; I wasn't sure even I could do it.

"Bella, help me!"

She dropped to her knees beside me, and so did River. The Terralings who'd come to fight at my side put their strength beside mine and with a creeping pace, we closed the wound in the earth, sealing the demons deep within, crushing their bodies.

A cheer went up around me. I looked and saw that there were only a few casualties, mostly bad wounds. How the hell had we stood against so many?

Bella reached up and touched my face, "Little sister, you are the reason. You united us and we worked together."

"Lark," Pamela's voice cracked on my name, fear chasing it. I spun on my knees to see her facing the direction of Rylee's farm. "The sun hasn't gone down, so why is the sky still black?"

I stood, chills racing through me. That was why it had been so easy to take out so many demons. It had nothing to do with me.

"It was a distraction. They were there to keep us busy while the rest attacked Rylee." The words slipped out of me as the horror of what was happening hit me square in the chest.

And now, Rylee was at the center of the true battle without me.

36
ALEX

Running flat out through the streets of Bismarck, I couldn't help but nip at the wolves around me, unable to contain myself. A few nipped back, but there were no serious bites involved. The energy around us was hot with excitement and the thrill of the hunt.

It seemed I wasn't the only one enjoying the breaking of this particular rule as our paws pounded the pavement. I kept my nose twitching, breathing in deeply, but it wasn't me who picked up the scent of the half-breed trolls.

A howl echoed from our left and the monster pack shifted as a unit toward the call. We leapt cars and dodged traffic as if the city was an obstacle course set up just for us. A few people stared and pointed, and then more. And more.

How were they even noticing so many of us? No time to stop and ask questions though. Not that I cared.

Tongue hanging out, I bolted to the front of the pack, wanting to get there first to see the half-breed trolls.

I skidded around the corner and found myself staring at a tattoo parlor that jogged a memory. Blind

Bats Tattoos had been rebuilt and looked as though whoever put it back together made an effort to have it look as rough as it did before.

Swallowing hard, I shifted and stepped forward. From above, Eve dropped me my clothes and I pulled them on quickly.

The auburn-furred wolf—Luca—shifted too, but didn't bother with clothes. He would have given Dox a run for his money in the height department, standing at least six-and-a-half feet.

His eyes, a light gray flicked to me. "Kid, there are a lot of them in there. Not sure there aren't straight trolls too; that would be bad for your health."

I stepped forward, my eyes on the doors of the parlor. "Yeah, I realize that."

"And you'd go in on your own anyway?"

I shrugged. "I don't expect anyone else to risk their life for me. That's not how I roll, man."

He laughed and fell into step beside me. "You're an odd one, Wolf."

"Man, have I heard that a time or two," I muttered, but didn't hold back the smile that tugged at my lips.

We reached the door and I knocked first.

Luca laughed at me. "Kick it down."

"Nah, we want to talk to them, not scare them," I said as the door cracked open and a human woman peered out. I drew in a deep breath. Not human, but her face looked it. "I need to talk to Tara. Please."

Luca shook his head, but I ignored him. The woman's face tightened and a flash of fear slid over her. "You can't. She's being interrogated."

My eyebrows shot up. "By whom?"

A tear trickled down her cheek and that was enough for me. I pushed the door open and ran into the shop. I knew where I was going. The idiot trolls had set things up exactly as they had before. I found the partition in the wall and was running through it, a stream of wolves behind me.

I knew why I was going in, but why the hell were they following me?

A whisper floated to my ear from a familiar voice . . . Giselle?

Because you gave them a cause to fight for. A reason to believe.

The ladder stuck out of the hole in the ground and I grabbed it, sliding down with my feet and hands on the sides. From there, I followed my nose, stripping as I went. As soon as the last piece of clothing was off, I shifted and galloped forward. A large cavern opened. In it was a slew of trolls, all in war gear.

On the floor, wrapped in nets and chains were at least a hundred half-breed trolls.

Snarling, I leapt at the closet troll, hamstringing him and dropping him to the ground before there was even a warning call let out. Around me the other wolves swarmed, teeth and claws driving the trolls back, tearing throats out. I bit and clawed my way to the half-breeds. Those under the nets struggled to get out.

"Here," I grabbed a knife off a troll's body, my long tipped claws wrapping easily around the handle, and then pushed it toward them. Scared, but determined, eyes looked back at me. As they cut themselves out, I launched into the skirmish once more. Swords and blades cut near to me, but I felt invincible, untouchable even.

Behind me came a bloodcurdling cry. I spun to see the half-breeds free and fighting the trolls with their bare hands. The wolves slipped in around them supporting them.

Working together, we drove the trolls out, killing as many as we could. Twenty or so of the wolves kept after the trolls, following them deep into the tunnels. I shifted and walked toward the half-breeds. Tara was amongst them, checking on the others, but I knew she wouldn't recognize me. She'd never seen me as anything but the stuck-between-forms-Alex.

"Tara."

She turned, her pale pink skin flush with excitement, and her eyes widened. "Do I know you?"

"Alex. I was with Liam and Rylee."

Her mouth dropped open. "The submissive wolf?"

I grinned at her and spread my hands wide. "The one and only."

She approached me, moving through her people. They watched her, as did I.

"You saved us. Why? Since when have supernaturals ever stood up for each other?" Her words were bitter and I knew why. The half-breeds had been all but treated as slaves, their children stolen and used in medical experiments, their woman raped by the full-blooded trolls.

"The world needs everyone to stand together, Tara. Rylee and Liam will be facing a horde of demons. We need your help."

She looked back at her people. "What can we do? There aren't many of us."

"You can fight," Luca said behind me. "You can fight and prove yourselves as you did here in the heat of battle. You are not a half-breed mistake, but a supernatural force to be reckoned with."

She shook her head, but I wouldn't give up.

"The demons will have trolls fighting alongside them, the same trolls who've been treating you like shit your whole life. They belong to Orion, the demon who is trying to take over the world. Trying to kill Rylee and Liam. Would you let them win?"

"Liam?" Tara slowly straightened and then nodded, her eyes hardening with determination. "I will come with you. I owe him my life."

Behind her, the other half-breeds nodded one by one. They would come; holy shit, we'd done it! I lifted up a hand and Tara matched my movement, high-fiving me. "Come on, then, we have demons to kill."

A grin lit her face. "We will show them not to mess with our world."

That's what I was hoping for.

But I had one last stop to make before I could go to Rylee. One last couple who I knew would fight for her.

I hoped there was enough time left.

Giving instructions to Luca on how to get to the farmhouse, I left him to organize things.

He grabbed my arm. "Where are you going?"

"One more set of reinforcements. We need every soul we can get at this point." Even two more people might be the tipping point in our favor.

Bursting out of the tattoo parlor, as I pulled my clothes back on, yet again, I flagged Eve down. She dropped to the pavement, her eyes wide as she took me in. "What happened?"

I looked down at myself, noticing the gore and viscera covering me for the first time. "We routed the trolls and the half-breeds are going to fight with us."

"That is the best news."

"But I have to stop at one more place, Eve. They will fight for Rylee, I'm sure of it." I climbed up onto her back and strapped myself into her harness. She launched into the sky.

"Where?"

"You know that motel on the outskirts of Bismarck?"

She bobbed her head. "You think that they will really fight for her?"

"Yes."

We fell silent as we skimmed the skies, Marco right behind us.

Something about the time with Eve felt strange and I couldn't put my finger on it.

The sensation registered as we circled downward toward the motel. It felt like this was the last ride we'd ever have together. My heart clenched and I forced the words out.

"Eve, I want you to know you're one of my best friends. And it has been the time of my life flying with you." I touched her back gently as she hopped on the pavement.

"Don't get morose on me, Alex." She sniffed. "We have lost enough people. Neither of us is going anywhere. Rylee needs us too much."

I hoped she was right. I ran to the motel office and burst through the door. John sat with his feet up on the desk, his beat up cowboy hat pulled down low.

"John, Rylee's in trouble, and she could use all the help she can get." It hadn't occurred to me until that moment that they would be of no real use being human.

He pushed his hat up with one finger and raised an eyebrow at me. "What you doing here, Wolf?"

"Rylee's in trouble and . . . wait, how did you know I was a wolf?" I stared at him as my mouth slowly dropped open. "You knew all along?"

He shrugged and a slow grin slid over his face. "Wolf, I can't come with you. Ry needs Mary and me here. You've got to trust me that we will do more good here than in the middle of that mess of demons."

I backed up. "Okay."

"I'll see you in a bit," he said, waving at me as he lowered his hat back down.

Running out of the office, I leapt up onto Eve's back. "So much for that."

"They won't come?" The despair in her voice clawed at me.

"He said they were needed here. Then he said he'd see me in a bit." The whole conversation, as short as it was, was strange.

"Then we need to go," she said as she launched once more into the sky, heading straight for the farm.

"Yes," I said softly breathing in the fresh air, filling my lungs with it, "I think you're right. It's time to go."

37
RYLEE

Jonathan pointed. "Which path do you want to see first?"

"Does it matter?"

He shrugged. "I don't know."

Left or right . . . did it matter? I looked at the path under my feet. The one to the left was made of perfectly in-line stones stretching out in front of us. Around each stone the grass was manicured and beautifully bright green. The other was overgrown with tangles of bushes and grass shooting up between the bricks. Most of the bricks were broken, some were completely missing, leaving gaps in the path.

"Let me guess, two states of mind?"

"If that is what you see, then that is what it is. I am just the facilitator here. This is your mind, this is your journey," he said, a smirk on his face.

The path to the right represented my inability to plan. No matter how hard I tried, I would find myself going by the seat of my pants. I took a step to the left and I was back in the barn.

Doran leaned over me. "Rylee, what did you learn?"

"We're going to do a play-by-play, understand?" I pushed to my feet, clutching at my stomach and the wound there.

He nodded. "You're the one in charge here, Rylee. And you know I like it like that." He winked at me and I laughed softly.

"Doran, will you never give up?"

"Nah, too much fun." He slipped an arm around my back and helped me stand. "What do we need to do?"

I directed those left in my care to their positions. "When the sun drops behind the horizon, we're going to do exactly as I planned. Everyone understand?"

They nodded, murmuring their assent.

The plan was to have the shamans holding the protective circle to let it drop and Ophelia would tear the barn right off us so we had a clear view of what we faced.

The vampires would rush me to the ceremonial slab, the shamans would set up another protective circle around us there, and I would end the game with Orion, complete the ceremony and save the world.

Easy as peach pie in the South.

I watched Berget and Faris for the first signal: the sun had gone down. Berget's blue eyes were on mine and I saw the flicker there a split second before she nodded.

"Now!"

Ophelia ripped the barn off. Or at least, half of it. The other half fell on top of Jonathan, crushing the kid. Doran scooped me into his arms and ran across the short distance to the burned out shell of my house. The ceremonial slab beckoned me.

I closed my eyes and trusted in the plan. For the first time, I had truly planned this out and it had to work. I looked over Doran's shoulder. "Where the fuck are the shamans?"

The barn wall collapsed on them, Rylee. I couldn't stop it. Ophelia's words turned into a scream of pain and I squirmed in Doran's arms. The rapid staccato of her heart pounded through my body. Slash after slash of red-hot fiery death lanced through me from her.

Like Blaz, I felt her slipping away, the pulse of her blood slowing as she fought.

Rylee, I can't hold them off. Ahh, my babies. My babies are the last.

"Put me down, they're killing her!"

One last shot, and Ophelia slipped from me, the bond shattering, and with it my will to fight. Not again. I was losing her like I was losing everyone around me.

"You can't save any of us if you don't do this!" Doran grabbed my arms, shaking me hard. But his back was turned to the demons and it was the last mistake he would ever make.

A sword sliced through his neck, taking his head off in a single clean swipe. His beautiful green eyes widened and a single tear fell from each as he air-kissed at me one last time.

I fell backward as his hands slipped from me. "Doran, no!" The words escaped me, even though I knew they were of no use. I fell through the air, backward, landing hard on the ceremonial slab, screaming his name. I loved him, he was my friend, and like Faris, he'd stolen a part of my heart somewhere along the way.

My head smashed into the hardened stone with a crack that I felt all the way through my skull. Warmth pooled under my neck and I lay there, looking up at the sky. The screams of my friends and family as they died trying to make sure I was able to do what I had to. But without them at my side, the ceremony would never take place.

I knew that for the truth it was; the purple skinned book of prophecies had made things very clear. I needed someone from each of the seven divisions of the supernatural world to help me with the ceremony or it would never be complete.

Around me, the world exploded in fire and earth, and chunks of ground raining down on my head. I closed my eyes, listening to my own heart slow.

"Rylee!"

Alex's voice cut through the fog of dying, but still I struggled to open my eyes.

"It's too late," I whispered.

"No, don't say that. You can't give up, boss." His arms circled around me and he pulled me up to his chest. "You can't give up, Rylee. That isn't you. Don't do this."

He whispered into my ears something important, something I didn't understand at first. "This isn't the way. Don't do this. Please." His voice cracked on the last word and I managed to open my eyes.

Tears streamed down my face, but they weren't my own. They were his as he stared down at me, clutching me to his chest. "Rylee."

"Alex, I'm sorry."

He pulled me tighter against him and I reached out for my other loved ones. Feeling for their threads as I Tracked them.

Gone.

Liam, Berget, Eve, Charlie, Calliope, Pamela. All gone, their lives cut short. I dared to reach for the babies. Zane was gone and his loss was a thousand times worse than saying goodbye to Milly. His life threads, I scrabbled for them as I howled to the night sky, but no sound came out. Not the babies, I couldn't lose the babies; they were all I had left to fight for.

In a last moment, I reached for Marcella. The only hope I had left.

"Oh, I'll be keeping her alive, Rylee. Don't you worry about that." Orion stepped into view, holding Marcella in his arms. She saw me, cried out, and reached her tiny hands toward me.

I couldn't move, and the tears on my face were now my own. "Ella."

"Momma." Her hands waved as she frantically reached for me.

Ah, the pain in my heart outstripped every pain I'd ever felt in my body as she cried for me, and Orion laughed, holding her away. "Now, I think we're about done here."

He held up a sword, twisting it one way and then the other. A sword I'd held before, years ago. "The elemental who had this on her, she was a true bitch to kill. Almost had me at the end, but you know what broke her?"

I stared hard at him. He grinned down at me, his bald head shinning from the fires that had sprung up around us. "I killed her familiar and her sister in one fell swoop." He made a kissing noise. "Their deaths broke her, and my demons swarmed her and brought me this sword."

Laying there on the slab with Alex still holding me tight, I dared to Track Lark.

She was right behind him. There was a quick twist and her spear point slammed through his heart, opening him up like a can of rotten fruit. His body fell to the ground as he clutched at the spear and Lark caught Marcella.

"Rylee, hang on," she said, dropping to her knees beside me. Marcella crawled onto my chest and lay her head by mine.

"Momma."

I wanted to reach up and touch her one last time, to do as Lark commanded.

But there was no hanging on. My heart stopped, Alex cried out, and the last thing I saw was Marcella's eyes as she touched my face and I slipped over the Veil.

38
RYLEE

I jerked out of the vision, my heart scrambling as if it were actually restarting. Jonathan touched my arm and I spun to face him. "Fucking hell, that was shitty."

"Yeah, I didn't think that path would be any good. It's not your style, despite how people want you to conform." His eyes flickered over me and then to the path on the right; the one that held no uniform steps, no obvious answer. "Do you want to see this?"

I backed away. "No. No, I don't." He was right. Everyone around me always wanted me to plan my way through a salvage, and every time I did, shit fell apart. People died. "I'll do this my way."

Jonathan grinned at me. "Then maybe you have a chance. Your heart hasn't failed you yet, has it?"

I realized here in this place, he wasn't a creepy kid with weird eyes anymore. He was actually quite handsome. He grinned a little wider. "Here, you see my spirit, as I see yours." He pointed behind me and I turned to see my reflection hovering in front of me.

"I don't look any different." The woman in front of me was dressed the same, her tri-colored eyes swirled, and her auburn hair fell over her shoulders.

Scars were visible on my arms and my white shirt was bright against the color of my hair and dark pants.

"That's because you have always been true to yourself, even when others tried to change you. That is your strength, Rylee of the Blood. You are a warrior, and you lead with your heart. Don't change that."

The vision broke apart and I opened my eyes back in the barn. Jonathan was sleeping in the hay beside me, snoring softly.

Doran leaned over me. "Rylee, what did you learn?"

A chill of déjà vu slid over me and I shook it off. Planning wasn't going to work, and maybe I'd already known that. "The only thing I need is one supernatural from each species at my side for the final ceremony." I ticked them off. "Doran, for the fanged. Ophelia, for the winged. Jonathan, for the psychics, Liam, for the furred, Lark, for the blooded, and Louisa, for the magicked." I had to pray Lark would get here in time to play her part.

Doran gave me a look, raising his eyebrows. "And the demons? They need a blade on you too, don't they?"

I swallowed hard and looked at my stomach, the wound still seeping. "Deanna already did it." Understanding hit me. She knew. She'd known a demon needed to cut me, and how else could that happen, safely? I closed my eyes for a moment and silently thanked her.

She'd given her life for mine. "Everyone get to the fucking ceremonial slab. That's the job, got it? Get there and stay alive."

Around me, they nodded. Liam crouched beside me and the world faded except for his eyes, blue rimmed in silvery gold. "Are you sure you don't want to plan this?"

I touched his face, leaned in, and kissed him softly. "Absolutely certain."

My instinct was to get up high on Ophelia and see what the fuck was going on.

I am here. The demons are massing, Rylee. This battle is going to push us all to our limits.

I had no fucking doubt about that. Standing, I looked over my head. I needed to get to the ceiling and then from there onto the roof so Ophelia could pick me up. Liam wrapped his arm around my waist and pulled me onto his back as if I were a child. "I see what you're up to. Let me help."

He climbed the beams that took us into the rafters. A few seconds alone, that was all we were going to get.

"I love you, Liam," I said softly, placing a kiss against the back of his neck. "With all I am."

"I know, Rylee."

"And I love Faris a little, too."

He grunted. "Yeah, I know that, too."

"And maybe even Doran a little."

From below us, Doran whooped. "I knew I'd win you over!"

I tried not to cringe, knowing that Berget also loved Doran. "I said only a little," I shouted down at him.

"I'll take it," he shouted back.

Underneath me, Liam chuckled. "Your heart is big enough to hold us all in it, within different capacities,

Rylee. I understand that. But I also know I am your mate; no matter what happens, we will be together."

I pressed my face against his back and breathed him in. "I don't want to do this without saying what I have to say."

We were under the trap door that led onto the roof. He pulled me around and into his arms. "Then say it, beautiful, and then let's kick demon ass."

I laughed despite the pain in my guts. I pressed my hands to either side of his face, no longer seeing Faris, but only seeing Liam and his soul shining through his eyes.

"No matter what happens, no matter how this plays out, I want you to know I wouldn't have lived this last year any other way."

His eyes searched mine and peace flowed through them. "Neither would I." He cleared his voice and Faris spoke softly. "Neither would I, Rylee."

I reached around his neck and pulled him tightly to me. "Bite me, Faris."

"That's rather rude."

"No, I mean it, bite me. Invoke the bite when, if, I yell for it." An insurance policy. In case things went sideways.

Who was I kidding? They'd be sideways two minutes into the battle, knowing my luck.

Outside the barn came a booming bellow that could be only one person.

Orion.

"Rylee, Tracker, Slayer, Blood of the Lost. Are you coming out to play? Or should I send my demons in to fetch you?"

Faris bit my neck, taking only a few mouthfuls. I let the pleasure wash through me; a reminder that life could be good and was worth fighting for to the very last breath.

He pulled back. "Go get him, Rylee."

One last kiss, a fleeting touch of our lips. I wasn't sure if it was Liam or Faris, and in that moment, it didn't matter. I loved them both. Just differently, like Liam said.

Liam gave me a boost, his hands tight on my ass as he lifted me over his head and out the trap door. The last of the sun caught his fingers, but he didn't jerk back. Only waited for me to scramble onto the roof on my own.

I didn't look back as I strode up the sloped roof, heading for the peak. At the top, I straddled the two sides and looked across my farm.

Or, should I say what was left of my farm? As far as I could see, which on the prairie is a long fucking way, was black with demons. Millions and millions of demons. As if we were in the center of a fucking anthill and we'd stirred up the nest by tossing rocks into it. I looked down at the base of the barn and the two shamans holding the circle of protection.

"Louisa, how you doing?"

"Rylee, we can't hold this much longer." The fatigue in her voice was no surprise.

Orion stood near the ceremonial slab and in his arms was a tiny, dark-haired little girl.

My blood ran cold and my heart went into overdrive. He held her up over his head. "I believe this is the prize you want. Yes or no?"

I sent a thought to Ophelia, a simple request.

The world and time narrowed to small flashes and tiny images. The tears on Marcella's cheeks.

The strain in Louisa's eyes as she looked up at me.

The beat of Ophelia's wings as she rose into the air.

The smell of demons heavy on the back of my throat.

For a moment, I felt a presence beside me. Giselle's spirit drifting close, and with it, her voice.

Follow your heart, Rylee.

Follow my heart. Marcella was my heart. The demons around us roared, the sound of their battle cries actually reverberating inside my chest. No more Immunity for me, and they knew it.

"Invoke the bite, Faris," I yelled. I needed all the strength I could get in order to reach Marcella. Even if that meant the wound from Deanna's strike healed.

A rush of power lit through me and I leapt from the top of the barn, landing in a crouch in front of Louisa. I pulled my two swords from my back and stood, holding one over my head and pointing the other at a grinning Orion.

"To me! Calliope, hold!"

From inside the barn came the battle cry of my family, my pack, and my heart swelled with hope.

We could do this. For the first time, I truly believed we had it in us to defeat Orion, despite the enormous odds against us.

I leapt forward, swinging my blades at the demons closest to the barn. They dissolved as my weapons touched them. Their eyes widened as they began to fall back. Cowards, they had no heart, and I had no doubt they would scatter.

Except I was wrong again. I battled into the heart of the mob, a ten-foot space around me, and my family followed. Berget and Liam moved up to my right side, Doran and Louisa were on the left.

Ophelia rained fire down on the ranks, turning piles of demons into melted puddles like wax crayons being pushed together in a hot pot.

The demons kept coming, flowing toward us and around us, like water. I reached out, Tracking all my people at the same time, their lives shining beacons that I held to as I destroyed every demon I came in contact with.

Crystal was the first of ours to fall. The blow caught her by surprise and I let out a scream as her death rocked through me.

"Rally! Calliope, now!" I yelled, and our circle shifted, pushing harder toward the burnt out shell of my old farmhouse.

Orion laughed. "You think you can make it through them? Rylee, you are a fool."

The unicorns burst out of the barn, their coats shimmering in the pale darkness like living lanterns. They drove forward, Calliope leading them in a V formation, driving hard through the heart of the demons. Tiomon swept by me and I grabbed her mane, launching onto her back.

"He has Marcella and Zane!"

Not for long. Tiomon's voice had a harsh edge to it I'd never felt from a unicorn. A righteous anger bled from her into me and I held onto it. I clamped my legs around her, and alone, we blasted through the demons.

Her horn stabbed and slashed, as did my swords, as we carved through them. Twice, I caught the edge of blades on my right leg. An arrow shot out of the horde and deep into Tiomon's shoulder.

But we didn't slow. Her hooves clattered on the edge of the cement as we scrambled up the back steps and onto what was left of the foundation of the farmhouse.

I leapt from her back, the burning fire in my leg telling me all I needed to know. The blades that had cut into me were poisoned, and for the first time in my life that meant something. What a great fucking time to lose my Immunity.

Tiomon reared up and then plunged forward, her head down as she charged Orion. With a roar, he tried to get out of her way, but holding two babies that wasn't going to happen.

He threw Zane first, tossing him high into the air above our heads.

"NO!" I was too far away, Zane would fall. He would be crushed against the broken timbers and cement. His green eyes found mine and he reached for me, the only mother he'd known. Child of my heart, but not of my blood.

A hair-raising screech snapped through the air, and as Zane fell, Eve swooped out of the night sky, catching him as carefully as if he were her own. From her back, Alex whooped. "Gots him!"

In the distance, came the growing howl of wolves rolling through the night air. Hundreds of wolves coming to our aid. But how the hell was that possible?

Eve screeched again and I glanced up to see Alex grinning down at me. "Reinforcements!"

I stumbled to one knee, the poison spreading fast despite Faris invoking the bite. Fucking hell. I stared at Orion as he tried to dodge one very pissed off unicorn. She darted in, her horn piercing his left shoulder, right over Marcella's head.

He screamed and I scrambled forward. With Tiomon keeping him busy, I had my shot at him.

A body slammed into me from the left, taking me down in a tumble of limbs. Around us, the horde roared and pulled back. Hot, rancid breath poured over me and a thick body pressed me into the ground. "War has come for you. Now what will you do?"

Tiomon's voice reached me. *I have her. Fight, Rylee, and fear not for your daughter. She is my heart mate and I will protect her.*

Relief flowed through me and I stared up at the demon on top of me. He looked like a politician I'd seen on TV once, with a weak chin and terrible hair that might as well have been a mop badly stitched on.

"Rhymes, really?" I drove my elbow up, catching War under the chin and knocking him off me.

But my blow was weak and he reeled back only a little.

"Oh, we aren't done yet." He laughed, pushing his hips against mine and it slammed home what he wanted to do. War wasn't just about fighting, it was about showing how strong you were over those who couldn't defend themselves. Rape, degradation, horror. They all made up war. I wrapped my legs around his waist and pulled him tight against me.

"You want a piece of this?"

I grabbed his ears and slammed my head forward, breaking his nose. He howled. Black blood poured from his mouth and busted face. I held onto his head as he writhed, trying to get away from me.

"What the fuck is wrong with you. I thought you wanted a piece of me?" I distantly realized that he was affecting me, making me do to him what he wanted to do to me. But I couldn't pull back.

Calm, Rylee. Feel the calm. These horsemen are tough because of how strong they are, but they can still be sent back. You know that. Ophelia was right, but I couldn't let go of him. If I did, I would be done in. The demons around us backed farther away, making room as if we were a show they didn't want to miss. But why wouldn't they take a shot at me now that I was down? At the edges of the circle, I caught the eyes of two demons with scars on their cheeks. Two parallel vertical lines with an intersecting dash.

Moloch's demons were helping in the only way they could, holding their own back. I hoped it was enough.

War stood and inadvertently took me with him. My legs trembled under the strain of holding me so tightly to him while the poison from the blades made my blood sluggish.

I bent backward as I pulled my whip free from my hip. War couldn't keep his hands to himself and he slid one palm up my belly.

What a fucking idiot.

Orion roared at him. "Kill her, you fool!"

"In my own time," War yelled back. "I want to make this last. I haven't had a woman in centuries who could—"

I sat up with the whip stretched between my two hands. "And you're not about to, you piece of shit." I wrapped it around his neck and yanked it tight as I let go of him, and my entire weight dropped to the ground. He let out a strangled scream that barely gurgled past his lips. Putting my boots to his shoulder, I straightened out, pulling for all I was worth. The demons around us still hadn't come any closer. Thank the gods for Moloch and his friends.

War clawed at the whip while I was killing his body. Why was he still here? "Go, would you, already!" I yelled at him.

A laugh that could only be Orion's reached me, and the crowd parted. I Tracked Marcella and Tiomon. For the moment, they were together and safe, but not very far away.

Which meant they were still in danger.

Orion leaned over me while I strangled his general. "Rylee, Rylee, Rylee. When will you learn that you are not meant to win this war?"

He kicked me hard in the hand closest to him, breaking bones. I clung to the whip with all I had left in me.

"Go, War. You've failed," I whispered thinking of Marcella and Zane. They did not need war in their lives, not ever. I gave myself over to the calm and the love of those two babies; to the purity of their innocence and their sweet souls. The whip began to glow, pulsing in time with my heart. The light as pure and clean as the love I had for those around me.

War's black eyes widened. "No," he mouthed as his body began to dissolve.

Orion let out a roar and booted the side of my head. The world spun, and I kept pushing War away with all the power of a Slayer I had in me.

The horde around us shifted, like storm clouds carrying the threat of an epic flood to wipe us off the face of the earth. Or maybe that was my eyes watering from the pain. Orion booted me again, but not as hard. I looked up at him, the blood trickling down the side of his face as he shook his head. The bond worked against him again.

He lifted his foot and I braced myself, but he stepped back. "Fucking manipulative bitch."

War glared down at me as his body turned into nothing but a distant, ugly memory.

I lay on the ground. "Sticks and fucking stones, Orion. And I will hurt you." I pushed myself up. The demons let out a series of low, angry hisses that filled the air like pissed off cicadas. But they didn't approach us. Moloch's demons held them back.

Orion spat on the ground in front of me. "You think I won't kill you now?"

I slowly reattached my whip to the left side of my belt and pulled my two blades. "I think you'll try."

My body hurt all over, and the poison was slowing me down. Faris's bite had faded, and while it had healed some things, I was not at my best.

And I was about to face the biggest, baddest demon of them all.

Fucking hell, it felt like a Monday hopped up on steroids.

39
LIAM

The number of demons was beyond staggering. He fought with his cutlass and fists, and picked up a short blade for his other hand somewhere in the melee. But they kept coming, the demons interchangeable as far as he was concerned. One downed body replaced by an upright one over and over.

He let out a grunt as he was hit from the side. The one good thing about Faris's body was that it took damage almost as well as a Guardian's. Almost.

There was a thundering of hooves and a bay unicorn slid to a stop in front of him.

Take your daughter, Wolf. The unicorn spun sideways showing him a tiny girl that had Rylee's eyes. Without hesitation he reached for her, pulling her tightly against his chest. His daughter.

A demon with long spider legs came at him from the left. He let out a snarl and cut off the two closest legs, unbalancing it. Marcella clung to him, but didn't cry. Didn't let out a peep.

I will guard this side of her, you guard the other. The unicorn said as she struck out, demolishing three demons with one well-placed kick.

Side by side they fought. Above them, Marco and Ophelia culled the horde while Eve flew high, protecting Zane. Doran, Louisa, and the other supernaturals held their own, but for how long? There was no way they could defeat this number of demons. No way at all.

Wolves darted in and out of the legs of the demons, taking them down in sneak attacks the fuckers never saw coming. Here and there, he even thought he saw the pale skin of a half-breed troll fighting. He didn't question why they were there, only knew that without them they would likely have fallen already.

Despite the shitty odds, they battled onward. Marcella tucked her head against his shoulder and closed her eyes, her lashes brushing against his skin like butterfly wings. As if she couldn't bear to see what was going on around them. He didn't blame her. If he could, he would have closed his eyes too, and wished the whole world away. Inside his head, Faris paced.

"You know, that's fucking irritating as hell," Liam grunted out as he took the head from another demon.

Nothing else I can do, is there? The vampire snapped at him, still pacing. *I'll admit, you are the better fighter when it comes to this sort of shit.*

Only a few days before, Liam would have gloated, but not now. There was too much riding on the outcome.

We have to get her to the ceremonial slab, Liam. That is the only way this is truly going to end.

"How do you suggest we do that?"

Do what I say, and we can all get out of here alive. I think.

"I'm listening, vampire."

Faris's plan, as he spun it, was simple and smacked of actually putting someone ahead of his own well-being. Liam liked it.

There was nothing he could do to help Rylee, though, until Marcella was safe. But where would his daughter be safe?

There was only one place left in the world he could think of.

"Alex, bring me the boy!" He slammed his shoulder into a demon as it reared back to strike at him. The unicorn behind him let out a grunt and he turned to see a demon on her back. Grabbing it by the ankle, he ripped it off her and used the half-beetle, half-man as a club to clear a bigger area in front of him.

Eve dropped low and Alex leapt off her back, Zane clinging to him.

"Boss?"

"We've got to get them out of here." He flipped his hand in front of him, opening the Veil to a tiny motel on the outskirts of Bismarck. Tiomon and Alex ran through first, and he was right behind.

But so were several demons, their headgear over seven feet tall, antennas waving around as they surveyed the place he'd inadvertently brought them. He closed the Veil before more could pour through, then spun around. The unicorn was already on them. She skewered the first one through the neck, the second through the chest, and the third in the belly. Then she turned to face him, her horn was as clean as if she'd not run three demons through in the space of as many heartbeats.

You believe this is a safe place?

He strode toward the office. "Yes. Though they won't know me in this body."

Alex jogged beside him, breathing hard. The kid had scratches all over his face and arms.

"You doing okay?"

"Huh? Yeah, I got banged up fighting on the way here."

Liam wanted to ask, but there was no time for small talk. He pushed the door to the office.

John, the owner of the motel looked up from under a beaten-down cowboy hat. He looked straight at Alex. "What did I tell you?"

Alex shifted his feet but said nothing.

Obviously, Liam was missing something, but again, no time. "John, I know this is a lot to ask, and you won't remember me, but—"

John waved a hand at him. "The babies can stay here with me and Mary. That's not a problem. You go and take care of our Ry. That *is* your job, isn't it, Wolf?"

Liam was taken aback. How could the old man possibly know about Rylee and the babies? Or the fact that he was a wolf?

Alex leaned forward and whispered. "Don't ask. I've got a feeling it'll blow your mind."

Liam looked down at Marcella, her face still curled into his shoulder. He ran a hand over her cheek. The first time he'd ever held her, and he had to give her away before he really could register she was in his arms. "Baby girl." She slowly lifted her head, blinking up at him. So beautiful, she had her mother's features already, though she had more of his coloring.

She reached up and brushed her tiny fingers over his lips, a tentative smile on her sweet mouth. He kissed her on the forehead, his throat tight. He couldn't say goodbye to her, not even as he handed her over to John. Mary, John's wife, stepped out of the back. Liam had never met her before, and even Rylee said she didn't come out of the back much when she was around. Mary's eyes met his, and he knew why she'd avoided Rylee.

"Here we go, give her to GG." She reached for Marcella and the little girl cooed and reached back for her.

"GG?" Liam said, forgetting for a split second there was a battle raging, and Rylee waiting on him.

Mary smiled, and the smile silenced all his questions, the resemblance was too strong to deny. "Great-grandma. Now, go and save our Ry, Wolf."

Alex gave Zane to John. "Liam, we need to get back there."

"I know." He couldn't take his eyes from Mary as he backed out the door. She smiled down at Marcella as she jiggled the little girl gently. He opened the door and the unicorn was still there, her head high as she scanned the area. "There's a unicorn outside to guard the babies."

John waved at him. "We know, Wolf. Now git."

He opened the Veil, feeling the pull on his soul as using it tore away another piece. Worth it for Marcella. Worth it for Rylee.

The slash in the Veil opened in the middle of the melee, closer to Doran. He and Alex leapt through, tackling the two demons who'd tried to get around him and to the other side of the Veil.

Liam pummeled the demon into the ground, then tore its head off with his bare hands.

Beside him, Alex had shifted and was snapping the neck of a demon with his teeth.

"Doran, time to get the girl," he shouted to the day-walking vampire.

Doran was in a pocket of demons about ten feet from them. "You got a plan?"

"Not really, Faris does." Liam took a step back, bracing himself for a split second. "Alex, with me?"

Alex was at his side in a flash. "Yuppy doody, boss."

He raised a hand. "Eve!"

The harpy swooped down and caught both him and Alex up in her talons.

"Where?"

"Rylee."

She tipped her wings and they were over a bare patch of ground, devoid of every demon except one.

Orion.

And he was beating the shit out of Rylee.

Eve let them go without asking, dropping them in front of Rylee. "Get him, Liam!" she screeched.

Liam landed in a crouch, his eyes locked on the glowing red orbs of the demon in front of him. Orion was breathing hard, blood ran down the side of his head, and his hand looked like it had been busted up. Alex ran to where Rylee lay on the ground. "She's alive."

"Well, well, well. If it isn't the martyr. Come to sacrifice yourself again, Wolf?"

Baring his teeth, a low rumbling growl slipped out of him. "Fuck you, demon."

"Now, now, is that the kind of language you want your daughter to learn? Where is the pretty little Marcella?" He looked around then back at Liam. "Naughty boy, you took her away, didn't you? Never fear, I'll find her soon enough."

Liam didn't hesitate. He leapt forward, tackling Orion to the ground. The demon was big, bulky, and physically dominating compared to the lean muscle that Faris's body carried. But Liam—and Faris—fought for someone they loved, giving him the strength he needed to overpower Orion.

He rolled the demon under him, straddling the fucker's chest. Yanking his cutlass free, he brought it down hard, aiming right for Orion's neck. He only hoped it would do more than slow the big bastard down to lose his head.

Something that smelled like it had been dead for months slammed into him, sweeping him away from the demon in the last second before his blade made contact. In the tumble through the air, he caught flashes of gray tattered skin and long, cracked claws. Liam hit the ground hard, rolling across the broken cornstalks, stopping only when he came to rest against Rylee's side.

She looked at him, her eyes swirling. "We're in deep shit this time, Liam."

"This time?"

"Well, you have to admit, all the other times we weren't outnumbered, not like this."

He choked out a laugh. "No, not exactly like this."

Around them the demons laughed. How long had they been fighting? Hours? It felt like it.

And there was no doubt in his mind that they were far from done.

40
PAMELA

We weren't going to make it in time to save Rylee. That was the only thought that rolled through my head, and I couldn't shake it no matter how hard I tried. The seething black mass of demons in front of us was too great. Was too much.

Lark's words to me echoed through my head.

"Let it all out," I whispered. For everything I was, and all those I loved, I would embrace everything in me. The light and the dark.

I opened myself to the magic like never before and it screamed through me like a maelstrom of epic proportions. Barely able to direct it, I didn't care if I lived past the battle. If we couldn't get to Rylee, it wouldn't matter what was left of me.

A scream ripped out of me as the magic exploded in a wave of pure power, dissolving the first lines of the demons. I didn't walk, but ran forward into the opening and did it again. And again.

And again.

41
LARK

I'd be damned if we didn't make it in time to save Rylee. Well and truly damned. Pamela was battling with all she had, and I would do no less. I embraced the power of Earth and Spirit and wove them together, making a deadly concoction.

I flexed my fingers as I unleashed my power right behind the wave of magic Pamela sent out.

Destroyer. That was my name.

And I would live up to it every time.

42
ALEX

I held my ground, putting my body against Rylee's, as if I could feed her my strength. I would give it all to save her.

No matter what it cost me.

43
RYLEE

What was left of my family, my pack, was grabbed and brought to the opening Orion had created around us. All except the unicorns, who were still fighting as fiercely as they ever had, alongside the werewolves and what was left of what looked like half-breed trolls.

Yet, if they continued for a month, they wouldn't be able to destroy all the demons.

Doran, Berget, Louisa, Mer, Charlie . . . they were shoved into the circle with us, still fighting. But it had been hours since we'd started the battle. Hours of fending off the never ending horde.

A whoosh of wings and Ophelia landed behind us, scattering demons left and right. She crouched over me, snaking her head toward Orion with her teeth open.

Before she could close her teeth, though, she was hit in the head by a club of a tail attached to a dragon bigger than her. A dragon that looked as though it had been dead for a long fucking time.

The heavy smack of bone on bone reverberated through the air, like a bell being rung. Ophelia shook her head and her legs wobbled.

Death dragon. Impossible to kill because they are already dead.

"Of course they are. Why the fuck would the world give us a break?" I said, pushing myself to my feet. Why indeed?

Orion spread his hands. "You are surrounded, Rylee. Your friends are dead, your shot at freeing the world gone. Do you surrender? I promise to not go too hard on you." The demons circling us laughed, as if Orion had told a particularly funny joke.

I looked at my family, met the gaze of each soul I held as dear to me as if we were all born under the same roof. And in them I saw my own defiance reflected. We knew we were surrounded, knew there was no way we could possibly out-fight the horde.

They knew, as did I, this was the end for us all.

I shook my head. "Orion, you are dumber than a bag of bent, useless nails. Fuck you."

"Yeah, yous fuckity fucker! We's never surrendering to yous!" Charlie yelled, shaking a tiny sword in his fist. Blood dripped down his upraised arm, and his limp was worse than ever. But he stood with me still.

"Kiss my assy ass," Alex snarled, his fur standing at attention along his spine as he stiff-legged walked toward Orion.

Mer, her eyes hard as stone, said, "Suck it, demon."

Doran laughed. "Bite me."

"Never." Berget shook her head, her long hair floating on the breeze as if she'd come from the salon only moments before.

Liam looked at me, but he spoke to Orion. "To the end, Rylee." My heart clenched, and I dared to Track

Marcella and Zane. Liam nodded as though he knew what I was doing.

"They're safe. I made sure of it. And the unicorn went with them."

Relief flowed over me, and with it a renewed surge of strength. My mind cleared as each of my people—my family—said their piece, and the world seemed to hold its breath. Orion shook his head, but he was grinning with uncontained glee. "Well then, I suppose we're almost done here."

The horde around us shifted, tensing, waiting for his call to finish us off. Orion lifted his hand, his red eyes glinting. "It's been a slice, Rylee. Let's do this again sometime."

Under my feet, the ground heaved, and I went to one knee, bracing myself. What the fuck was he doing now?

Orion whipped around, his back to me. "No!"

Behind him, the demons fell in a wave of earth that exploded in every direction, followed by a flame caught up into a tornado that danced through the horde as though picking partners.

I stared as the demons split apart, and opened a perfect aisle for us to see down.

Lark ran toward us, and she was not alone.

The elementals ranged out to all sides of her, and Pamela was with her, flinging fireballs and exploding the earth with every step she took.

Maybe we could pull this crazy-ass thing off.

I swung out my two swords, my broken fingers crying out for me to stop, but I knew an opening when I saw one and rushed Orion while his back was turned, attention on the incoming elementals. Leaping up, I came down hard, driving both swords into his back. "Go, get the fuck out of here."

Orion screamed as he fell under my sword, but he didn't dissolve. He spun, backhanding me and sending me flying into the first line of demons. They caught me gently and I saw the scars. Saw the demons attached to them nod. "Get him, Tracker." They threw me back toward Orion. Like it was a sporting event, and I was the ball to catch and toss between opponents.

Around us, the demons scattered, bleating like an oversized herd of sheep as the elementals cut into them. Though they weren't able to send the demons back, they were able to slow them, giving everyone a much needed breather.

Orion stared down at me as he pulled the two swords from his back, yanking them out. With a casual indifference, he held them out in front of him, then brought them down hard over his knee, snapping them in half. "You won't be needing these."

Shit, without my swords I was down to my whip and crossbow. Both good weapons, but not in close quarters. I scrambled to my feet, and Liam moved to my side. Orion spared him a look. "And you won't be needing that, either."

He took the broken tip of one of my swords and flung it toward Liam, driving it right through his heart. My mind stuttered; silver-edged swords could kill vampires. Liam was trapped in Faris's body—a vampire.

Liam slumped, his fingers touching the edge of the sword. His eyes flicked up to mine and he whispered my name. "Rylee."

No. Not again, I could not do this again. "You hang the fuck on, wolf; I'm not losing you twice!"

I reached down and jerked the blade out of him, cutting my hand open as I did. He grunted, but I looked away as I spun with the broken blade.

From the corner of my eye, Lark stepped into the circle. "Rylee, use this." She pushed something toward me.

A blade. One I'd used before. My hand was slick with blood, but the grip on the handle was perfect. "Get Pam. Liam needs help."

"You got it." She scooped him up under the arms and dragged him backward, away from Orion. I couldn't even watch them go. I didn't dare turn my back on Orion, as he'd so stupidly done with me.

I gripped the sword and swirled it once. It seemed to whine with eagerness as I swirled it through the air, hungry to bite into something. Orion's eyes narrowed. "It doesn't matter what the blade is, you are going to be the one to die first. Not me. Isn't that right?"

He glanced to the left, and I followed his gaze. The final one of the four horsemen, Death—an older woman with graying hair pulled back so tightly, it gave her a free facelift—nodded. "The Tracker will die. I see it. And when she dies, Orion, so will you."

He grunted. "I know. But my people will be free."

She laughed. "Your people? Ah, Orion, you always were a dreamer. We are no more your people, than we are hers." She pointed at me and I took a step back. I couldn't help it. I didn't know if she was really Death or not, but I didn't want to take the chance and find out the hard way.

A roar lifted the air around us and the death dragon swooped out of the sky, its claws narrowly missing me as I dropped to my belly. The corn stalks under me flattened and a few silk strands tickled my face. I rolled in time to see Death picked up by her dragon.

Orion was gone. Again. "Motherfucker!" I screamed as I pushed to my feet. "Ophelia!"

The dragon snaked her head toward me and I grabbed the scales on the back of her neck as she leapt into the sky and flipped me into the air. I landed near enough to the harness, but didn't use it; instead, standing on her back, balancing. The poison from the demon blades, the wounds to my hands, the kicks to my head—every injury fought to pull me down.

You have strength still, Rylee. Center yourself, draw on your core. You are a warrior. Do not let the wounds define you.

Her words seemed to help block the pain and I refocused on the dragon flying ahead of us. One more horseman and we'd be down to Orion.

I pulled my crossbow off and raised it, sighting down the shaft.

I had only ten bolts, and they had to count.

"Ophelia, we need to take Death out before I can truly deal with Orion. He's using her to stay alive, despite the injuries I inflict." At least, that was what I suspected was happening.

Agreed. She snaked her neck out and roared, the sound shimmering over the horde below us. A battle cry, a charge of dragons. I felt the emotion from her, calling out the dragon that carried Death.

The demons fell back from her wings sweeping toward the ground, and the unicorns used the opening to push our people toward Orion at the ceremonial slab; a few feet at most, but it was in the right direction.

Death looked at me, her eyes a bottomless pit of darkness that, even in the growing night, were fearsome and black.

The death dragon lifted its rotting head and roared back at Ophelia.

Challenge accepted, dumbass. The beast launched toward us, Death never taking her eyes from me.

"You will die, Blood of the Lost. And with your death, we will rule."

I smiled at her, and flipped her off. "Fuck you."

Ophelia laughed and let out a roar. *Yes, fuck you.*

The dragons rose together, high into the skies above the battlefield. Lightning arced around us, dancing through the clouds, thunder chasing the forked death. I tucked my feet into the harness, wrapping the leather around my ankles, as Ophelia's muscles bunched under me, her intent flowing through my mind.

She reared back and then shot forward like a slingshot, using her head as a battering ram right into the solar plexus of the death dragon. It grabbed at her, raking his claws down her sides, aiming for her wings. She tucked her wings back, keeping them safe; but also then taking away any lift we had. The two dragons spiraled downward, picking up speed with each loop we spun in the air. I went to my knees and slid my hands into the harness, clinging for all I was worth as the G-force continued to pick up.

The speed was too much and I slipped. "Ophelia!"

I've got you.

A front claw shot out and caught me as I was ripped from her back. She rolled in the air and the world inverted. I lost all sense of time and space for a few seconds. I couldn't make heads nor tails of where we were until Ophelia got us straightened out and was winging after Death and her dragon, who seemed to be heading for the hills.

"We can't leave the battle!" I yelled.

If we don't take them out, Orion can't be killed; I believe you may be right about that.

I couldn't help the groan that slipped out of me. "Then let's kick it into high gear, 'Phelia."

Stretching herself out, she shot after the death dragon. Within seconds, she had its tail in her mouth and she back winged hard enough to yank it to a stop. The death dragon spun in the air, its mouth open and jagged teeth coming straight for Ophelia. She flipped me into the air, toward the dragon's back.

I will keep him busy; you take care of Death.

"Deal," I yelled as I ran up the death dragon's spine. Death waited for me, calmly.

I held up my sword, waiting for her to lift a weapon. She didn't move. "What are you waiting for, Slayer?"

I paused. "You aren't going to fight?"

"No. The words I spoke were for Orion's ears, so he would not know what I planned. I do not wish Orion to win this battle. We do not belong here. And as long as I am alive, only a Slayer can kill a demon and send it back to the seventh Veil. You can injure the bodies they are in, but all that does is slow them down. Your people will die if I am not sent back." She shook her head slowly, reached up, and pulled her hair loose from the overly tight bun. On her face, a pale scar emerged of two lines intersected by a single dash. She was one of Moloch's friends. "My death will mean that you will truly have a chance at stopping this madness."

In that light, the way her hair curled softly in waves around her face, she looked like Anna, the necromancer who'd stolen dying children to raise as her own. She knew she needed to die for the greater good, and had offered herself to me.

Now Death was doing the same. Her dragon slowly landed. She reached down and patted him. "It's all right. This is the way it must be, my friend."

We landed and she slid off the dragon's back. I looked to Ophelia. She was to my left and I could tell she didn't trust this anymore than I did. But it looked like Death truly was one of those demons Moloch had spoken about. A demon who wasn't all bad.

Death went to her knees and bowed her head. "Do it now, Slayer. Save this world and ours. I will not die like the others, but be reborn on the other side of the Veil."

I raised my sword, the blade lighting up the sky like a beacon of hope as my emotions raged through me. I whispered a single word. "Peace." The blade cut through the air in a flash of light like a falling star, and the back of her neck held no resistance to the edge. A blinding flash of light rippled out from the contact between blade and bone. Death was swallowed in a tiny super nova, her dragon dissolving the same time she did.

I put a hand to my eyes. "Fuck, that was bright."

Ophelia scooped me up and put me on her back. *Hurry, the night is fading. The time of the ceremony is now. We must get you back.*

Already?

I gripped the harness for all I was worth, my heart beating harder than it had probably in my entire life. This was it, the moment was now, whether I was ready or not.

I took a deep breath, held it for a moment and slowly let it out. "Then let's end this shit."

44
LARK

Beside me, Pamela healed Liam, though I could see the toll it took on her. Her lips were pressed tightly together in a thin line as she closed the wound. He sat up, reaching for his cutlass before Pamela's hands had even fallen from his chest.

Around us, the demons began to die as they fought our allies. Not dissolve, not go down in a massive twitching of limbs that could re-spawn. No, they were dying, and the elementals roared with a fierce and wild glee.

Fiametta met my eye and nodded, pride filling her face; her fire elementals were a wicked force to be reckoned with, and were showing how very dangerous they were. From the weakest of them to the strongest, they'd blasted a line through the demons in order to get me to Rylee in time, to get the sword into her hands.

Somewhere behind me, Finley worked with her Undines, and they in turn were assisting the queen of the Sylphs. I was still surprised she'd come. Mind you, she'd stayed as far away from me as possible, but that was fine.

A swirl of a black cloak ten feet from me drew my eye. Blackbird had come as he'd sworn, and as I stared, he killed the demons around him. I hesitated, my spear in my hands as I considered running him through.

The time is not now, child. For this moment he stands with you, and has earned his life. The mother goddess spoke firmly to me, as if perhaps I wouldn't listen. It would not be the first time I'd ignored her.

"Until tomorrow then," I breathed the words out, spun, and took a demon's oversized rat head from his shoulders.

Rylee and Ophelia winged above us, heading for the ceremonial slab. Orion was hot on her heels, ripping through his own people to get to the slab before her. I gathered the power of Spirit, but held back at the last second. I could not use it, the fear of what it would do to me stopping me.

A demon that looked like he'd possessed an ogre's hulking mass roared at me. I screamed back at him, driving the shaft of my spear into his groin and dropping him to his knees. On his back was a black and gnarled bow that I ripped off. Kicking him in the neck, I pushed him the rest of the way over and took his arrows as well.

Orion mounted the steps of the burnt farmhouse.

Rylee dropped from Ophelia's back, not seeing him or his raised sword.

I lifted the bow and sighted the arrow staring at the back of his neck where it joined the base of his skull. I released the bowstring and the arrow flew straight and true, slamming through him.

My vision blurred as I was tackled by two demons at once. "We've got her. Master will like us for this. Blackbirdy, we's got her!"

Hell no, this was not happening.

I called the earth up under us, pulling all three of us down deep. With very little effort, I pushed myself back out and shook the loose dirt off. The two demons were buried; the tips of their fingers the only thing visible.

"Blackbird, you bastard." I snarled. The time was soon coming that I would have to deal with him.

Not yet.

No, I was rather busy making sure the world didn't get overrun by demons. But as soon as that was done with . . . Blackbird would get his comeuppance.

One way or another.

45
RYLEE

I spun as Orion came at me, his sword over his head, already in a downswing toward me. There was no way I'd get my weapon up in time. The moment slowed, and I stared up at him.

But at the last second of his swing, his whole body jerked as though he'd touched an open electric line.

"No, I won't let you win," he spit out, blood flecking his lips. He twitched and turned sideways, the arrow protruding from the back of his spine dancing like it was a fishing line with a large catch. Lark saw me, gave me a nod, and then was tackled to the ground by a couple of hulking demons.

I raised the katana. Orion was dying, and I needed a wound from a demon to kick-start the ceremony; but I finally realized it couldn't be just any demon. It had to be Orion, or this wasn't going to work. That was what Deanna hadn't understood either. As much as she'd tried to help me, she'd only ended up killing herself by letting the demon in.

"If you don't want me to win, then you'd better take a swing at me, you fucking idiot," I snapped, bringing his attention back to me. His red eyes were clouded with a gray fog as death crawled up and over him.

Fuck. I was running out of time. The night was beginning to fade, the distant light of the dawn coming faster than I could believe.

Orion reached around and pulled the arrowhead from his neck, and his eyes cleared. "You didn't think a single arrow could actually down me, did you? Who is the idiot now?"

Oh, fuck.

Here it was, the moment I'd been trying to make happen all along.

I had a moment of fear that Doran hadn't listened to Charlie when I'd sent the brownie with instructions for how to set up things. Because it wasn't just my blood needed to send the demons back and close the Veil.

It was Orion's, too.

Spinning, I leapt over a burnt-out timber into the well of the house. The ceremonial slab had been cleaned off, and its placement was under what would've been my bedroom.

I stood in the middle, and breathed out a sigh of relief. The ropes were in place as I'd asked Doran to do. Orion came at me.

We circled the thick slab, the details of it searing my brain. The depressions under the seven points where blood would be drawn from me, the channels that would take that blood into the earth and seal the Veil. The section pushed out to the left would be for Orion's body.

"This game has gone on long enough." Orion lunged at me, his sword tip missing me under the chin as I backpedaled, forgetting I needed him to cut into me. But it had to be the right place. Seven points: both arms, both legs, my heart, neck, and belly. Belly was for the demons.

"I agree. But it has never been a game to me."

Orion seemed perplexed by my words. "A game is a game. There are winners and losers."

"But if you're a loser, is it a game?" I stepped toward him, the katana arcing through the last of the night air, faster than any blade I'd ever used. I followed it up with a roundhouse, catching Orion in the side of the head. He reeled back and off the slab. Too far. I needed him up there with me. I folded my arms over my chest and snorted. "So you want to rule the world, but you can't fight without your voodoo magic?"

Snarling, his face twisting into a grimace that let his true colors show. He clambered onto the slab with me, the monster in him glimmering through the thin Veil of humanity he held over himself like a cloak.

Back and forth, we fought, our weapons never drawing blood as we pushed each other to the limit. Other demons came close, but none stepped in to help him. At one point, he saw me looking.

"If I can't kill you on my own, I am no leader," he said, then spit at my feet a glob of black saliva.

What he said hit me hard, right in the heart. I wasn't alone.

That was what Lark had been saying all along. That even the smallest piece of the puzzle like Jonathan was important to make this picture whole.

I didn't have to do this alone, so why was I trying so hard to?

"LIAM!" I screamed his name, knowing he would hear me no matter how far away he was. "ALEX. BERGET. DORAN. PAMELA. LARK. EVE. OPHELIA. PETA. CHARLIE. WILL. JONATHAN. CALLIOPE."

The names of my family, the ones I loved beyond anything this world could ever offer me. Orion's eyes widened. "That's cheating!" He lunged forward, his sword aimed for my belly. I spread my arms wide and let it drive into me.

The blade slid through me to the hilt. I stared up at Orion, the physical pain nothing to the echoes of what was coming. "No. This is family. And I don't have to do this on my own," I said. Alex tackled him from behind, dropping him to the slab with a meaty thunk. Liam was right on top of him, then Doran for good measure. Pamela was there at my side, breathless with exertion as she wove a spell around Orion. "I don't know how well it will hold." She looked at me, her face paling. "I have to heal you, Rylee."

I shook my head. "No. Don't heal me, no matter what happens." Dropping to my knees, struggling to breathe around the gut wound, I scooped up one end of the rope Doran had placed earlier when prepping the slab. "These will hold the big bastard."

I made a slipknot and put it over Orion's left wrist. Lark copied for his right wrist and ankle. Peta fought beside her, slashing any demon that got too close. Berget caught me as I slumped backward and onto my ass, the gut wound finally taking me down.

"You're almost done, Rylee," she whispered into my ear. I nodded, the sword slipping from my fingers. I touched the wound at my stomach and Pamela rushed to me. I shook my head.

"No, this has to bleed."

Around us the air shifted and a thunderstorm rolled in at a speed that was anything but natural. Lark came to my side and put a hand to my cheek. "The elementals are turning on each other."

I stared up at her in shock. "They're what?"

"I knew this would happen. They bought us the time we needed, but I never expected them to play nice for this long."

Peta shook her head, her green eyes sorrowful. "Stupid idiots, they will pay for this one day."

The storm broke over us, big fat raindrops falling on my upturned face as Lark scooped me up and laid me on the slab beside Orion. He thrashed, but the ropes held him.

"Ropes made from unicorn hair," I whispered to him with a smile. I lay there, feeling the time slip away. "Lark, you know what has to happen?"

She bent over me, her eyes brimming with tears. "I do." She touched my cheek gently and stood back. "Say your goodbyes."

Pamela startled like she'd been shot in the ass. "Goodbyes? No, this is—"

There was no chance for her to say anything else. The demons around us were no longer held back by Lark's groups. The few elementals left—Cactus, Lark, and her sister Belladonna—were the only ones who'd stayed. The remaining wolves and half-breed trolls circled tightly around us, but their numbers had been easily cut in half.

Lark held my hand. "I can't help them and do the ceremony. There is no time for anything else."

I nodded, a warm fatigue spilling over me. The wound in my stomach was bad. "You'd better hurry then, I'm not sure there is going to be much blood left in me."

Lark nodded and let me go. "Cactus, Bella, Pamela. Make a circle, hold them as long as you can."

Not too long, though. It wouldn't be too long and this would be done. My family would be safe.

The world would be safe.

Marcella would be safe.

46
LARK

The ceremony was simple. Seven points of the body bled out into the slab, a single invocation spoken over each participant and the blood would be drawn out of them in a rush like water receding ahead of a tsunami.

I looked up at Eve hovering above us, out of range of the demons' arrows and spears. "Harpy, bring me the boy, Jonathan."

She let out a screech and shot into the fading darkness.

Peta stayed close to me, her strength helping me focus my mind on what had to be done. "Thank you," I whispered. She gave a soft mewl of acknowledgment, but said nothing. No doubt she was picking up the tumultuous emotions swirling through me.

At the altar, I bent over the demon first. He glared up at me. "Blackbird isn't done with you yet, chicky."

Taking the katana I'd made ten years prior for Rylee, before I ever knew her, before I ever knew what my role would be, I sliced it across each of his wrists in a vertical slash. I moved to his legs, then his belly, one cut over his heart, and then paused at his throat. "Any last words?"

"You've not seen the last of us. Demons will not be held back, not even if you close the Veil. We'll find a way. We always do."

I refused to admit his words chilled me to the bone. Shrugging, I slid the katana across his throat and spoke the invocation. "*Signantes velum.*"

A bolt of lightning ripped out of the sky and drove through his body, superheating his blood. The black liquid poured out of him so fast his skin shriveled and tightened over his face and chest, until he was nothing but a wizened body that looked as though it had been mummified for a thousand years.

"Tell me that isn't going to happen to me," Rylee whispered, her eyes locked on Orion—or what was left of him—beside her on the slab.

"It's not. That was because he has no soul." I tried not to hear the sounds of the battle around us. Alex pressed close to her on the other side.

"I'm here, Rylee. To the end, whatever that is."

I shook my head. "You can't touch her once the ceremony begins, Alex. No one can until her blood is drained, or their fate will be tangled with hers. She dies, you die, understand?"

He looked at me, his golden eyes wide and brimming with tears. "Then don't let her die, Lark."

My jaw tight, I nodded. "I'm going to be doing my best not to let that happen."

Cactus grunted. "Hurry, Lark, we're losing ground."

Hurry, hurry. I called Berget over. "We start with you. The fanged must make their mark. You have to say, 'for the fanged, you bleed.'" I handed her the katana and then pointed at Rylee's left wrist.

This was about to get very, very real.

47
RYLEE

I stared up at Berget and gave her a smile. "It's okay."

She shook her head, tears falling from her pristine blue eyes. "No, I just got you back."

"I know." I wouldn't lie, not now.

She dropped to her knees beside me on the slab, her arms going around my neck. "I love you, Rylee."

"I love you, too, baby sister. Look after Marcella for me, help her be strong and kind. And maybe not as much of a potty mouth as me."

Sobbing, she pulled back from me and put the katana against my left wrist. Holding her lips between her teeth she drew the blade over my skin. I didn't even feel it, wouldn't have known I was wounded except for the warmth trickling down my arm. "For the fanged, you bleed."

Lark touched her on the shoulder. "Hold the circle, keep the demons at bay."

Berget stumbled back and leapt into the fray with a war cry that made me think the demons had best run from her.

"Ophelia," Lark said, and my dragon—yes, my dragon, not my father's any longer—reached out with the tip of her claw and cut my left leg. "For the winged, you bleed."

As if on cue, Eve swooped low and dropped Jonathan right at my feet. Lark handed him the blade and he cut into my right leg. "For the psychics, you bleed."

Lark took the katana from him. She looked at me. "Pamela or Louisa?"

"I will do it," Pamela said, striding over to us. Gods, she made me proud.

She took a deep breath and took the katana, her words shaking. "Rylee, you know you aren't going to die. You can't."

I smiled up at her. "I love you, Pam. You are my other little sister. Look out for each other."

"Love is the key," she whispered. "It always was. You loved me, and that brought me back from the darkness. You never gave up. Please don't give up, Rylee." She leaned over and slid the blade over my right wrist. "For the magicked, you bleed."

She kissed her fingers and then held her palm up to me. I couldn't move and I hated I was going to break a promise to her. To all of them.

Lark's voice softened. Alex hadn't moved from my side, not during the whole time. "For the furred, Alex. Can you do it?"

He swallowed hard and his tears spilled over onto his cheeks. "Yes. Though I will hate myself forever for taking part in this."

"Hey," I said softly, hiccupping around the sobs reverberating through my chest. "Don't you dare change, Alex. Not for a split second."

He held the katana carefully, putting the tip over my heart and drawing a line across it. "For the furred, you bleed."

Lark took the blade from him and shooed him backward.

Tears dripped from her eyes, down her cheeks, and splashed onto the slab beside my head. "Goodbye, my friend."

"See you on the flip side, Lark."

She drew the blade across my throat. "Rylee of the Blood. For the world, you bleed. For the world, you sacrifice. For the world, you die."

I closed my eyes, the rush of warmth flowing over me as my blood slipped from my veins. Liam cried out and Lark yelled at him not to touch me. We'd said our goodbyes; not to say I wouldn't have liked to hold him again. To whisper one last time that I loved him.

But if I did that, I might not ever let him go, or let any of them go, for that matter. Beside me, Alex sobbed, his cries turning into howls that shattered the night air, and another piece of my heart broke.

I didn't want to go. Didn't want to leave any of them behind.

Around me the world faded and the Veil slipped over me, flashes of each level as I slid through. Their meaning becoming known to me.

The first Veil hid the unseen world of the supernatural. The second level was of dreams and visions. I'd been there more than a time or two. The third Veil carried ghosts that couldn't move on for one reason or another.

The fourth Veil stumped me, and I stayed for a moment to take it in. Books were everywhere, like a giant library that contained everything ever written in the world, both human and supernatural; a place to seek answers, I understood.

The fifth level was a dungeon . . . a place of penance for supernatural assholes. Several trolls hissed at me, including a one-eyed, dual-dicked prick I knew all too fucking well. I flipped him off as I passed into the sixth Veil.

The realm of heroes, those who would stand between the world and the evil that would swallow it whole.

I stopped moving and stared at the first person, unable to believe what I was seeing.

"Dox." I whispered his name and he gave a roar, scooping me into one of his infamous hugs, his blue-skinned arms squeezing me hard enough he should have cracked ribs. I hugged him back, unable to stop the tears. "Dox, you're going to be a father."

"Rylee, I know. I know." He set me down, grinning. The triplets, Sla, Lop, and Dev surrounded us, laughing, their smiles infectious. Their violet skin the same shade as Sas's, but their attitudes couldn't have been more different from hers. They each slapped me on the back.

"Goose feathers and fuck a duck, you did good, Tracker," one of them said, and I shook my head. I would never get the hang of their cursing.

"Thanks."

A laugh I would know if my ears were plugged made me push past them. Giselle smiled at me and held out her arms. "Well done, Rylee girl. I knew you wouldn't falter."

I buried my face in her neck, unashamed to cry in front of her. Of all the people in my life, she'd been there from the beginning. From the first salvage. From the first betrayal, and the first broken promises. The mother of my heart and the one who understood why I did what I did.

"Hush, you're here now, and it won't be long before you can rest." She smoothed the hair back from my face. I looked up, wiped my face, and sniffed.

"You mean it's not finished?"

She shook her head and pointed at the horizon behind us. "You have to close the Veil still, my girl."

She turned so I could look past her. Beyond her, the horizon seethed with darkness, glimmering and moving like a giant snake that had twisted its coils in on itself. From the ground, it rose far into the sky. It was a solid wall that seemed to have no end.

Here and there were flashes of bright light, like grenades popping within the darkness, and they lit up with thousands upon thousands of red gleaming eyes. That was the barrier between us and the seventh Veil, where the demons were supposed to be caged.

Giselle didn't let me go. "We are with you, Rylee. The battle will rage on both sides of the Veil. It is why you had to lose so many of your friends and finest warriors. You need an army here, as well."

"It's why I was not afraid to die," Milly said softly, and I spun to face her.

Her bright green eyes were clear of Orion's influence for the first time since I'd known her. But her being in the sixth level surprised me. "You aren't in the fifth level doing penance? Not that I want you to be!"

She shook her head. "No. I was a child when Orion took control of me. I fought where I could and that was enough to bring me here." I grabbed her and hugged her tightly. Another coming home. A friend I thought lost forever only to find her again.

An arm slid across my shoulders and a rough voice spoke. "Niece. Tell me the babies are safe."

I turned and let Erik hold me, seeing again his death at the hands of the mob of trolls and how he'd protected Marcella with his own body. "They are. Liam got them out of the battle."

A big sigh slipped out of him. "Good. I could never forgive myself if something happened to them."

"Thank you, Uncle," I said softly. "You gave your life for her."

He grinned. "I wouldn't have done it for just anyone."

Frank was next, tucking his hands into his pockets. I held out a hand to him and hugged him, then kissed him hard on the lips. "That's from Pamela."

He blushed. "Is she . . . okay?"

"She will be. She's a tough girl, and she loved you."

He smiled, and I could see how easy it would be for her to fall for him. "I know. It's why this was worth it."

Love, it all came back to love.

I looked around us, unable to believe how many friends we'd lost. Deanna was there too, as were all the shamans who'd died. The coven of witches, and most of the supernatural world who'd died at the hands of Orion's pox.

On this side of the Veil, there were more supernaturals to fight for us than on the other side.

Giselle's words, what she'd said, actually sunk in. "Warriors. You said they came here to fight . . . ." I couldn't breathe past the single possibility that lay ahead of me.

My mentor smiled and Erik gave a laugh. "Yeah, those two have been waiting a long time to see you. Go." He pushed me and I started running in the direction he shoved. I ran, hopping on one leg and then the other to try and see farther past all the people who'd come to greet me. The supernaturals around me parted, letting me through.

Ahead of me, two figures approached me at a walk.

He was tall, had light auburn hair, and moved a lot like a younger version of Erik. I knew his name was Bram, but that was it.

She could have been my mirror reflection except for the pitch-black hair. Her eyes met mine, tri-colors swirling. Green, gold, and brown, like mine. I skidded to a stop, but she kept coming forward. Elle, her name was Elle. My mother.

"Rylee," she said my name, and I put my hands to the back of my head.

"Is this happening?"

A smile quirked her lips. "What did you think would happen if you died? That you would be left alone in the darkness? You've touched too many lives, Rylee. And you have made us so proud."

She reached out to me and touched my cheek. I fell into her arms, and then my father wrapped his arms around me. Their strength was my strength, their hearts beat in time with mine.

For a few moments, I could be a child, protected from the world by parents who loved her.

Bram pulled back first, his eyes sparkling with humor. "Time to kill the demons, daughter."

Daughter. Damn, that sounded nice.

"Yes, but how are we going to get all the way over there?" I pointed at the blackness. As big and obvious as it was, it had to be at least a hundred miles away.

He grinned. "All the warriors come here . . . even those we don't expect sometimes."

A bellowing roar that put Dox's cry to shame shook the air, and I was running from my parents toward the blue, black, and silver dragon as he dropped toward me. Blaz, his wings shimmering in the bright sunlight, landed in front of me. He snaked his head out and I grabbed his face as best I could, another tiny piece of my heart healing. All the loss of the last year made sense, and even though they hurt me, I understood why.

"Rylee, you're almost done."

I looked up at him. "Your voice isn't in my head."

"Not here." He grinned and winked one golden eye at me. He bent his front leg and I scrambled onto his back. No harness, but I wasn't worried.

Other dragons dropped out of the sky, and across the open plain came the thundering of hooves. The warriors and heroes around me mounted, but they didn't move forward. Their eyes all rested on me.

I lifted my hand into the sky, and slowly made a fist, but the words clogged in my throat. What the fuck was I doing? What would happen to these people I loved so dearly if they died a second time fighting for me? Would their souls be destroyed? I couldn't bear it if that was the case.

"It's not like the other side, Rylee," my mother said as she climbed up behind me and settled on Blaz's back. Mom looked at me with a wry twist on her lips. "This isn't going to be a battle like all those you've faced so far."

I swallowed hard. "You're here, why is no one looking to you?"

"Because it is not my blood sealing the Veil. You have to direct it. That is the last thing you must do. We will guard your flank and your back as you face Orion one last time."

She scooted closer and wrapped her arms around me. "I'm sorry, but I can't believe I'm holding you again. It's been so long since I said goodbye."

Blaz looked back at me and I nodded. He launched into the air and I held my mother's arms to me, thinking of Marcella. Perhaps one day I'd get the chance to hold her again, after she crossed the Veil.

As I stared at the seething darkness in front of us, I could only hope that was the case. That I didn't fuck up this last step and doom the world to the demons.

No pressure, no pressure at all.

48
LIAM

He couldn't hear Rylee's heart beating, and he thought perhaps his own had stopped. This was not how it was supposed to happen. Lurching toward her, he didn't see Alex until the kid stood up and blocked him. "Lark said you can't touch her."

"I'll fucking well touch her if I want," he snarled. But Alex didn't back down.

"Boss, Lark is trying to help her." Alex pushed him back hard enough to make him stumble.

Liam reluctantly looked away from Rylee's pale face. Lark was on her knees, her arms raised over her head as her whole body shook. "What's she doing?"

Lark spoke softly. "I'm holding her spirit. Her body is close to true death, but if I can hang onto her long enough . . . ."

Faris leapt forward, shoving Liam aside. "You can put her back?"

Sweat dripped down the back of her neck and into her shirt. "Yes."

"What can we do to help?"

"Right now, keep the demons off me. I need all my strength for this."

Faris spun and Liam let him lead. The vampire leapt toward the demons, tearing heads off with his bare hands and eviscerating any that got within even twenty feet of the slab and Rylee's body. Liam egged him on, giving him whatever strength of spirit he could.

Anything to keep Rylee safe.

49
LARK

I'd lied to Liam to keep him out of my way. I wasn't at all sure I could put Rylee back into her body, but it was the only thing I could try. Holding onto her spirit was like wrestling with the wind. Her strength was still there, and though she wasn't exactly fighting me, she wasn't helping, either.

All around us, the demons kept coming. Though they were mortal now, and easier to kill, the sheer numbers would eventually overwhelm us. Even as I thought that, another of our people went down. The shaman, Louisa, and then the ogre, Mer.

The blond leader of the vampire nation, Doran, glanced at me. His green eyes met mine and in that split second I knew . . . he could help me.

"Doran, to me. Now!"

He didn't hesitate and leaped the distance between us in two jumps. Our ranks tightened, the circle around us smaller from losing the shaman, ogre, and now Doran to my command. The wolves were down to only a few dozen and the half-breed trolls were down to less than ten.

"Elemental, I never thought I'd see you again. What am I saying? I knew we'd run into each other." He gave me a wink, though it looked like an effort.

"Old history," I spit out. "Not the time to discuss it."

He grinned at me, but it was forced. "She's fighting you, isn't she?"

"Not intentionally. It's in her nature to be difficult. Her spirit is strong and wants to move through the Veil, to pass over, and I'm about the only thing holding her here." I wriggled my fingers, hooking them deeper into her spirit. Though she was deep in the Veil, I could feel her, but was barely able to hang onto her.

"When I bring her back, she will be bloodless."

"Which means she won't survive even if you can hang onto her." He put a hand to my lower back and a flood of energy ripped through me.

"Thanks."

"No problem." He leaned closer, looking Rylee over before letting out a slow breath. "Bloodless. Are you sure? Every last drop?"

"That's the rules of the game, vampire," I whispered, trying to conserve the energy he'd given me.

"Then I think . . . maybe I might be able to help."

What in the seven hells was he talking about?

It took my fatigued brain more than a few beats to pick up what he was laying down. "Are you goose shitting on me?"

His grin was crooked and his eyes glittered. "Not even for a second."

Mother goddess . . . there was a chance. Not a good one, and she might be pissed as hell if we managed it . . . but a chance.

"Do it. When the time comes, do it," I said, digging into her spirit, holding it tighter. I bowed my head.

"Not without a fight, Rylee. We aren't letting you go without a knockdown, drag out, black-and-blue fight."

I only could hope she would not want to kill us for what we'd done to her.

Of course, that was if she survived at all.

50
RYLEE

Blaz's wings beat in time with my heart. My mother sat behind me, and I was heading into my last battle with Orion.

Yet there was no fear in me. The other dragons around us in the air sparkled with vibrant colors in every shade and hue. Below on the plains, the unicorns galloped, keeping up with the dragons easily. Their horns glinted, and more than one let out a whinny that sounded more like battle cries than a gentle call.

"How do I close the Veil?" The question burst out of me as I realized that was the one part missing in the book of prophecy. "There was not a fucking thing about this bit."

"No one could have possibly known, Ry," Mom said. "The prophecy could only take you so far, you have to do the rest."

"Did you know, when you had me, that this would be my fate?" I turned to look her in the eye and was surprised to see her crying. "Did you?"

"No, my girl. I never had a clue. I was young and foolish, and the world was mine to explore. I had no idea there was more to our blood until it was too late. Until you were already on your way." She took a slow breath. "But even with the little time I had, the small amount I held you in my arms . . . I would do it all again in an instant."

I smiled at her, truly understanding. For Marcella, I would do it all again. For all those I'd loved along the way, the pain was worth it.

Blaz let out a cough, interrupting us. "Here we go, Rylee."

"But what do I do?" I yelped as he drew parallel with the undulating darkness. Staring into it, I could see it was the physical barrier between the demons' level and their access into the other levels, and from there into the world. Instinct took over and I reached for the darkness, but it was too far away. "I need you to land, Blaz."

"You got it." He tucked his wings and dove down as the first thread of the blackened Veil shot out and tried to grab him.

He spun as we plummeted, missing the tendril easily. "Whatever you need to do, do it fast," Blaz yelled back at me. From the black Veil, demons began to wriggle through. The heroes didn't back down, but went into the battle in full warrior mode. Dox, Sla, Lop, and Dev took on the demons with a fervor that only ogres could produce, and as they fought, Mer's spirit flickered into existence. She didn't hesitate, but stepped in with them, as though she hadn't just been slaughtered on the other side.

"You ready?" Blaz asked.

"Nope." I shifted my weight, looking for my weapons. But I had nothing on me. Not a single blade.

Fucking hell.

We landed and I was already sliding off before he came to a full stop.

My mom jumped off with me, and ran to where my father waited for her. They stood side by side, cutting a swath through the demons as though they were taking a walk in the park. Erik was on the other side of my mom, never moving far from her, reminding me that he had loved her first.

There were no demons coming for me this time, though. They avoided me like I didn't exist. Only one demon faced me.

Orion stood within the darkness, glaring out at me. "I will always be stronger than you. Which means no matter how this plays out, you will lose."

Is that what this was about? A fucking pissing contest?

I doubted it. I put my hand into the darkness, thinking I could hold myself out.

I was wrong and the black Veil sucked me in with one gulp, my ears ringing with Orion's laughter as my family and loved ones battled behind me, yet again.

51
LARK

Rylee's spirit began to slip through my fingers. "I'm losing her," I yelled, knowing it would distract everyone around me, but not caring. The Veil hadn't closed yet, which meant she was still fighting to end this. If Rylee couldn't finish what she started, we were all dead.

Calliope, the young leader of the unicorns swept in to me first. Her white coat was splotched with blood, heavy down her chest, but none of it looked to be hers.

We can hold the line on our own, but not for long. Minutes. Is that enough?

"It will have to be."

She let out a shrill whinny, and the remaining unicorns circled us and the burnt out farmhouse, keeping the demons at bay. I looked up into the sky. "Eve, we will need you too. You and Ophelia have ties to Rylee. We need everyone who loves her."

Alex drew closer to me, his hands hovering over Rylee. "Can I touch her now?"

Jaw clenched, I nodded. "In a minute, yes. We have to, if we're going to hold her." I dropped my hands first, pressing them against her bare belly. My spirit blended with Rylee's and I gave her all I had, feeling the dip in my own life force as I pumped it into her.

I fed my emotions and thoughts into her: how I wished we'd had more time together. How proud I was that she was my friend. How I trusted her to complete the monstrous task laid at her feet alone. "You can do this, Rylee."

Pamela was there beside me, her hands clutching Rylee's opposite hand, and holding it to her cheek. "Believe, Rylee. You have to believe."

Liam dropped to his knees and cupped Rylee's face with his hands, bent over and kissed her softly. He whispered something in her ear, something too soft for even me to hear.

Eve was next, dropping behind me and reaching out with a talon. She clutched Rylee's leg. "Hang on, Rylee. A little longer."

Ophelia clawed at Orion's body and pulled him out of the way, then laid her head on the slab so her muzzle was pressed against Rylee's other leg. *Rylee, you promised me you wouldn't die. You must come back.*

Doran laid his hand over Rylee's heart. "You are stronger than him, Rylee. You always have been."

Will, the panther shifter, slid close and dropped a hand to touch her. "Come on, Rylee, you can do this."

India, the little spirit seeker that had remained glued to Calliope's side, knelt beside Liam and touched Rylee's face. "Your spirit is stronger than his, Rylee."

Charlie wrapped his hands around her right arm. "Come on, lass. You bees everything this world has waited for. Don't yous doubt it for a second."

Alex waited until everyone else was holding her, the battle around them ebbing and flowing, the circle contracting. I looked at him. "Now, Alex. You are the last, and perhaps the lynchpin to this moment. She is bound to you like no other. Not even Liam."

He nodded, let out a slow breath, shifted and then lay his head over her chest, his black fur covering her. His words were the simplest, and yet I knew as he did, they were more powerful than anything else he could have said.

He let out a deep throated whine and closed his eyes.

"Alex loves Rylee."

52
ALEX

Wherever Rylee was going, I was going. My choice. My decision. I'd promised her I would stay to the end. I would hold to that promise no matter where it took me.

I clung to her, knowing only that I couldn't go on if she wasn't with us. The whine slipped past my lips; pain, fear, and utter desperation. She couldn't leave this world.

I wouldn't let her.

53
LIAM

He held her face gently, his lips pressed against her forehead. His love was all he had to offer her.

Faris closed his eyes. Love, who would have thought he would find it now, and with Rylee?

Liam smiled as Faris's thoughts flowed over him. But that wasn't what caught his attention. Around them, the sky was lightening.

He tensed and looked at Berget. She shook her head, but her eyes were scared. "We can't let her go."

"I know," he said softly, reaching out and taking her hand. "Faris, you understand what this means?"

The vampire let out a sigh. *That we're both idiots, willing to die for her.*

Liam couldn't help the smile that curved his lips. "That's love, my friend."

Faris startled. *Friend.*

"What would you call us?"

More like brothers at this point. The vampire grunted. Liam couldn't argue. He looked past the circle of unicorns to the sky. The faintest hint of pink tinged the lower horizon in the east. Liam wasn't terribly worried. A strange sense of peace flowed over him.

He'd left her once and found her again, and he had to believe this wasn't the end for them.

What fear Faris had eased at the thought. *Yes, I think you're right. We won't lose her.*

Their bond was too strong. He swallowed hard and turned his head, inadvertently catching Lark's eye. She stared at him, then her head snapped around to the horizon.

"Marco! Get the blackout curtains, something, anything to cover the vamps!"

The remaining Harpy let out a shriek of acknowledgment, but already Liam could feel his skin heating up.

"Berget." Lark shifted and pretty much laid on top of the smaller vampire. Berget curled up under her, but didn't take her hands from her sister. None of them could, not as long as Rylee was still fighting to end it.

"Faris, can you open the Veil?" Doran asked, his green eyes swirling with ideas.

Liam shook his head. "No. Not without taking my hands from her."

The others threw out idea after idea, but Liam already knew the outcome.

And so did Faris.

The sun slid upward and the first rays hit him hard, like being dipped in burning oil.

He bit down on the scream that roared up his throat. Around him the clatter of voices, the whoosh of wings, the scream for him to get under cover.

Too late, seconds and inches too late. Faris breathed through him, a peace that the vampire hadn't known for hundreds of years and his voice broke on his final words.

"To live for love is a blessing, but to die for love? I see, now, to die for love is an honor."

54
RYLEE

The black Veil, the seventh Veil and the only thing between the world and the demons at the moment, sucked me in with a rather large belch. I stood in front of Orion, seeing the glow of his aura around his body for the first time. It wasn't black, but a bright pulsing silver that beat in time with his heart. I looked down at myself. A dim thread of gold ran around my body, also beating in time with my heart.

"You see, you aren't strong enough." Orion laughed, stalking toward me. He grabbed my hands and linked our fingers together before I could jerk away from him. I stilled my initial instinct to fight him and locked my fingers around his. His grip was dry and cold, and he squeezed until my knuckles popped, forcing me to one knee.

I shook my head. "No, I'm not strong enough; you're right."

His eyes widened. "You admit it?"

Slowly, I lifted my eyes to his. "Not on my own, I'm not." Around me the flicker of spirits whispered. Lark, Pamela, Berget, Doran, Eve, Ophelia, Charlie, Will, India.

Liam and Faris.

Alex.

They were indistinct and yet their strength fed mine. The pulsing band of gold grew around me until it was three times the size of Orion's.

He snarled, "That is not fair."

"All's fair in love and war, asshole," I bit out, using the strength they gave me to stand and push Orion to his knees. Around me, the Veil flickered, and I saw it for the first time. It was built of threads, not unlike those I Tracked for a salvage.

Using my ability, I Tracked the Veil, and the world around me opened like a map unfolding. Each piece of the Veil lay out in front of me as simply as a drawing. I let go of one of Orion's hands so I could run my fingers through the threads around me, plucking at them like a harp. They were all intertwined, but I could fix that.

But that would mean letting go of Orion completely and exposing myself to him.

I swallowed hard, and unlinked our fingers. He leapt toward me, and I braced myself. But the blow never came.

A black, furred figure slammed into him. "No hurts Ryleeeeeeeeeee!"

"Alex, no!"

He glanced back at me, golden eyes glowing in the darkness. "I gots it, boss. You take care of the Veil."

Shaking, I watched with my mouth hanging open as Alex dodged Orion's blows while driving him farther from me. Did that mean Alex had died on the other side?

Between Alex and me ran a gold thread—the bond between us. His heart beat in time with mine; a steady pulse that reverberated his strength and love through me.

I lifted my hands and closed my eyes, seeing the Veil. As quickly as I could, I pulled the threads apart, untangling them from one another. Those that went to the first six levels, I left alone, smoothing them out. They were needed. There was still a place for them in the world.

Alex let out a howl that was cut off as quickly as it started. Tears slipped down my face as I grasped the threads of the seventh Veil and began to tie it off. Knot after knot, I tightened the threads in on themselves, over and over again. The bundle of threads vibrated in my hands and I stared at it, knowing I wasn't quite done. There was one thing left to finalize this sealing of the Veil.

"You fucking little bitch!" Orion screamed at me and I looked up. I was no longer within the darkness, but Orion was.

Alex lay at my feet in his wolf form, his sides heaving. "Finish it, boss."

Orion hammered his hands on the now solid wall between us. "Fucking little bitch!"

I flipped him off. "You're repeating yourself, demon. A sign of dementia, perhaps?"

The black Veil shivered and the demons behind me screamed as they were sucked into the seventh Veil, one by one. Their bodies popping as they slid through, like mosquitos hitting a bug zapper. I waited, feeling the demons careening along the threads as they were sucked in from the world.

A vacuum of epic proportions.

Hands touched my shoulders and I knew without looking it was my mom and dad. "Rylee, a life is the final key."

Alex sat up, shifting into his human form. "Her life, or any life?"

Elle stared at him. "Her blood started the ceremony. She was needed because she was the only one who could see the threads of the Veil and untwist them. The Blood of the Lost created the seven Veils, so it took someone of the same heritage to fix them." She was avoiding the question. Alex stared her down.

"Any life, or just hers?"

Elle's eyes never left his and her unwillingness to look my way freaked me out. "You are correct, wolf. Any life will do, now."

"No, Alex. You aren't doing this." I shook my head and tried to back away.

He stood and held his hands out to me. "Rylee, Giselle said I was the lynchpin, and so did Lark. This is the last thing I can do to keep my family safe. To keep those I love from facing this kind of darkness ever again. I can be the lynch pin to keeping your life intact."

I shook my head, unable to see past the sudden onslaught of tears. "Alex, you can't. Without you there, my life won't be intact."

Yet, already I knew he'd set his mind on it. "I can. I do this because I love you, Rylee. You were my only friend and you believed in me when no one else did. You took me in and saved me." He wrapped his arms around me and I sobbed into his chest, clinging to him.

"Alex."

"No, this is the way it's supposed to be. I can do something no one else can. I can give you back to the world. I can give you back to Marcella and Liam. To all of them. They need you more than they need me and we both know it."

He kissed the top of my head and I clung to him harder. Not Alex, anyone but him. But that wasn't true, either, I didn't want to lose any of my family.

"I can't let you do this. I am the one who is supposed to die. Not you."

He shook me lightly, and for the first time I truly knew he was no longer submissive. "You can and you will. For Marcella, if for no one else, you will let me do this. We both know this is the right way. But you have to promise me something," he said, pulling back from me. Tears streamed down his face too, soaking his cheeks and chest where they dripped. Damn him, he was right. For Marcella, I would let him go.

"Anything," I whispered through the pain and the tears.

He gave me a quirky smile and for a moment I thought his tongue would loll out. "I want you to go into the desert, get one of those fucking rabbits, and roast it over an open fire for me."

A sob escaped me, and with it, I lost my ability to speak in coherent sentences. He stepped back, glancing at Elle. "I have to touch the Veil now, don't I?"

From the corner of my eye I saw her nod. Alex lifted my hands, kissed them both, and then gave me a wobbling smile. "Don't tell Pamela how I felt about her. She's lost enough."

"I won't," I whispered.

He swallowed hard. "I love you, Rylee."

"I love you, Alex." I couldn't stop the cry as he stepped backward and into the black Veil. A burst of light exploded outward like a supernova. We were thrown back, and I hit the ground hard, feeling it dig into me like a slab of rock. I tried to open my eyes, but wasn't able to even blink. Voices surrounded me; first, those I'd been reunited with, and one new one that sent my heart into overdrive.

"It's okay, baby girl. Go, we'll be here when it's your time," Mom said, and she pressed a kiss against my forehead.

"Alex knew it wasn't your time to let go. Tell Ophelia . . . tell her I loved her," Blaz whispered in my ear.

"Tracker. Your damn wolf was right. Love is worth dying for." Faris breathed over me and I forced my eyes open, though it took all my strength to do it. My heart leaped at the sight of him until I realized what it meant.

Faris was dead. Liam was Faris.

"No, no. I can't lose you too!" I screamed the words and his arms slid around me, pulling me to his chest.

"Ah, you don't know how long I've waited to know for sure you loved me. That it wasn't just the wolf you wanted."

A hiccupping sob escaped me and I'd thought I was through all the tears in my body, but I was wrong again. I held him, feeling the strength in his body as he bent his lips to mine. A kiss that was for the first time free of manipulation or lies.

Just Faris.

"Damn you for making me love you too," I whispered.

He laughed softly. "I could say the same. But I won't. Your love . . . I think it might have saved me from penance."

Faris ran a finger under my eye, swiping away the tears. "Don't cry for me, Rylee. You were a blessing and a curse, and I am grateful for both." His blue eyes glimmered with unshed tears. "Maybe I can find my mother and sister now."

Sniffing, I nodded. "Then this is goodbye."

He tipped his head to one side and smiled, not a single fang showing. "Perhaps. Perhaps not. It's hard to say in this world of ours, don't you think?"

My laugh turned into another sob. "I don't know anymore, so many people gone, lost."

"Willingly, Rylee. We all went willingly." He tucked a finger under my chin. "Remember that, we would all do it again to be at your side. To fight for you. To love you." He leaned in and kissed me again, soft and gentle, as sweet a kiss as I'd ever tasted. Then he stood and stepped back. "Get out of here, Tracker, you aren't ready for this adventure . . . not yet."

My eyes slipped shut again. But Liam didn't come to say his goodbye and my heart lurched. Perhaps that was my penance for letting Alex go. For allowing him to take my place so I could go home to Marcella and Zane.

They all came to me, my friends, all those I'd lost until their voices blended into one thing.

We love you, Rylee. But it isn't your time yet. Not yet.

Their voices faded and new ones slipped in and became those I'd left behind.

Doran's voice was the first I heard. "She's going to kick my ass for this."

"I'll take the blame. Do it," Lark snapped.

A rush of warmth filled my mouth and I swallowed instinctively. Gulp after gulp of sweet liquid flowed down my throat until my belly was full. I turned my head. "No more."

Lips brushed against mine. "I have to seal it with a kiss. The kiss you owe me."

Doran pressed his mouth against mine, his fangs pressing into my skin. I groaned, but not out of pleasure. My body hurt all over, and I struggled to open my eyes.

"Give it a minute, Rylee." Doran pushed on my shoulders, holding me to the ground. "Don't move too fast."

I opened my eyes, staring up at an early morning sky. There were no sounds of battle, no demons leering over us. Blinking slowly, I looked around at the faces peering back at me.

Pamela, Ophelia, Eve, Marco, Doran, Charlie, and Will. Calliope and her Crush of Unicorns, India at her side. Jonathan behind Lark. The weight on my chest though wasn't entirely from Doran. Black fur filled my vision as I looked down to see Alex seemingly asleep on me.

My shoulder's shook as I ran my hands through his fur. "Damn you for leaving me, Alex."

I cried until there were no tears left. There was nothing anyone could say. I'd lost him. And I'd lost Liam again. Whatever we'd gained in saving the world, I wasn't entirely sure it was worth it. How could this world exist properly without my two boys?

Without the laughter that Alex pulled from me in my darkest hours?

Slowly, I sat up, and Doran pulled Alex from me, gently laying him at my side. I buried my fingers into his long fur, knowing that soon enough I wouldn't even have that.

Lark shook her head. "Holy hell, Rylee, I wasn't sure it would work."

"How?" I whispered. "All my blood was gone, wasn't it?"

Doran cleared his throat. "Well, that is true. But it is also the last step to becoming a vampire. You have to be drained of every last drop of blood before you can be turned. Essentially, you have to die in order to be reborn."

My eyebrows shot to my hairline and with them I shot to my feet. Not possible, it wasn't possible. "I'm standing in the sunlight."

He shrugged. "You're a new breed of vampire. Like me."

I stumbled back and fell over a lump on the ground. Berget's voice snapped out. "Ow! Not funny."

I crouched. "Berget?"

"Yeah, I got stuffed undercover again." Her voice wasn't really irritated. "Rylee? Is it really you?"

"Yes." I couldn't manage more than that, so I put a hand on her back, giving her a light pat.

I looked around, searching for Faris's body. But of course, it wouldn't be there, but burned up in ash. Was I not to be able to even bury Liam?

I Tracked him, reaching for the threads that would at least tell me he was truly gone.

And felt nothing. Not that there were no threads, but I couldn't Track anything. Hands shaking, I held them out. "I can't feel anyone."

Lark stepped closer and took my hand. "You were drained of all your blood, Rylee. The Blood of the Lost is gone, and with it, your abilities. At least, that's what I think has happened."

I couldn't help feeling I was missing a part of me. That which made me *me* was gone. Yet I couldn't be angry; I'd been given a second chance.

"Thank you." I looked to Doran, then Lark. To each of them. "I could never have stood against him without you."

Doran caught me first in his arms and that quickly turned into a group hug as everyone got in on it. Pamela was crying, her face pressed against me.

"Alex would have loved this."

A laugh that turned into a sob escaped me. "Yeah, he would have."

I held them tightly, my family. The ones who'd survived and I was grateful for all I had. Though we'd lost so much, I knew I couldn't dishonor the sacrifices made by being ungrateful. By wanting more than I'd been given.

I closed my eyes and held tightly to them.

To those I could still hold onto.

55
LIAM

Faris shook his head. "You lucky bastard. The sunlight burned me out of you."

Liam frowned. "What are you talking about?'

"YOU aren't a vampire. You never were. You were just inhabiting my body." Faris gave a rueful smile and shook his head. "Which means when the sunlight hit us, I was fried. But you got to keep on living. So I'll tell you this now, you'd better stick it out with Rylee, because I think she's got a thing for that body you're in."

"You died for her."

The vampire snorted and spoke over his shoulder as he walked away, heading into a fog that swam up between them. "Yeah, I guess I did. Maybe you and I aren't so different after all, Wolf."

"Wait." The word slipped out of him as he tried to open his closed eyes. He made himself open them, but it was like prying apart two pieces of paper glued together. There was no answer to his request, not even a snotty reply.

Faris was gone, and for the first time in months, Liam was alone in his head.

"What the hell," he murmured, sitting up, pushing the heavy curtain off his body before he thought better of it.

The sunlight spilled over his face and he drew in a slow, even breath. His heart beat, almost frantically, and a distant urge to run and hide from the bright light bit at him. Leftover muscle memory from hundreds of years living in the darkness. He looked down at his body.

His body.

Not Faris's any longer. He shoved the curtain the rest of the way off and stood. The slab was bare. Rylee's body and Orion's were gone.

Fear clutched at his heart with icy fingers, and despite the warm sun, he was cold all the way to his core. He ran forward searching for a sign of what had happened. So much blood . . . .

"She's in the barn."

He spun to see Lark standing behind him. How the hell had she snuck up on him? Why didn't he hear her? Or smell her for that matter?

The realization hit him like a hammer between the eyes.

He was human again. That was the only answer.

"Is she . . . alive?"

Lark smiled, though it was tired and full of sorrow. "In a manner of speaking. And you aren't human, Wolf. You never were. Let your body catch up to the soul that it now contains; your senses will come back."

A barking laugh rolled toward them and Griffin strolled up behind Lark, slinging an arm over her shoulders. "Listen to her, yeah? She's a smart girl."

Liam stared at the older man. "Am I still a guardian?"

Griffin shrugged. "As much as you ever were. The wolf is a part of you. Don't matter what your body looks like, yeah? And that wee girl of yours . . . she's going to be walking in your footsteps soon enough, so don't forget the training that old coot Peter gave you."

He nodded. Peter . . . the old werewolf deep in the wilds of Russia had given him insight into what he was capable of . . . and he'd bound Rylee's soul to him.

Griffin turned away, and Liam couldn't help but grab his arm. "You're leaving already?"

Grunting, Griffin swatted his hand away. "You remember Catya? She needs me more than you do, yeah?"

Catya, the littlest werewolf Liam had ever met with a heart of pure gold. "I'm sorry."

With a wink, Griffin shifted into his wolf form and loped away.

Lark waved at Liam. "We can talk later. Go to her; she thinks you're lost to her."

Liam nodded and jogged to where the barn, re-markably enough, still stood. Pushing the door open, the flood of smells assaulted his nose. Hay and mold, sweating bodies, and . . . take-out Chinese. Lark wasn't kidding about his senses coming back; they felt even keener than before. He sniffed loudly. "Any of that left?"

Absolute silence met his words and he looked right at her. Her eyes . . . they were the first thing he noticed. No longer tri-colored, but a perfect hazel with flecks of green and a slight rim of gold around the edge. No swirling of her emotions showed in their depths as she stood and stumbled toward him.

"Adamson, please tell me you don't plan on saving the world again anytime soon."

A sob spilled out of her and he caught her up, crushing her to his chest. "I'm here, and I'm not going anywhere." Her grip tightened on him to the point that his ribs creaked. "Ease up, beautiful."

She loosened her hold and stared up at him. He bent his head, kissing her hard, his tongue darting into her mouth and brushing against . . . he jerked his head back unable to stop himself. "What happened?"

Her eyes narrowed and he braced himself for an onslaught from her.

He was right to be wary. Even without the telltale swirling of colors in her eyes, he knew he'd pushed a sore spot, right off the bat.

For a moment, he thought Faris would give him shit for screwing up already. Of course, the vampire was gone. Which mean Liam was on his own.

56
RYLEE

"What do you mean, what happened? Were you not there?" I couldn't help the snap to my tone. I was scared. What if he didn't want me now that I was no longer a Tracker? Now that I was something different.

He cupped my face. "I was there, but apparently, I missed the finale. Doran, you want to explain since I can smell you on her lips?"

I jerked away from him. "How about I explain?"

His lips twitched and I realized we'd both changed so much in the last months . . . but I would never stop loving him. I only hoped he felt the same.

"Spit it out, Adamson," he growled, but there was a teasing light in his eyes and on his lips.

A breath I didn't realize I was holding slid out of me. "My blood was gone; they had to replace it with something, didn't they?"

"So Doran offered?"

Doran laughed softly. "She owed me a kiss."

Liam seemed to be thinking it through, and for a moment, I thought he was listening to Faris. That maybe that brassy vampire wasn't gone. "You only owed him one, right?" He slid his arms around me and pulled me to him once more. I smiled up at him.

"Yeah, only one."

"Good, because I'm staking my claim on these lips for the rest of forever."

I grimaced. "Maybe staking isn't the word you should use."

Laughing, he pressed his lips to mine and I fell into the kiss, peace rolling through me.

We'd done it. We'd defeated Orion.

It was time to go home.

But first, we had two little people to pick up.

My heart skipped a beat and I grabbed Liam's hand. "Marcella and Zane."

"I left them with John and Mary, at the hotel. And you are not going to believe what I found out," he said and laughed again. "Seriously, Rylee. You aren't going to fucking well believe it."

"As long as it's a good surprise, I don't care."

I grabbed him and pulled him toward the barn door with me. He looked around, his eyes sweeping those who were left.

"No." The word whispered out of him and his feet stopped moving. "Tell me he's off scrounging for rabbits."

My heart clenched and I closed my eyes. "He gave his life for me. So that I could have a second chance."

Liam dropped his head until his chin touched his chest. Tears slipped down his cheeks and I wrapped my arms around him. So many tears, too many. The barn door opened and Lark stepped inside.

"We have visitors." Her voice was dull. I wasn't the only one who had been pushed to their limit. All of us had been forced to face things we'd been afraid of.

"Tell me they're good visitors."

She nodded. "They are."

Liam turned and tipped his head. "Sounds like your Jeep."

My Jeep? How the hell could that be?

I walked out of the barn and stared as a Jeep bounced down the driveway, coming to a stop near the remainder of the house. John stepped out first, then went to the back and opened the door. "Finding car seats was a bit of a pain with the blackout, you know."

I jogged to his side and reached past him to my girl. Marcella saw me and squealed, wriggling in her seat like mad as she lifted her hands to me. I had the buckles off and pulled her into my arms in a flash, the new speed I'd acquired like having a bite constantly invoked.

I breathed her smell in, held her out, and stared at her beautiful face. She laughed and touched my face, running her hands over my wet cheeks.

John laughed. "Don't forget this little man." He handed me Zane and I kissed the little boy who'd so deftly stolen my heart. Doran once said I would love another . . . that had been Marcella he'd spoken of, I was sure. Yet as I held Zane, I knew I loved him as much as I loved her.

Then there was Faris.

I fought the tears as I thought of him, telling me he loved me, and he was leaving. He'd died protecting me; because of love.

Zane clung to me. "Mama."

Liam held out his hands and Marcella went to him, snuggling herself into his neck. He didn't look anywhere near the FBI agent I'd met eleven years ago. He'd changed in every way someone could.

And yet . . . he was everything I needed to forge this new life ahead of us.

John touched my arm. "Ry." I turned to see him smiling, his eyes watering. "You look a great deal like our Elena. I've wanted to tell you that since we met."

Elena that was my mother's . . . "Elle?"

Mary stepped out from around the Jeep and smiled at me. I'd only seen glimpses of her in the past when I'd gone to the hotel.

Now I knew why. She was an older version of my mother, down to the dark hair and slim build, the angle of her jaw and shape of her nose.

I swallowed hard at what was being offered to me. Family. "Why didn't you ever say anything?"

John shrugged. "I'm not your real grandfather, Ry. He passed on not long after your mother was conceived."

Lark moved up beside me. "He was my uncle. He was killed because he was a Spirit elemental."

Mary nodded slowly. "That he was. John found me after the accident and helped me heal. I'm sorry we never told you, Rylee, who we were. We were afraid you wouldn't believe us. So many times people didn't believe us." Her eyes went to his, and I suspected a story there, an explanation for doing things the way they did. Perhaps another time they would tell me.

Lark touched my arm and then tipped her head to the side. "Rylee, I have to go. There are other problems waiting on me." Right behind her Jonathan fidgeted, his eyes still as screwball as ever.

"She's right, she has to go. So do I. I have to go with her." Jonathan's hands twitched as though he were holding a pencil, writing in the air. I wasn't going to be sad to see him go.

I shifted Zane on my hip. The little boy wrapped his arms and legs tightly around me. "What can I do to help?"

She shook her head. "This is not your fight, my friend. Though, I thank you for the offer. Perhaps we will meet again."

Her words had the feeling of a final goodbye. "Just like that."

She shrugged and looked over her shoulder. Cactus and the other elementals who'd stayed were standing in a group, waiting for her. "No. I think we will meet again, Rylee. But not for a long time." Gently, she brushed a hand over Zane's head. He smiled up at her, his dimples flashing. "These two are going to be trouble, you know that, right?"

I laughed. "I have no doubt about it. Call on me, Lark. I will do everything I can to help you." With my free arm, I pulled her into a hug and squeezed her as tightly as I dared. "Thank you does not begin to cover things."

"Oh, hell," she muttered, "what's family for if not to get you out of a jam once in a while?"

Smiling, she backed away from me, her one hand raised in farewell. Pausing, she locked eyes with me. "Two last things. Watch the sword, Rylee. An elemental named Blackbird may try and take it from you. I suggest you hide it." Her eyes swept past me, looking over my shoulder. "Pamela, in five years, come to the Rim."

I turned in time to see Pamela nod, a faint, tired smile on her lips.

When I turned back, Lark, Jonathan, and the other elementals were gone.

"Goodbye, Lark," I whispered into the air and I was sure she whispered back on the wind.

Goodbye, Rylee. And good luck. You're going to need it in your new life.

57
RYLEE

The following weeks were hectic as we all tried to settle into something that resembled a normal life.

While we'd fought for the survival of the world, human technology had shut down completely. All that supernatural energy from the demons had put everything on the blink, and the humans had gone into panic mode. Three days they were without power and electricity.

Three days, and the fools lost their minds rioting and burning the shit out of things. The pox was gone as if it had never been, and a lot of people were saying that it was all a terrorist plot to wipe out whoever it was terrorists were after. Conspiracy theories ran rampant on every channel.

"What's wrong with them?" Pamela asked once our TV turned back on and a news channel showed the extensive damage.

"I don't know. But if this is how they react when things go sideways, it's all the more reason to keep the supernatural from them," I said softly.

The Tamoskin Crush went back to the badlands, Calliope in the lead and Tiomon promising to come back for Marcella when the time was right. India went with them, though I tried to get her to stay with us.

"My human family is dead, Rylee." Her hand wove into Calliope's mane. "I . . . I can't go back to pretending I'm something I'm not."

I pulled her into a hug. "We're right here, India."

She smiled up at me, her light auburn hair catching the light and her hazel eyes twinkling. "I will come see you often. The spirits are going to be drawn to you, Rylee. Your calling has shifted, I think."

With a quick leap that belied the fact that she was so tiny, she mounted on one of the older unicorns. Seconds later, the Crush was gone in a flash of golden horns and thundering hooves.

To be honest, I was hoping it was going to be a long, long time before Tiomon decided Marcella needed her. Because I had a feeling that when the unicorn showed up on my doorstep, trouble wouldn't be far behind her back hooves.

Doran stayed for a week, making sure I got the hang of my new life. "I'm your sponsor; I have to see you can handle things without me around."

Liam snorted. "Her sponsor? This isn't AA."

The cheeky-assed vampire grinned at him, green eyes sparkling. "I could sponsor you, too, if you like."

Liam shook his head and walked away, though not before I saw his lips twitch as he fought a smile of his own.

"I think one set of fangs is enough in the family, thanks," I muttered, running my tongue over my newly acquired teeth.

Eve and Marco set up a clutch not far from where Calliope and her herd ran. They decided to raise their species together, to start fresh. Watching them bridge the gap between the age-old enemies, I knew Eve and Calliope had the hearts for it to work.

Will and what was left of his Destruction headed back to England; Deanna had been wrong about his death. Though looking into his eyes as he said his goodbyes, it was easy to see that a part of him had died during the battle. Pamela shook his hand when he moved to hug her and I fought a smile. Once he'd sent her into a blushing stammer. She'd grown up a lot, and apparently left her crush on him behind.

He hugged me gently. "Rylee. Take care of yourself."

"You too, Will." I let him go. Perhaps I would see him again, but I had a feeling my time across the water was done.

At least for the foreseeable future.

The Veil was once more open—minus the connection to the seventh Veil—and working smoothly. The mineshaft—after the doorways were unsealed—was an easy way to travel.

Charlie was hailed as a hero by his fellow brownies and asked to lead them, an honor he couldn't turn down. "Yous sees, Rylee girl, they no longer thinks of me as a liability." He tapped his wooden leg.

I blinked several times. "Is that why you didn't have much to do with them? I didn't realize—" All the years we'd worked together on salvages, he never spoke of his kind. I realized that to take Zane as he had to protect him would have been a monumental task. Yet he'd done it.

He waved me to silence. "They's don't likes to admit they be so damn critical. But it bees the truth. I thinks I can change that now." He grinned at me and I bent to hug him.

No more words between us. There was no need. He turned, stepped through the door to Liam's house, and was gone. Would I see him again? The question wandered through my head, but I had no answer. Things were changing so fast, I wasn't sure what would shift next.

When we were able to tally the supernaturals left, I wasn't sure I'd saved enough of us. Species had been nearly wiped out by the pox, and those remaining had fought with us, cutting their numbers further.

In some cases, like Eve and Marco, there was only a pair of each species left. Sas, as far as we knew, was the only ogre left.

Do you still wish to get the children from her? Ophelia asked me about a week after we'd closed the seventh Veil. I nodded slowly and scrubbed my hands over my face. To be honest, I'd lost my desire to wipe Sas from the face of the earth. "I think we have to at least see what the hell she's up to. If she really is the last ogre, then we need to make sure she's alive."

"Agreed," Liam said moving beside me. He knew me well enough not to fill in what I wasn't saying. Though the pain of Blaz's death still clung to me, the anger had faded. Unless Dox's and the triplets' children were in danger, I wouldn't be taking them from their mother.

Even if she was a total bitch.

That didn't mean we could just leave her out there alone. For Dox, I would check in on his child. With the nice weather, we'd stayed out on the farm, roughing it with tents and the barn as cover. Pamela stayed behind to see if she could track down any supernaturals that survived the pox. So far, she'd only found a handful, but she wasn't deterred.

Gathering up Marcella and Zane, Liam and I packed for the trip to find Sas.

Ophelia flew the four of us to the West Coast. The trip was not rushed and we took our time, letting the babies play along the way at different stops.

Partway to our destination, I went for a solo flight with Ophelia, scouting out the area. At least, that was what I told her. "Ophelia, I saw Blaz on the other side."

Her wings slowed and she stilled under me as if we weren't hovering far above the ground.

You did?

This was something I hadn't spoken about to anyone, not even Liam. I would perhaps one day, but not yet. I opened myself up to her, and let her see my memories. Let her see those who'd passed so they could fight for me on the other side of the Veil.

Let her see Blaz's face as he'd spoken to me. "Tell Ophelia I love her."

The dragon below me let out a cry of pain, and yet there was a flood of joy as well. To be loved, even to lose it, was a blessing I knew all too well. I pressed my hands against her, tears trickling down my face. Shit, I'd cried more in the last week then I'd probably cried my whole life.

Thank you, Rylee. You are right. Love is a blessing that can help us face the darkest hours of our lives. Your love and the bond between us has healed the madness that was eating at me. And Blaz's love . . . it will buoy me when I feel like sinking.

We spoke no more of Blaz, but I knew we'd have another trip to make soon enough. There was the clutch of eggs Ophelia had hidden away from the demons.

Reaching Mount Hood, Ophelia circled the green spot that Lark created, and through our bond, I could easily feel her heartache. This was the spot we'd lost Blaz, and she was seeing his grave for the first time.

She winged down slowly, landing on the edge of the blooming trees. Marcella was strapped to my chest in a baby carrier, and Zane was strapped to Liam's back in another. We slid off the dragon and landed lightly. Liam lifted his head and took in a long breath.

"Something is dead in there. Hours at most."

Well shit, that couldn't be good. I unbuckled Marcella from my back and put her on the ground at Ophelia's feet with a couple of toys. Liam followed suit, putting Zane close to Marcella. The two screeched as they fought over a toy they both wanted.

"'Phelia, you know what to do if it goes sideways."

Of course. The babies will come first.

Liam and I pulled our weapons and crept into the trees. I tried not to put too much stock into the fact Liam had kept Faris's cutlass. Perhaps it was a way to honor the vampire's sacrifice.

My thoughts scattered as we pushed through a tall section of brush. At the edge of a clear pool, Sas lay on her side with her back to us, her violet skin from her back gone. Arrows fletched with demon insignias had been driven through her spine in several places

Liam took a long deep breath. "Witches did this. They tried to make it look like a demon hit, though."

A healthy squall of a child had me running toward Sas before I thought better of it.

In the crook of her curved body lay three ogre babies. Two violet and one the exact shade of Dox's blue. I bent and scooped up the blue ogre babe and Liam caught up the other two. Smiling, he shook his head. "Looks like you aren't done collecting lost souls, my love."

I rocked the boy in my arms. "Apparently not."

We left Sas to rot, not bothering to bury her. Considering all she'd done, it was a fairly light penance. Wrapping the tiny boys (tiny being a relative term since they were already the size of Marcella and Zane, who had eight and nine months on them, respectively) into blankets, Ophelia took us into the closest city and dropped us off. Juggling five babies, I let Liam do all the shopping. He brought back a minivan filled with baby seats.

We loaded them up and headed home, the interior of the van replete with five screaming babies who took turns seeing who could out yell who.

"So, as the Tracker who stopped a demon horde, does this feel like something of a letdown?" Liam spoke loudly to be heard over the kids.

Perhaps if I hadn't experienced all the death that had come for me and my friends, or maybe if I hadn't seen how dark it could be when all hope was lost, the moment might have felt like it was never going to end.

"Not in the least," I said softly, knowing he could hear me. "Not in the least."

Six months later . . . .

Pamela jiggled the two violet boys on either side of her hips as they tried to use her as a climbing apparatus. "Bam, Rut, stop pulling my hair!"

Marcella toddled toward me, Zane right beside her as I lowered Kav to the floor, his blue skin still baby soft. "Put them down. They want to wrestle, let them go at each other."

With a sigh, she did as I said, and the three ogre babies immediately crawled all over each other, squealing and laughing. Zane joined in—he was big enough to hold his own—but Marcella held back, watching, her eyes never leaving the four boys.

Ophelia had gone to her babies and brought the eggs back to the farm one by one. Three eggs, one with a hairline crack in it. Though she said it wasn't a problem, I knew she was worried. I couldn't do anything to help, though I couldn't help but worry with her. Only time would tell if the worry had any merit.

We had settled into Liam's old house, but it was barely big enough, and we were talking about moving. He started up his own business, and he and Pamela were working to follow up leads on cold cases that could have a supernatural bend. A part of me wanted to rebuild out on the farm, despite the things that had happened there. The bloodshed was that of our friends and family. If it meant their spirits were closer, I didn't mind in the least.

As for me, I'd been stuck in mommy mode for long enough that it was easy to forget there was anything else. That I'd ever been anything but this herder of children.

That didn't mean I'd given up my workout routine, or my weapons training.

I wasn't an idiot.

A single knock of the door was about to change all that. Three sharp raps snapped my head up and I flared my nostrils, but I all I got was human floating under the door. "Go ahead and get it, Pam. I think it's safe."

She went to the door and opened it slowly. A young man who couldn't have been more than twenty stood on the doorstep. He was built lean and gangly, and for a second my heart skipped a beat, thinking it was Alex. That he'd come back to us. The kid cleared his throat and a thick accent coated his words.

European from what I could detect, but couldn't pin down where on the continent. "I'm sorry, but I have heard this is where the Tracker lives. And maybe she could help me. My family needs help. Are you her? Rylee Adamson?"

He looked past Pamela to me, and the need to do something, anything, to ease his pain rose in me. The Blood of the Lost was no longer in me, but my heart was my heart, and it beat to help others. There was nothing I could do about it.

"No, I'm sorry. My name is Rylee O'Shea." I held out a hand and he shook it slowly. "And I am a Day-walking vampire."

ABOUT THE AUTHOR

Shannon Mayer is the *USA Today* bestselling author of the Rylee Adamson novels, the Elemental series, and numerous paranormal romance, urban fantasy, mystery, and suspense novels. She lives in the southwestern tip of Canada with her husband, son, and numerous other animals.